Also by Nicole Galland

I, Iago
Crossed
Revenge of the Rose
The Fool's Tale

Godiva

For Jamil + Jenny –
Enjoy the ride!
Much love
Nicki

Godiva

NICOLE GALLAND

Nicole Galland

WILLIAM MORROW
An Imprint of HarperCollinsPublishers

P.S.™ is a trademark of HarperCollins Publishers.

HarperCollins books may be purchased for educational, business, or sales promotional use. For information please write: Special Markets Department, HarperCollins Publishers, 10 East 53rd Street, New York, NY 10022.

FIRST EDITION

Designed by Diahann Sturge

Library of Congress Cataloging-in-Publication Data has been applied for.

ISBN 978-0-06-202688-0

13 14 15 16 17 ov/rrd 10 9 8 7 6 5 4 3 2

For Maureen and Alan Crumpler

Historical Note

In the year of our Lord 1040, the Dane named Harthacnut became king of England. Although the English were expecting him to have the throne—following in the rocky wake of his father and his brother—he approached their shores with more than threescore warships, and landed as if he meant to conquer the island. This was insult enough, but Harthacnut's impudence went further. To furnish this extravagant army that he did not need, he revived a war tax on his new subjects so harsh that it impoverished all of them. This tax was called the heregeld.

In the year of our Lord 1041, in the stormy depths of autumn, two of Harthacnut's men rode to the town of Worcester, in Mercia, to collect the heregeld there. The people refused to pay it and they murdered the two tax collectors to clearly express their outrage.

In response, Harthacnut harried Worcester, meaning, with advance warning so the people themselves might flee, he sent men to raze the town.

But not just any men.

To demonstrate that his word was law, Harthacnut ordered the three great earls of the kingdom to destroy Worcester in their own persons, with the work of their own men. Had they refused, that fleet of warships would indeed have disgorged its mercenary troops, and England would have tumbled into chaos once again. Sickened by the task, the earls obeyed their new king.

Leofric of Mercia (in whose realm Worcester lay) was one of those three great earls who were ordered to raze the town. To be ordered by one's superior to harm one's own people was a loathsome thing.

Soon after the Worcester tragedy, this Danish king of England died, a young man whose dark soul had eaten him away from the inside. He left no heir of his body. But after great political intrigue and machinations, Harthacnut's half brother Edward ascended the throne of England. He was placed there by the three great earls (none of whom were fond of him) because they could not find a better choice.

Edward was not the despot his brother had been. He returned power to the Great Council, giving the nobility and the Catholic Church a say in how the kingdom was ruled. But he had spent twenty-five years on the Continent, in Normandy, and it had shaped him deeply. He did not understand their Saxon ways. He did not understand their history. He did not understand their outrage over the heregeld.

He retained those foreign mercenaries, even in their idleness, and did not rescind the heregeld.

At least, not soon enough.

Godiva

Part 1

CHAPTER 1

Gloucester

I n the time it took Godiva to wrest a concession from the young man, she could have as easily spun a skein of yarn. She did not much like spinning yarn; wresting concessions from young men, however, was agreeable enough. Gloucester's dank great hall proved especially agreeable for concession-wresting; this was her third today. But Sweyn, who was absurdly handsome and had the intensity of a catamount, was her perennial favorite. At the moment she had him against a wall. The hall was full, bustling with men and women of rank, and he was certain they were all laughing at him.

"I concede that *perhaps*," Sweyn allowed, at last, "*accidentally*, my herders might have strayed over the border. A bit. In that one valley."

"Thus accounting for . . . ?" she prompted.

"Thus accounting for Mercian sheep," he acknowledged, "ending up as mutton on Herefordshire tables."

Her golden-green eyes, framed by her glittering veil, blinked expectantly. This was about more than poached mutton, and they both knew it, but each hoped to avoid saying so outright.

"And, of course, I shall make amends for that," he said urgently into the silence.

The countess Godiva relaxed and smiled. "In what manner?"

"If you give me an accounting of the missing flocks, I will replace them."

"That's an excellent beginning," she approved. With confiding tone she added, "But he'll want more than that as recompense. Of course."

"Of course." Sweyn watched her sparrowlike hand flutter toward the spot on his chest where his leather cloak hung open. She watched him watching her; she could smell the mix of pleasure and dismay her movement elicited in him. It was a scent she was familiar with. "Lady Countess, pray but tell me what he wants."

She stood up straighter, enough that he could breathe without inhaling her perfume. She clasped her hands together at her heart, her bracelets clinking importantly against her necklaces. "I suspect he shall like to hear that you will express your regret and replace the missing sheep twice over. That would be so very generous of you."

"Oh, 'tis nothing," said Sweyn, trying to maintain a shred of dignity.

"And I think perhaps building palisades, or earthworks that are defensible from our side, not yours, just to remind your naughty . . . shepherds . . . not to wander so far into Leofric's land again."

He stiffened, resisting, as she looked at him with one fine pale eyebrow cocked in warning. He frowned.

"Shall I call him over to ask if he would like that, or shall you trust my judgment on it?" Her fingers probed between the two sides of his cloak, coming to rest delicately beneath them on the decorative seam of his tunic. He pulled away, as if shocked by the touch. "I'll build the palisades," he offered almost desperately.

"And sign your mark to such a promise? Just so there is no confusion as to what we have discussed?"

"Yes," he growled.

"And might you show me the progress, if we meet seasonally at the border?"

"Very well," he said, a chastised child.

"Lovely," she said. She moved her small hand so that the flat of her palm rested on his chest. He inhaled sharply, at which she smiled apologetically. Then unnecessarily lowering her voice she added, "What a shame Leofric will not be able to join us. Will you mind terribly a rendezvous with me alone?"

"You alone with half a dozen of your husband's armed men, Countess. And no doubt a priest."

"I shall send them all on an errand for an evening," she whispered.

"Your methods of persuasion should be outlawed," Sweyn said. "And I am not the only one to think so." His handsome head nodded slightly to his right, and she glanced in that direction without quite turning her head.

When she saw whom he referred to, she pulled away from him on reflex, almost guiltily.

The redoubtable Abbess of Leominster was eyeing them from the Holy Corner of the king's drab wattle-and-daub hall, where all the religious congregated between sessions of the Great Council. Godiva could tell it was the abbess by her remarkably erect carriage, and because there was no decoration whatsoever on her garments, hanging shapeless and dark about her. It was too dim to read the Face Superior—what little of it showed—but Godiva, knowing her so well, could guess her thoughts.

To avoid dwelling on them, Godiva turned her head in the other direction and saw her husband's broad, slightly slouching silhouette near the hall door. He too had been eyeing them.

She stepped back from Sweyn abruptly again, as if they had been practicing a dance move and the musician had suddenly been shot. "Thank you, darling Hereford, I shall have His Majesty's cleric take down your mark this evening after whatever tries to pass as supper." And then, dropping all pretense of playfulness, she asked him firmly, but not unkindly: "Was not this better than Leofric accusing you before the Council of armed incursions?"

Before he could answer, she swirled to her right and walked, graceful and swift, toward the hall door where Leofric of Mercia awaited her.

Sweyn watched after her a moment, and then ruefully rubbed his face with both hands. *Someday she will be old,* he reminded himself. *And will stop having this effect on everyone.*

He glanced guiltily at the abbess, but could not read her expression in the dim light.

"And he will himself build the palisades for us," she said, her cheek resting on Leofric's bare chest. "Under our supervision. Defensible from our side only. He will sign his mark to it tonight."

"How great a danger do you rate him?"

She grimaced dismissively. "'Tis nothing serious. An impulsive youthful escapade in amorality, nothing strategic or even considered. Let it go, love. I've scared him into knowing better."

They were naked together, wrapped in Leofric's woolen mantle, in the feed room of the king's stables.

"I am too old for this," he said, regarding the setting of this clandestine tryst during the Great Council's dinner break.

"No you are not, you're merely spoiled from so many nights in feather beds," she said with breezy affection. "Also," she continued, fidgeting with the Woden amulet around his neck, "it is only nine men-at-arms that the redheaded thane at the Northumbrian border has to call upon for service, not fifteen as he told you. One from Wessex, if that makes any difference."

"It doesn't—but he admitted to *fewer* men? I'd think he'd have exaggerated to impress you."

"Oh, no, he claims he has no *need* of more men than that. He does all the heavy soldiering himself, whatever that is supposed to mean. If I'm ever widowed or deserted, he'd be honored to show me what a *man* he is."

"Of course he would." His hand absently, affectionately, closed over hers, his rough thumb caressing her soft knuckles.

"I love the way your skin smells," she said, "as if you have been out in the moors in the rain when the gorse is blooming."

"The gorse is always blooming," Leofric said, now stroking her pale hair. "Save your seductive commentary for the men who cannot have you."

"And you assume you can have me, just like that?" She grinned up at him. "You do not believe you must needs earn me?"

He harrumphed. "A good thing I do not, as I would fail in the attempt, grey as I am."

Godiva shifted within the woolen cloak, wishing the boards beneath them were cushioned with some hay. She tugged at his beard. "This is not grey, but silver." She smiled with a girlish overbite, a private affectionate expression she saved just for him. "Yours is the silver that purchases my heart."

"Spare me your poetic hogwash," he said, sounding pleased, and kissed her.

In the time it takes to jog a mile, they were clothed again, oat husks swatted briskly off each other, and strolling back into the great hall. Here men and women were still milling and mulling in the lee of what had passed as Lenten dinner. Some of the more devout were praying at portable altars the king had set up around the perimeters of the hall. The trestle tables were being set away, the slops distributed for pigs and servants. Servants lifted and moved the benches and the few stools to create an awkward oblong corral with the king's high-backed painted chair nearest to the fire pit. Lords, ladies, bishops, thanes, and all their retinues were moving like contrasting tides, some inward bound, some outward, some busy, some waiting. The earnest and abashed young Sweyn of Hereford had doffed his leather cape to demonstrate some wrestling moves to an admiring thane. In a few moments the final session of the Great Council would convene. And then eventually, thank God, adjourn.

"There you are." She heard the abbess's resonant alto. Godiva smiled and turned toward the voice, oddly maternal in one so young and delicate.

"Edey," she said, kissing Edgiva's cheek.

Abbess Edgiva kissed her back without smiling, then glanced at Leofric, her expression questioning.

"Yes, I saw her with Sweyn," he assured Edgiva. "In fact, I set her on him. I noticed you watching like an anxious chaperone from a distance. Just as the fellow himself is now watching us anxiously. Do not turn, he's directly behind you, Mother."

"Perhaps he worries you are cross at him," Godiva said to her husband.

"About poaching our sheep?" Leofric said drily.

"About Godiva throwing herself at him in view of you," Edgiva corrected.

"Oh, that," said Leofric dismissively.

"I will never understand you two," the abbess said, blue eyes glancing from one to the other. "I believe you are devoted in your marriage, and yet Godiva behaves like a heathen strumpet almost daily."

"I do *not*," Godiva rebuked her affectionately. "I simply find flirting an effective way of getting a man's complete attention while conveniently disarming him at the same time."

"It is remarkable," Leofric assured the abbess, "what crumbs of information men share with her that never would they share with me."

"It is because you are not as pretty as I am," Godiva said.

The abbess pursed her lips to repress both a grudging smile and chastisement. Her fingers—strong fingers, so out of place in a woman of such physical refinement—worried the rosary hanging from her undertunic. Godiva always suspected this was just a nervous habit, and that she would find as much comfort in worrying a river stone or an amulet of polished oak.

"My behavior hardly differs from your own, Edey," the countess said. Sweyn had dismissed his wrestling partner and was indeed staring at them, apparently fighting off the urge to fidget, inching toward them. She pretended not to notice. "I use my beauty and you use your righteous gift of rhetoric, each to persuade men to behave as we believe they ought."

"I persuade by winning over their higher faculties," Edgiva retorted, "You, my daughter, appeal to their basest impulses."

"We both achieve results, so what does it matter which means we use? We are neither of us abusing anyone."

Although they had this conversation nearly every time they saw each other, Edgiva plunged into it again: "Are not you abusing your marriage vows with such behavior?"

"On the contrary, I applaud her skill," said Leofric heartily. "While I exert my might and my right, she exercises subtler influence over the workings of the world."

"I have nipped in the bud illicit affairs that might have destabilized the kingdom," Godiva offered as example.

"You have promoted friendly marriages," Leofric added agreeably.

"I have negotiated the fostering of noble scions."

"Indeed you have. You," he concluded, gazing at her with such admiration it almost made the abbess blush, "are a self-appointed matchmaker, not only of marriage but of harmonious relationships of all kinds. It is"—here he turned his attention back to Edgiva—"a talent inborn and unteachable, and rarer than military skill or political savvy. I would be a fool to consider it abuse."

"Why thank you, husband." As if noticing the Earl of Hereford for the first time, she called out genially, "Earl Sweyn, how do you? Join us. We have quite concluded complaining of you. I believe we are about to begin complaining of me."

The young man reddened to his ears, and with leather cape draped over one arm, and a grim smile, he began to walk toward them, as casually as he could manage it, but looking as if he did not really wish to arrive.

"You are not always so enamored of her," Edgiva was meanwhile insisting to Leofric. "I have heard you groan about her behavior often enough."

"Yes," Godiva agreed comfortably. "Occasionally he even wants to divorce me."

"Occasionally you are very foolish with your . . . talents," Leofric said. "Remember with King Harold's—"

"Will you never let me live that down?" Godiva sighed.

"You propositioned Harold Harefoot?" the abbess demanded, eyes widening.

"Of course not," Godiva said in a disgusted voice. And then brightening, she pitched her voice just over Edgiva's shoulder: "Welcome, Sweyn. You are arrived in good time to hear my husband thoroughly embarrass me. I believe you will enjoy the story."

The abbess's face had grown stony, and she took a step away with the gravity of a religious ritual. Leofric, desiring an attentive audience, reached out and rested an avuncular hand on the arm of Sweyn, who, dressed all in fawn-colored leather, now looked like a trapped deer.

"When Godiva was still young," Leofric began, "Harold Harefoot was the king, and one of his housecarls took an interest in her."

"I remember this," Edgiva said, relenting, returning her attention to them.

"Understand, I had nothing to gain from his interest," Godiva told Sweyn emphatically. "He was no threat to either Leofric or me; there was no information, favor, or agreement we wanted from him. There was no reason to encourage him."

"Not that Godiva *always* needs a reason to encourage men," said Leofric cheerfully, smiling at Sweyn, whose blush was now so deep it verged on purple.

"But he was very forward," said Godiva, also to Sweyn. "He actually intended to get under my skirts, where I had no intention of allowing him."

Leofric continued: "After dinner, somehow—she claims she knows not how this happened—"

"And I don't!" said Godiva. "Only that I was exceptionally naive and foolish—"

"Pinned, she was pinned against the outer wall of the stable," her husband continued. "She was trying to stop him, of course, because she did not want to be fined for allowing a man to grope her in public—"

"That was not my prime concern—"

"—but he would not be dissuaded. He told her that I already knew myself to be a cuckold and I would not care, which is not true, by the way," he said, a confiding aside to Sweyn, who looked so mortified that Godiva genuinely felt pity for him. She pressed a ringed hand against Leofric's hand to stop him, and took over the storytelling.

"I started to say 'I am not a whore,' but as I spoke the words I realized he would disregard that. So I decided to try a trick I learned from Edgiva—"

The abbess gasped, mortified. "What?" she demanded, crossing herself and turning almost as violet as Sweyn—at whom she glanced nervously. "I have *never*—"

"I mean the trick of indirect resistance," said Godiva. "Your hallmark tactic. That is all. Calm down, Mother." It was a rare treat to tell Edey to calm down, Edey being perhaps the calmest woman she had ever known. Turning her attention to Sweyn, and ignoring his blush, Godiva continued, "Since I could not overpower him and since I could not change his belief in what I was, I decided to use his perception of me against him. So I kept speaking, and what I said was, 'I am not a whore . . . whom you can afford.'"

"She said, 'I am sitting on a gold mine and there is a high charge to enter it,'" chuckled Leofric. "'You must pay the master of the mine—my husband. In person. With gold. And he has the privilege of witnessing it.' All of this, she said to the cur." He delivered this again to Sweyn, who appeared increasingly con- founded.

"And he looked just as you do now, Sweyn," Godiva said. "So I continued, 'Shall we seek him out? Come quickly, do let's find him!' He was so confused, I was able to push past him and back into the courtyard, where there were more people. He gave me a wide berth the rest of the Council. But that is not the best piece of the story." She gave him an expectant look.

"Pray continue," Sweyn said dutifully, clearly wishing he had never left off wrestling.

"I told both of these two about it that evening. Mother here grinned about it despite herself, although she was shocked." She winked at Edgiva, who reddened and looked away again. "But Leofric? Oh, dear. He groaned and rubbed his fingers at his tem- ples as he always does when he is distressed, and told me I would create the most atrocious trouble for both of us and he would divorce me if I did not cease flirting."

"In my experience, you have not obeyed him," Sweyn ob- served, embarrassed.

"But hear the coda," Godiva said, in a triumphantly concluding tone. "The next day, I charmed an elderly Danish lord into forgetting he was not supposed to tell any Britons how many new warships King Harold was to build, and certainly could see no harm in sharing that number with a young lady who was staring at him adoringly and trying to speak Danish. Leofric was grateful, and lifted his censure."

"Ah," said Sweyn, at a loss for further commentary.

The horn sounded near the king's chair to announce the recommencement of the Council, and Sweyn nearly swooned with relief.

CHAPTER 2

Gloucester

It was an hour later and the countess Godiva was bored almost to nausea.

At the time the Great Council was called in Gloucester, the ruling couple of Mercia had been in the small, recently resettled hamlet known as Coventry in one of Godiva's estates. With Leofric, whose wealth dwarfed hers, she had just endowed a new Benedictine monastery there. They had done so mostly because King Edward had—the moment he'd been crowned three years ago—expressed a desire to build a monastery there himself, and the ruling couple decided they would rather be patrons of a minster in their territory than allow the king that chance. Edward had been quite irritable about this, claiming sorrow not to found such an auspiciously sited abbey himself.

"The site is auspicious chiefly for being deep in the bowels of my earldom," Leofric had muttered to his wife. "An excellent harbor for his spies."

So they had leapt into building the monastery, although they usually saved their patronage for monasteries placed in other people's territories (providing an excellent harbor for *Leofric's* spies).

From Coventry to Gloucester was two days' ride in summer, but this being early spring and the nights still long, they had given themselves a leisurely three days for it. Godiva wished they had given themselves a fortnight and missed the Council entirely.

The crush of well-dressed bodies, Lenten-lean, provided heat in the smoky great hall. But not everyone was given to perfumery, and once they were settled onto benches, it was a pungent gathering. There had been such fuss about positioning. Only earls and bishops warranted stools; the rest made shift cramped together on benches. The king was flanked by two of his three great earls: Godwin to his right, Siward to his left. Leofric of Mercia had chosen not to play the game of who-sits-where and quietly joined his wife on a bench among the lesser gentry.

Only out of love, Godiva now forced her attention to the end of the hall where the Abbess of Leominster, poised and elegant, had risen to address her uncle, the king, comfortably situated in the room's only chair.

There stood her childhood friend; there sat the king, who always looked irked when a woman stood to speak; and to either side of him, sat the men Godiva liked to call "those other earls."

Godwin was that famous Godwin of Wessex: the most powerful man in England, more powerful than the king himself, and father of young Sweyn. He was tall and leathery faced with shoulders one could break rocks against.

Siward's eke-name was "the Stout." And not without reason.

But he was rumored to have pagan tendencies, and Godiva found that endearing.

Mother Edgiva declaimed gracefully, despite the shapeless dark robes that left nothing visible but the center of her face. Her voice resonated in the deeper tones of a woman twice her age. Godiva had always loved that voice and admired Edgiva in her rhetorical ecstasy. She had been pontificating gently since she was five, and she grew more splendid at it yearly.

And yet Godiva, in her red and gold and green layers of double-girdled tunics, her large gold and garnet necklaces weighing on her neck, clanking gently against her enormous circular pure-gold Byzantine brooch . . . Godiva remained bored almost to nausea. She already knew the intention of Edey's speech. At every Great Council, the abbess chronically agitated on behalf of those who had no direct voice here. This was foolhardy. Godiva cared about such people too, but lecturing about them to this Council was a waste of time.

". . . abolish the heregeld and dispense with the mercenary bodyguard," Edgiva was saying this time. "They are a reminder of a barbaric king and his barbaric rule. You cannot claim to have advanced the monarchy if you do not forswear them."

Of all the suggestions Edgiva had ever made at council, thought Godiva—giving slaves the rights of serfs, allowing priests' wives the same religious status as nuns, returning to certain elements of Roman governmental policies—this was by far the most unlikely.

"But Mother Edgiva," said King Edward, with a cloying smile, relaxing into his fur-trimmed leather cloak. "I do not tax the clergy or the Church. Your abbey is safe enough."

"I do not protest it for myself," she said. "I protest it surely on behalf of England." Her somberly sweet face, bright eyes, thick dark brows, turned to stare at the crowded hall. "Will none of you stand up with me on this? It is your subjects who suffer under the tax."

Her eyes rested meaningfully on Leofric, who frowned and looked straight at the floor. Godiva subtly stroked the back of his broad hand.

Rooted as an oak tree, slender as a sapling, Mother Edgiva began her litany: "We are battle-scarred from decades of invasions and strife. If we do not thrive, the invaders will come again. But we can only thrive by having a healthy population to provide food and materials and services to each other and to us. It is one thing to levy taxes that give rulers the means to care for their charges. But the heregeld was invoked by a despot, to pay his soldiers to keep all of us in submission to him. The perversion of that alone should make an enlightened monarch abolish it at once."

There was murmuring around the room, at this unsubtle slight to His Majesty. His Majesty scowled at the back of Edgiva's head, but said nothing. Serenely, as if oblivious to having just insulted Godwin's Anointed, she continued. "There should be no need to raise monies to pay mercenaries to protect His Majesty from his own subjects. The heregeld is obsolete and should be abolished."

There was a moment of silence. Then:

"Allow me the presumption, Mother, of explaining our silence."

Earl Sweyn of Hereford stood up, the eldest son of the most powerful man in England, and brother to the king by marriage.

He had regained the composure Godiva had robbed him of earlier, and had pushed his very short leather cloak back over his broad shoulders, drawing attention to their broadness. *Nicely done,* thought Godiva, who wished her handsome, broad-shouldered husband attended likewise to his presentation.

Sweyn strode to the open center of the gathering, toward Mother Edgiva and the king. "Mother, King Edward sits precariously on his throne, and we precariously keep him there. If I may be blunt, Your Majesty."

Edward gave him an annoyed look, but also an allowing gesture.

"This is not the reign of Harthacnut, for which we all rejoice, but His Majesty requires a whiff of despotism for just a few more years yet, lest he be perceived as ineffective, and slip off that throne we've placed him on."

This evoked murmurings from around the circle. Edward's expressionless face seemed suddenly made of stone.

"However, Mother . . ." Sweyn took another step toward her. It appeared to Godiva that the abbess—his senior by a decade—blushed slightly. "Once he has proven himself a goodly king, who knows himself a goodly king and therefore not needful of tyranny, I vow to instantly join your protest of what is, indeed, a heinous and unjust tax."

Then he abruptly fell on one knee at Edgiva's feet. She tensed, and her upright bearing grew even more upright. He grabbed her hand and pressed his lips to the back of it, met her eyes, and said, "If you scribe a petition, I swear upon my own paternity, Holy Mother, I shall be the first to put my mark to it when the time is ripe."

A murmuring rippled in the crowd, and Edgiva's face pinked.

"How gallant!" Godiva whispered to Leofric, from behind one yellow fluted sleeve.

"This is no time for amusements, Godiva," Leofric said. "He is challenging me." He rose. With deliberate steps he crossed the circle, somber and simple in his long wool cloak. The crowd hushed. This man carried the weight of a ruined town on his shoulders, and everyone there knew it.

"Likewise, in the name of Christ and Woden both, my support, Mother Abbess," he said, taking Edgiva's hand from Sweyn's grasp, and pressing his own lips to it. "When it is timely."

He turned his gaze to his chief rival and ally: Sweyn's father, Godwin.

Godwin, Earl of Wessex, dressed entirely in leather and violet, stood up from his stool to King Edward's right. He took Edgiva's hand from Leofric and kissed it without looking at her. "I match your oath," he said. Then, offering Edgiva's hand, as if it were a delicacy, he asked Earl Siward the Stout, "Will you join us?"

Siward stood in his northern weave of colors and received, then kissed, Edgiva's hand.

All eyes turned to the king, whose blue eyes glittered out from under frowning brows. Then:

"Excellent!" said Edward in a confoundingly cheerful tone.

He stood up from the chair, gangly tall, dressed in bright embroidered silks all trimmed with ermine, and reached to take Edgiva's hand from Siward. "I would be pleased to feel that I could safely repeal the heregeld. I leave it to you all to make that a possibility," he crooned in a slightly nasal tenor voice. Then he awkwardly flourished the abbess's hand, presenting it to the assembled lords and ladies and bishops as if it were a signed charter.

Edgiva's face had darkened, and now her brows pushed toward each other beneath her veil. "Do not belittle me, my lords," she ordered sharply, and retrieved her hand from her uncle. The lordly clutch of them unclutched somewhat, each taking a small step back. "You have just turned my request into an exercise in etiquette, in which each of you has spoken words that make you sound quite noble and yet not one of you has actually said anything at all. The situation is precisely what it was before I stood up to speak about it."

"I do not think so," said Edward. "For myself, I swear on the blood of Christ that I will think hard on how my earls might help me to feel more secure." Despite his pleasant expression, his tone was sinister. "I encourage them to do likewise."

Edgiva blinked and looked away. "Then I have nothing more to say, Your Majesty," she said in a flat voice. Underneath the discreet dark wimple and veil, her jaw was clenching with annoyance.

The earls of Wessex, Northumbria, and Mercia kissed the king's hand and returned to their seats. Sweyn stood up, paused a moment, as if to make sure everybody saw him, then bowed once more toward Edgiva. "Your servant ever, Mother," he said. He turned back toward his seat, providing Godiva with an excellent view of his attractive backside as he returned briskly to his place on the bench.

She glanced at Edgiva. Edgiva was looking at his attractive backside, too. And blushing.

"Edey has fallen for Sweyn," Godiva whispered confidingly to Leofric as he settled beside her.

"Stop that," he growled. "This is not the time."

"I think it is *exactly* the time," she replied pertly. She shifted her weight slightly, ruing the hard wooden bench, longing to arch and stretch her lower back. "Can you imagine a more beneficial match for us? My closest friend marries your rival's son, whose land borders ours? He is young and strong and able to fight off the Welsh and—"

"And she is an abbess, Godiva. She is not marrying *anyone*."

"She can leave the Church."

Leofric shot her a sardonic stare. "She glances at Sweyn's buttocks and so you think she will foreswear her sacred oaths?"

"So you noticed her looking at them too," said Godiva, as if that settled it.

CHAPTER 3

After several more catatonic hours of charters being witnessed and signed, and copies cut at odd angles from one large piece of parchment; of arguments resolved, appeals heard, declarations and resolutions drafted; of Edward (to Godiva's mind) reveling in a bias toward all churchmen's petitions and against all women's, finally the bells tolled for Vespers and the Great Council adjourned. The hall emptied out with a rapidity reflecting how fetid the air had become. Leofric went in search of his son Alfgar, who was attending as a thane; Godiva wished to join them, but there was something more urgent that required her attention first.

She allowed herself a luxurious, broad-armed stretch, sensing everyone in her vicinity giving her a passing glance. They all looked stiff and calcified inside their winter leathers; she loved the feline feeling of her garments. Even King Edward—who flashed her an unaccountably surly look as he passed by toward his private chambers—was not as comfortable in his furs as she was in all her silk.

Edgiva and Godiva, from years of habit, found each other just outside the main hall entrance. The sky was grey, the air moist and chill, but it was such a welcome change from inside the hall that it lightened them as if it were a sparkling midsummer morning. They stood together in silence, left hands lightly clasped, Godiva's fragile-looking one in Edgiva's sturdy one. They watched the straggling noblemen and noblewomen and bishops exit into the wan spring afternoon, taking in lungfuls of cool, clean air.

When traffic had drained beside the doorway, Edgiva dropped her friend's hand and gave her a solemn look. Godiva steeled herself for rebuke.

"You did not stand up with me," Edgiva said.

"Everyone knows our history. My support would bear no weight beyond a childish loyalty to you."

"Or a wifely loyalty to your husband," Edgiva returned without rancor. "Which is your Christian duty. When Leofric stood up, why did you not join him?"

"Because I knew what he was up to," Godiva said. "He wanted to put it to Godwin and Fatty—"

"His name is Siward—"

"He wanted what you wanted—for all three of them to equally endorse you. I'd have interrupted the *rhythm* of that," said Godiva. "But surely now that they have all pledged, it will be easier next time for you to rouse more people—"

"Starting with you, the wife of one of the earls."

"Please stop scolding me," Godiva said. "You do always *scold* me."

Edgiva softened her tone. "I do, yes, and I should not. But

it hurts my heart that you do not bother to use your position to forward a cause so obviously right. And so dear to me."

The lady of Mercia felt petulant, and then felt shame for feeling petulant. "Very well. Not only shall I support you next chance, I will see to it that others do as well. I think you should follow young Sweyn's suggestion. Charter a petition." Godiva grinned conspiringly. "And I shall convince all the lords to put their marks to it."

Edgiva's lovely blue eyes rolled in the direction of her thick dark brows, barely visible beneath her veil. "Convince," she echoed. "I know what that means."

"Never mind, then," said Godiva quickly. "I do not meddle where I am not asked to."

Edgiva looked abashed. "I am sorry to sound critical. Of course I would be grateful, although you know that I . . ." She hesitated.

"—Judge me," Godiva concluded for her firmly, without bitterness. "Yes, I know you judge me for my methods."

Edgiva winced. "Judgment is a harsh word," she said softly. "I leave judgment to God."

"Really? I leave it to you."

Edgiva closed her eyes and took a moment to consider her words. "That is a failing in me, if I have treated you as if I were your judge."

"I forgive you," Godiva said, thrown. If Godiva herself were as impeccable as Edgiva, she would cling to that distinction dearly, and deny any insult to her reputation. But Edey—in such a collected, reasoned Edey manner—resisted nothing, including Godiva's occasional complaints.

A fawn-toned figure stopped just outside the doorway, behind Edgiva. "Greetings," Godiva said cheerily to Sweyn. Edgiva turned in his direction, then immediately stopped and turned back toward Godiva. The color rose on her face.

Sweyn's eyes moved between them for a moment—that is, between Godiva's face and the back of Mother Edgiva's veiled head—and then with a careful smile, he took a step to join them. "I am quite beyond my depth in the presence of the two most beautiful ladies of the Council."

Edgiva blushed further and licked her lips. Godiva saw her check the urge to cross herself; instead, her left hand reached for her rosary, and nervously she fingered the fragrant pink beads. She studied the ground by her feet, as if hoping to find there written directions for conducting herself.

"You were a good man to stand up with me today," she said, not turning even a little bit toward Sweyn. "Although your father and the others made it a mockery, I am grateful for your action."

"They did not mock it, Mother," consoled Sweyn. "Of course they are genuine in wishing the heregeld to be abolished. I know no living soul who favors it. Even Edward himself, I think, finds it an unfortunate relic."

"So why does he not renounce it?" Edgiva demanded.

"For a king to renounce a source of control over his subjects is not a small thing," Sweyn said. "Especially for this king. He would need to replace it with some other means of control."

Godiva stopped listening to their conversation; she was rather watching them both.

She knew Sweyn's postures very well. There was a certain movement of his lower torso, a subtle arching of his back and hips, that Godiva could always elicit from him when she put her mind to it. The unspoken truth of this subtle movement was: *I will agree to whatever you ask, if you will only place yourself closer to me.* It did not matter that no man could actually have her. It was a natural response, etched into men by the most ancient of gods. Encouraging it was a kind of sacrament, an homage to the dance between body and soul. And, of course, a useful political tool for a woman surrounded by men.

But for all that, he was a sharp fellow, Sweyn. The first year of his earldom, he was malleable as clay and blushed through numerous erections Godiva pretended not to notice. The second year, he was a little cannier, and it required a brushing of her skirt against his outer thigh to get his full attention. Even then, she had failed to dissuade him from aligning himself with a certain Welsh prince whom Leofric detested. This year, his third in power, she'd had to be extremely forward when confronting him about the border violations. But eventually she'd coaxed from him that subtle arching of the hips, which always meant she could now press her advantage and get what she was after.

Now, he was arching his hips directly in Edgiva's direction, and Edgiva was not even looking at him.

She was not looking at him for the same reason that he was arching his hips at her.

Godiva had not seen it coming, but nothing under heaven was clearer to her. As a witness, she found it intoxicating. Excitement fluttered in her stomach, and she wished Leofric were there to hold her round the middle.

"I was telling Edgiva that if she follows your advice and creates a formal petition, I will help persuade the thanes and lesser earls to put their mark to it," she offered, interrupting their discussion.

Sweyn gave her the weary smile of the vanquished. "I predict you will be effective," he said.

Godiva fluttered her lashes at him playfully. Edgiva, still examining the ground, asked, "Are you fluttering your lashes now, Godiva?"

"Would you be disappointed if I weren't?"

"Not really," Edgiva said.

There was a silence, uncomfortable to earl and abbess, entertaining to Godiva. Somewhere across the courtyard, a goose honked suddenly, and several voices laughed in reaction.

"Well. I must find Leofric and Alfgar," Godiva said suddenly. "I bid you both Godspeed."

"I shall go with you," Edgiva said anxiously, her pitch rising almost to regular female tones. "I must thank Leofric for his support as well." She excused herself from Sweyn, having never once turned in his direction.

Godiva strode off through the crowded yard, intending to exit the manor property and stroll around the green, where she supposed her menfolk would be. It would be a wonderful change from the cooping-up of the last few days. There would likely be as many pigs as people in the streets, but at least the pigs would make less noise and smell more wholesome. And there would be trees and other reassurances of the natural world to keep the spectacle of human politics in perspective.

Edgiva followed close beside her.

"He is in deep," Godiva said, with a mischievous glance at Edgiva. The abbess's face paled.

"What mean you?" she demanded.

"Sweyn. He is utterly in love with you."

The abbess looked panicked and crossed herself. "That is terrible," she said, avoiding Godiva's eyes. "I am an abbess; it is terrible."

"Yes, it is terrible that you're an abbess, since that will complicate your marrying him."

Not quite to the manor gate, Edgiva stopped midstride and all her weight shifted to her back foot. *"What?"*

Godiva turned to her, smiling. "Edey, it is plain as wheat. There is a *glow* around the two of you. The spirits of the unborn babes who want you as their parents are shrieking at you to disrobe."

This brought an extraordinary look to Edgiva's face; Godiva had never so successfully horrified her.

"How can you say that to me?" Edgiva finally hissed, and her face crumpled.

"I'm sorry," Godiva said at once. "I did not realize you . . . realized." A pause, as two minor countesses minced by, eyeing them curiously. Once they were out of earshot, she asked, "When did this happen?"

Edgiva shook her head. "Suddenly. These past few days. From the moment I arrived and saw him. The last time our paths crossed, when he came to the abbey to receive a Bible from my nuns a month ago, there was no such attraction. I cannot fathom the reason for the change."

"Has anything happened between you?" Godiva asked hopefully.

The abbess glared and made a gesture to Godiva to speak softer. "Of course not!" she whispered. "I would not allow it."

"Has he tried?"

Edgiva raised her hands to cover her face and took a deep, unsteady breath. "I do not understand why God is testing me this way," she said in her low voice.

"So he *has* tried. What has he done? Edey, tell me what he's done, and I'll tell you what it means."

She lowered her hands and frowned at Godiva. "There are no *acts*. There is nothing in particular worth description."

She glanced uncomfortably about at the bustle around them: servants running in and out of the gate, a groom adjusting a horse's saddle as the rider waited huffing, a creaky wagon full of food being inspected by the porter while thanes and their wives skirted small piles of manure to get out of the yard. A small clutch of priests were debating something boring in low rumbling tones nearby; Edgiva looked especially wary of their proximity.

"There are only looks," she whispered, "and . . . gestures . . . and moving his body nearer to mine than is required, and . . ." She was flustered. "He offers to help me with things, mad things a nobleman would never help an abbess with—would you like company while you are praying, do you keep incense burning in your tent, and do you need me to help you light it—"

Godiva giggled.

"And I so desire to say yes! It terrifies me. It is an alien and heinous thing."

"It is natural and only right!" Godiva countered. "The world must be peopled—"

"But not by *me*," Edgiva said fiercely.

"Perhaps you are mistaken about that."

The abbess glanced nervously at the religious men again. "I took holy vows—"

"Edey, you were raised in that abbey," said Godiva, with impatient affection. "It is the only home you've known. Nobody ever asked you if you felt a calling; from the moment you arrived on English soil, barely out of swaddling clothes, it was understood that Queen Emma's granddaughter Edgiva would be the next Abbess of Leominster. You were never given a choice."

"Whoever is?" Edgiva argued. "You were not asked if you would *like* to marry and—"

"It is my choice to stay married," Godiva argued back. "Leofric and I could each divorce the other if we so chose. Our vows to each other were no less holy than yours were to the Church, but if either of us decides it is folly to remain together, we have the right to untie our knot. You should have the same right. The Church can toss you out if you displease her; why cannot you toss out the Church?"

Edgiva huffed with an anxious exasperation. "Because I've no wish to. This is mad. Even for you, this is mad. You haven't ever fathomed my devotion, which is very deep and very real, even if I chafe sometimes at the constrictions of its outer forms. Just because I am tempted to sin does not mean I have lost my calling. Indeed, I become more aware of my vocation because of it."

"Well of course you do, since your vocation is the only thing that makes your desire a sin," Godiva said reasonably.

"That is mere rhetoric, and faulty rhetoric at that," Edgiva said. She began to walk off, as if toward the stables. "It was foolish of me to confess anything to you. You are not the proper partner for this conversation."

"I agree," Godiva said, rushing to walk beside her still. "Shall I fetch Sweyn instead?"

The abbess's face reddened all the more. "I must keep a distance from him until I am able to return to Leominster," she said. "Will you help me with that?"

"Would you not rather I spend my energies convincing the lords to condemn the heregeld?" Godiva said.

Edgiva, failing to find levity in any of this, fretted thoughtfully. "The heregeld is most important," she declared in her mellifluous, omnipotent voice, composed again.

"Well," said Godiva. "Since you say so, I'll get right to it."

CHAPTER 4

Godiva had arrived here with three goals, all of which she had accomplished to Leofric's satisfaction.

First, she had elicited Sweyn's promise to contain his "poachers."

Next, she had convinced the thane of Hedingelei to send his son to Abingdon for fosterage, so that the boy's travel would all be through Mercia, although Hedingelei was under Siward and Abingdon under Godwin. Both households would want passage to be safe, and so they would be friendly toward Leofric and encourage their overlords to be so too.

Finally, there was upset between an abbot and a noblewoman, both Mercian; each intended to use the occasion of the Council to appeal their case to Leofric behind the other's back. Godiva had subtly mediated their argument without either of them realizing it, and as soon as they were feeling generous toward each other, she sent Leofric's son Alfgar to adjudicate their argument. They resolved their differences; Alfgar was honored to have had a chance to play his father's deputy; and Leofric was relieved to be excused from dealing with the problem himself.

So she was free now, on this final night before the lords and ladies of the land disassembled, to pursue Edgiva's project: the petition to abolish the heregeld. There were dozens of lords she could charm, but that was inefficient. So after parting from Edgiva in the courtyard, she did not go out to the green in search of Leofric, but rather returned to the manor hall.

It was emptier in here than she had seen it since their arrival. Some household servants were taking advantage of the quiet to mend benches broken by the collective weight of all those noble buttocks; other servants were bringing in wood. Countess Godiva regarded the room for a moment, then walked straight toward a familiar figure in the king's livery.

"How does one obtain a private audience with His Majesty?" she asked Alden, royal chamberlain.

She had known Alden for years. They were fond of each other. Not given to women himself, he knew her behavior for what it was and occasionally placed wagers with select friends as to her success in certain enterprises.

Alden asked her to wait and efficiently scurried to the far end of the hall, disappearing through a curtain covering a bolted door. A moment later, he appeared and gestured for her to join him.

He led her through the door into the royal bedchamber where Edward and his bride, Edith, were resting before supper. Edith was dressed in layers of pink silk that Godiva found unfortunate for her complexion. Standing around the periphery of the room, bored but obsequious, were several of His Majesty's favorite housecarls; the thane who guarded the royal wardrobe;

His Majesty's treasurer, Odo of Winchester; a bishop she did not know; and two hooded ladies in blue waiting upon Her Majesty.

Gloucester being an infrequent stop on Edward's circuit, the room lacked the ravishing adornments Godiva expected; indeed, it was plainer than Leofric's chambers in Brom Legge. A crucifix mounted on one wall and painted eggs along the one windowsill were the only decoration in an otherwise drab space. The room was candlelit and crowded. This would not work to her advantage, especially with Edith glaring at her.

Edith was a mystery Godiva could not decipher. A decade earlier, while Edward was still peacefully cloistered on the Continent, his brother Alfred had left Normandy to claim the English throne. Earl Godwin had shown up to meet Alfred when he landed on the shores of Sussex. He had welcomed Alfred and his bodyguards, accompanied them inland, swearing all of England eagerly awaited to put Alfred (son of a former king) on the throne . . . and then, even as he spoke these words, Godwin's men killed Alfred's guards as Godwin took Alfred hostage, blinded him, and piously sent him off to die in a monastery in the Fens.

This had made an impression on Alfred's brother Edward.

Now, eleven years and several dead sovereigns later, Edward was on the throne, and Godwin's own daughter Edith was his wife. How pleased could either Edith or Edward be about this marriage? Godiva was still trying, and failing, to determine that.

Now she bowed low, rose, and said, "Your Majesty."

"Yes?" Edward said curtly, from the bed.

She was not sure how she would have proceeded, had not she

been abetted by Fate in the form of Sweyn Godwinson, with his jaunty flung-back cloak, who appeared at the door that very moment and said, "Sister!" to the queen, and entered, without waiting for permission.

Edith turned her hawk stare from Godiva to her brother. "Sweyn," she said carefully.

"Sister, you asked to see the new Bible from Leominster, and Mother Edgiva has just delivered it to me. I am about to send it home to Hereford, where you seldom come, so this may be your last chance to see the excellent penmanship of the nuns. It is rare to have a manuscript illuminated by sisters, sister." He grinned at her, and said with the coaxing tease of a brother, "I think you would appreciate it."

Edith got to her feet and went somewhat icily with her brother. Sweyn dared to wink one soft brown eye at Godiva before he left, which made her heart leap a little, pleasantly: he was removing the queen because he had, somehow, intuited Godiva would appeal privately to the king about the heregeld, and he wanted to assist her. No, not really—he wanted to assist Edgiva. Godiva would mention that to her.

Edith's two women went as well, which seemed to dismay Edward, as the lady of Mercia was now the only woman in a private room with him and his men.

"Your Majesty," she said with another bow. "I thank you much for meeting me during your period of leisure."

"What would you?" he asked brusquely. "Between your friend and your husband I am quite worn down."

"I was remiss in my behavior today, at Council," she said, eyes downcast, fingers playing with the ruby on her heaviest gold chain, not unlike how Edgiva fidgeted with her rosary. "I should have spoken plainly at a certain moment, but was too cowardly to do so."

"You wish me to abolish the heregeld," he interrupted tiredly.

"More than that," she offered. "I wish to suggest how you may immediately render it unnecessary."

"I already know how to do that," Edward said stiffly to his bed's wool canopy. "I need only admit that your husband and the others hold all the power. I need only yield the slightest interest in actually ruling."

"That is not what I was going to say at all," Godiva assured him.

"They placed me on the throne as their puppet, and I am dangerously close to being, in fact, nothing but their puppet. I have almost nothing of my own; I should take something from the earls just to demonstrate my power. To give up the heregeld is to give up my own forces, which is to give up even the *appearance* of power."

She took an urgent step closer, so that she was nearly towering over the mattress. He glowered, and the housecarls shifted their weight forward. Instantly she sank to her knees, her pale gold-green eyes blinking up at him, framed by the gold-and-scarlet veil. The room smelled, for some reason, like drying hay. "You were never their puppet, sire," she said firmly. "I think you do not realize how much power you truly have. You were—and are—the only choice for the throne. You have no heirs yet, sire, nor is there anyone fool enough to supplant you. Godwin is the only man with the means to try, but if he did that, my husband and Siward would join to defeat him. Your kingship is the only means to keep the balance."

He gave her a puzzled blue-eyed frown. "Exactly. That is why I require the heregeld. How can you say these things and then suggest I abolish the only way I have of securing my position, woman?"

"You miss my meaning, sire. Abolishing the heregeld now would be an act of brilliant statesmanship, for you would be telling all the earls that you know they will keep you on your throne, *even without* a private army to protect you." She leaned in slightly closer to him and rested her hand upon the woolen bedcover. Alden cleared his throat warningly and the frowning housecarls took a step toward her; she withdrew her hand and pressed it to her chest, again fingering her necklaces. "Disband your mercenary bodyguard. Rely on the *fyrd*—your lords, and their men under them—to perform defense, as it was in our fathers' fathers' time, stretching back to the days of Rome. Behave as if you've nothing to fear from your earls—what could demonstrate more strength than that?"

Edward glanced over her head into the dusky corner of the small room. He was considering it. Edgiva would be so pleased with her!

"Not to mention the adoration you would receive," she added, "from all corners of England. Tell the masses their lords are such loyal and devoted subjects to your rule that it is now possible to do away with the heregeld. Then, the lords are pleased because you have extolled them to their people. The people are pleased because you have guaranteed them calm and safety. The lords *and* the people are pleased because the heregeld goes away. Everyone is satisfied."

Edward huffed, sardonically, and returned his watery gaze to her face. "There is no event in history in which *everyone* is satisfied," he informed her.

"The few who are not, they are malcontents who never will

be satisfied anyhow," she argued. "And who, if they wanted to sow discord, would do so even if you had the largest mercenary bodyguard in all of Christendom." She caught herself, realized she had been earnest and hearty where usually she would be deliberate and coy. She had actually used a tone with him she only ever used with Leofric, a voice nearly male, in that it was not deliberately feminine. It was not her coaxing voice.

She took a moment, to regain her coaxing voice.

She slowed her speaking, and fixed her gaze on his lips. "Those who matter will be very . . . satisfied with you," she said coaxingly. "Speaking as one of them, I swear it." Here she carefully lowered her chin but kept her eyes lifted up, and met his. She began to reach out toward the coverlet again, but thought better of it. Instead she leaned her upright body toward the bed.

He looked at her a long moment without speaking. The room was very still. "It would *satisfy* you?" he asked.

She smiled. "Yes, sire," she said, lowering her voice to near a whisper. "It would satisfy me greatly." She immediately blushed—being able to blush at will was a tremendous advantage for her, and the shade of red in this particular veil always made the blush look deeper. She sat back a little and shifted her shoulders. "And I am sure many others as well, sire," she added. Here she glanced over her left shoulder and smiled winsomely at Odo of Winchester.

Edward considered her. "I hear something untoward in your tone," he warned.

She blushed again, this time without meaning to. "I am sure I do not know what Your Majesty mea—" she stammered.

"Stop that," Edward interrupted harshly. He sat up, right suddenly, glaring at her. "You know precisely what I mean."

The bishop and a thane or two coughed, shifted their weight, frowned ponderously.

She opened her mouth in protest, reconsidered, and pressed her lips shut. She was blushing so intensely the skin around her nose ached. She clutched her hands together, almost prayerlike, at her breast, and bowed her head. "I am sure Your Majesty will be generous enough to disregard any . . . untoward comments I appeared to have been making."

"I would do that willingly, with a generous heart, if I thought your shame at this moment were sincere," Edward said harshly. He swung his long legs around so that his feet were on the floor by her; she jerked away from him, as if he might strike her. "But I have seen you, Godiva; I have watched how you speak to men when you want something from them. I can count the different shades of red you turn, depending on your purpose—which is usually Leofric's purpose. The argument you've brought to me is not unsound—you may tell your beloved Edgiva as much, for I am sure she is the author of it. It does not give me the power to actually hobble the great earls, and I need that more than anything, but as I said: it is not unsound. Sadly, the very fact you are delivering it in this *manner* that you do requires me to shun it."

"What manner?" she demanded, looking up at him, hands still clasped before her chest worrying the rubies on her necklace.

Edward said stonily, "If you had trusted your argument enough to simply tell it to me, I would heartily have heard it. But now, to accept your argument is to accept the manner of its presentation, and I'll not do that. I will not have you say that you seduced me into listening to you."

"Your Majesty!" she protested. Quickly she collected her three layers of silk tunic-skirts and rose to standing.

"None of that, Godiva," he said in a disgusted, nasal tenor voice.

"I would never say that—"

He stood up and towered over her; she winced from the suddenness of it. He was a tall man and spoke directly downward to the top of her head. "Of course you would not *say* it. You would *imply* it. You are a mistress of the indirect, do you think I do not know it? I've watched you at your work, Godiva, I know your rule. If your plea includes so much as an inviting smile, I must reject the plea, or I will be perceived as having fallen for the smile."

"Perceived by whom?" she demanded, trying to think how to salvage this. She had not expected any such astuteness from him; he had seemed socially inept in the past.

Edward sat on the bed again and gestured around the room. "You have done it before witnesses! Foolish woman, that is your great error. You shall get no satisfaction from me. You are dismissed. See her out, Alden, and then explain to me why you let her enter in the first place."

And with that he lay back on the bed, brought his muddy boots upon the gold coverlet, and closed his eyes.

CHAPTER 5

Having failed to attain royal endorsement, Godiva now pursued the ecclesiastical.

Only the three great earls and the two archbishops were accommodated, all together with their retinues, in the hall. The rest of the Council attendees brought tents and pavilions and made shift in the courtyard or out on the green. Happily the weather had been agreeable for March, but Godiva was glad not to be among those awakening with cold dew on her face. On the other hand, it would have been a welcome change to go out into the clear air more regularly, rather than continually inhaling everybody else's exhales, as they had been.

However, having cleansed their lungs, most of the attending bishops retreated to the Holy Corner of the hall until dinnertime, enjoying the respite from Compline services and their more trying Lenten duties. Some half-score men in unseasonably vibrant silk dalmatics, albs, and hooded mantles, their necks and shoulders weighed down by chains and rosaries that put Godiva's to shame, stood about together muttering importantly. Near them, a half-dozen women in darker but still highly decorated garments, far too decorated for Lent—even Godiva knew that—clustered together around the celestially contained Mother Edgiva of Leominster.

Edgiva stood out for being starkly unadorned. She was always uncompromising in her costume. *She looks like the Virgin Mary dressed in mourning,* thought Godiva, reflexively checking that her own veil showed off her pale forehead. The other religious women wanted Edgiva's attention; there was an adoration there which she either did not notice or ignored. If Godiva did not know her so well, she would think her friend was lost in prayer.

But Edgiva seldom prayed—not in private, not the way the nuns had taught them to as young girls. She led her congregation through certain accepted sections of the daily services, but left to her own time she was more likely to be fretting silently about the rights of slaves than about her own immortal soul. To her, that was a kind of prayer. She would cross herself and count her rosary, but Godiva was certain that was no more "religious" than the way she herself fidgeted with her jewelry. Godiva decided that Edey was probably now fretting about the heregeld. Or perhaps Sweyn's attractive backside. She returned her attention to the prelates.

The man Godiva most wished to speak with was her friend, the sternly handsome, reed-slender Shepherd of Worcester, Bishop Lyfing. But Lyfing lay ailing in Tavistock Abbey; his subordinate, Aldred, was at the Council in his stead.

Lyfing and the ruling couple of Mercia had, for years, shared prejudices and preferences. King Harthacnut, almost as soon as he was crowned, had removed Lyfing from the Worcester see, accusing the bishop of murder. He restored Lyfing to Worcester just in time for Harthacnut to raze the town for its infamous tax refusal. There were probably no men alive who spat on Harthacnut's memory more than Lyfing and Leofric when they were in their cups together.

Besides his political alliance with Leofric, Bishop Lyfing was one of the few men of the cloth not appalled by Countess Godiva's industrious eyelash-batting. Other bishops endured her methods because she and Leofric sagely made enormous donations to several outlying religious houses. But Lyfing was indulgent of Godiva's mischievousness. He understood her. He was himself unorthodox to a degree his peers found alarming. He was not a dogmatic man; indeed, he regularly performed the Land Ceremony Charm with the farmers around Worcester. He saw it as a way to infuse Christianity into paganism, while other Church authorities saw it as a dangerous incursion of paganism into the lives of Christians. Many were the bishops who would have rejoiced at his expulsion, but preoccupied with their own machinations, they settled for spreading gossip about him in the hope that Rome might take an interest. The gossip—that Lyfing was a heathen-lover, a heretic, a pluralist—fell indifferently on the ears of his flock. To those he shepherded, Lyfing was known and beloved chiefly for consoling and rebuilding Worcester after the heregeld razing.

Godiva was very fond of Lyfing. And she knew that he would sign a petition.

But his deputy, Aldred . . . Brother Aldred was a different creature, their physical contrast a living metaphor. There was Lyfing's sleek frame and calm deportment—"flexible as a blade of grass no wind can bend," as Leofric oft said of him—and then there was his deputy's thickset, ungraceful carriage, suggesting a heavy tree that even a breeze could buffet.

Aldred had attended the Great Council for three years now—as long as Sweyn had been an earl, as long as Edward had been king. He had always attended as Lyfing's subordinate. When Lyfing was absent for illness, Aldred always deflected, refusing ever to take a position on behalf of his superior. He had signed his name as a witness to charters, but on anything requiring policy, he declined to give counsel. Godiva and Leofric had no idea where he stood on anything. Leofric hypothesized that perhaps he was spineless by nature and thus could not stand at all.

He was certain to be the next Bishop of Worcester. Surely *any* Bishop of Worcester would want to see the heregeld abolished. How to make such a quiet, retiring one speak up, then? Godiva wondered.

Brother Aldred was just past the prime of life. He was from a wealthy Devonshire family and held estates from the Church, so he was not in need of material largesse and therefore he could not be bribed or rewarded. His face was pink and pudgy and his hair a thinning mouse brown, his body mercifully indistinct beneath his vestments. But he seemed comfortable in his homeliness, so appealing to his vanity would get her nowhere, and besides, after the embarrassment with Edward, she did not want to be called out for eyelash-batting. She would have to appeal to his sense of righteousness. She hoped he had one.

She glanced at the men of the Holy Corner. Brother Aldred was not among them. She wandered the crowded hall, ill-lit with rush lights and growing pungent again as people brought the twilight and their own odors back inside with them, and finally found him near the entrance to the kitchens.

Servants had pitched tents outside the hall to accommodate the extra food and preparation to feed so many bellies, even in this lean season. Aldred had taken it upon himself to hear confession of the kitchen workers. Perhaps this assured him a better selection of the wrinkled parsnips and salted trout. He'd set a stool near to the kitchen screen, where he was sheepishly examining several crudely half-painted eggs that had been set down, almost carelessly, upon a pile of strewing herbs. Servants scurried to make way around him; he was in the way and did not realize it, he was so self-absorbed. Important to know.

She pulled her scarlet veil modestly down over her brow, which felt slightly claustrophobic, as it had all those childhood years in Leominster Abbey. She commanded his attention with a nod and a smile. He stood when he saw her, but seemed unwilling to forsake his prime spot by the screen. For the sake of the servants as much as her own, Godiva gestured him to cross toward her, closer to the central fire pit.

"Your Eminence," she said with a smile as he waddled in her direction. "I wish to speak to you on behalf of my foster-sister, Edgiva of Leominster. She is seeking a quorum of wise men who might, at the next Council, beseech His Majesty to abolish the heregeld. She is concerned that nobody is willing to do anything about this."

He gave her a distracted smile. "Countess, do not disturb yourself about it. There was great promise today in the earls' oaths."

"I do not think so," Godiva said. "And I believe that if His Eminence Lyfing had been here, he would have stood with Edgiva."

"He has not done so in the past," said Aldred thoughtfully, fingering his rosary as if the gesture were a nervous tic.

"His Majesty has not been married in the past," Godiva pointed out. "The marriage changes things. There will surely be an heir soon, and by marrying Edith he has healed his relationship with Godwin, which was the most volatile obstacle of his reign. So I do not agree with Sweyn about the need for despotism."

He gave her a look. Godiva was familiar with that look. It was the look men gave her upon realizing she had enough intelligence to actually speak of things. "The young earl made a valid point," he countered, almost apologetically. "We are not yet recovered from the turmoils of a generation. Naturally the king wants to maintain an independent army."

"Until the mercenary army is eliminated, there is no possible way for the earls to trust the king—partly because of what happened at Worcester, partly because it upsets the natural order of the kingdom. He should surround himself only with his own men and the men his earls and thanes provide him. His army should be *us*, not *them*. Lyfing said exactly that to me. Has not the bishop ever said as much to you?"

"No," said Aldred, embarrassed. He added, hurriedly, "His Eminence and I seldom discuss political matters. Until he raised me to subordinate bishop, I was an abbot, and cloistered, and not much concerned with secular matters of any sort."

Godiva doubted this was true—she could not imagine any powerful family allowing even its least-promising member to grow up ignorant of politics. But it was typical of Aldred, to decline adding his own voice to any matter.

"Well, I have had conversations with His Eminence on this topic," she said. "You would be acting in his interests and supporting his beliefs to add your name to a rostrum of great men who would see the tax repealed." She gave him her ingenuous-yet-serious look and repressed an instinct to smile coyly.

He looked thoughtful. "I try to please His Eminence in all ways," he said.

"Then you had best support this petition of Edgiva's," she advised.

He pursed his lips. "I suppose I am willing, *conditionally*, to have my name associated with those who would beseech the king."

Success! She repressed an urge to cackle gleefully. "I will let the abbess know at once," she said quickly. "I am sure she will want to express her thanks to you most fervently. As do I." That had been so effortless.

"But I will not put my mark to a petition until I have spoken personally with His Eminence once I am home to Tavistock."

"Do you not think it wise counsel?" she said, surprised. "After all, what is your opinion of His Majesty?"

"I do not see why that matters," Aldred said uncomfortably, his large cheeks reddening a bit. He had not once met her gaze fully. "I myself am . . . waiting to see what Edward makes of himself," he added with excessive neutrality.

"As am I," she said, reassuringly. "As is Leofric. And everyone else here, I am sure. Of course," she added brightly, "if he does abolish the heregeld he will make friends much faster than if he doesn't."

"Yes," said Aldred, blowing out air from between fat pink lips. "But it is an enormous thing to demand of a monarch who is trying to establish his own power. And he is, you know, preoccupied with establishing his own power."

She considered him. Might he be won by appealing not to his sense of justice, but rather to his ambition? She did not like to play that card—the only man's ambition she approved of was her husband's—but she wanted his support for Edgiva.

"Perhaps you might make yourself useful to His Majesty and encourage him to feel at ease with this proposal. It seems to me he has yet to take any particular Saxon prelate as a favorite. It might be in your interest to present yourself as a friendly counselor."

He looked startled, and then blushed. "I forget you are a woman of the world," he said, awkwardly. "I do not think that way. If His Majesty were to call upon me for assistance, I would of course be honored to assist him, but I am not as yet convinced he is made of such material as I would choose to align with." For the first time he met her gaze. She was surprised to see his piggy eyes were a startlingly strong, deep brown, expressive and intense. For a moment she could imagine an earnest, insecure, intelligent child who chose the Church for refuge and Lyfing for a father. "Do not forget, my lady, I have been at Bishop Lyfing's elbow for years now. It would take a man of tremendous integrity to win my confidence as much as Lyfing ever did."

"How dear of you to say so!" she said, warmly. This meant more to her even than Edgiva's petition. "There are so few who will admit to his goodness so freely; it is not in style to do so. You gladden me to speak this." She grabbed both of his hands in both of hers, and pulled him to her and kissed him briefly upon the lips.

"What an appalling act of harlotry, under my roof, against a man of the Church," said an angry, nasal voice behind her. Shocked, she released the bishop's hands and spun around to see long-legged Edward staring at her.

Aldred stumbled backward and nearly stepped into the fire pit, gasping. "Sire, she was only expressing—" he began, grasping his rosary so hard Godiva worried he might crush the beads.

"Do not make excuses for her," Edward said in a voice simmering with disgust. "You are enough of an innocent not to realize her power over—"

"I was thanking him for his good words about a man we both respect," Godiva interrupted.

"That is not how one publicly thanks a bishop for *anything*," said Edward fiercely. He returned his attention to Aldred. "Whatever she was trying to convince you of, dismiss it. Go off into some corner and pray or meditate awhile, and when your senses are quite cleared of her lascivious shadow, ask yourself to reconsider what she was trying to convince you of, and see then, in the clear light of reason, if it is something you in fact believe."

"Of course it will be," said Godiva impatiently, and Aldred, looking hapless, crossed himself.

Edward grabbed her wimple-covered chin harshly between his gloved finger and thumb. "Stop talking, Countess," he advised. He released her. She brought her hand to her face, in part to stop her own mouth from saying something else she would regret. All the muscles of her rib cage tightened, and she could not breathe.

Edward turned and walked away.

CHAPTER 6

T hat evening, after the wan Lenten supper of unseasoned oysters and drab root vegetables, just before the evening exodus to tents and pavilions in the courtyard, Godiva again approached the Holy Corner. She and Aldred awkwardly ignored each other. But then, with the beaming excitement of a child, she gestured Edgiva to come toward the corner where Leofric's entourage would sleep.

"I have won over two thanes and an earl," she whispered, with delighted pride. "And my stepson Alfgar, of course, will do whatever I ask of him."

Edgiva gave her a quizzical, indulgent smile. "To what have you won them?" she asked in her placid alto.

"To you!" Godiva said. At Edgiva's surprise, she continued: "They did not understand how they could have missed the importance of supporting your exhortations, but by heaven—"

"With the prompting of your eyelash-batting—"

"They suddenly understood it very clearly, and they have

sworn on their very testicles that they will put their mark to a petition." She had resorted to flirtation for the thanes, but she'd done it cunningly, where Edward would not catch her.

Now she gestured, as if handing her friend a large invisible gift. She was glowing. Edgiva gazed at her, trying to tamp her emotions; finally, lips pursed, she shook her head, and allowed a maternal chuckle to escape her.

"You are quite the remarkable creature," she said. "I was afraid you would go straight to Edward."

"I did," she confessed, sobering.

Edgiva's eyebrows almost imperceptibly lowered. "And?" she said.

Godiva shook her head. "It did not go well. He is not so easy to fell with my particular ax."

"I could have told you that."

"I should have known it. I pride myself on my ability to read anyone that way."

"How bad was the damage? Have you marred my chances to convince him in a more straightforward manner?" Edgiva was not accusing, only strategizing.

"Well . . . ," Godiva said, shamed, "he ordered Aldred to refute me."

"Ahhh." A dry smile. "So you wooed Brother Aldred too."

"I did," Godiva confessed. "Although with him I was not woo-ish."

"Whatever you did was a waste of time. Aldred never takes a stand on anything."

"I thought I might . . . well, anyhow, I didn't. I couldn't. Worse, Edward misconstrued what he saw and did not like it." With a frown, she took Edgiva's strong hand and squeezed it, then brought it to her lips. "Edey, I shall never forgive myself if you lose support just because I have been acting like . . . well, like myself."

Edgiva sighed. "My dearest friend." To Godiva's tremendous relief, the abbess put an arm around her shoulders and pulled her close in an embrace. Her habit, so coarse compared to Godiva's own silk weaves, smelled of myrrh and smoke. "You mean well. I love you for it. Only, sister, you must not always try so hard. You know you get yourself in trouble."

Godiva raised her brows. "When trouble finds me, I outwit it," she declared. "I attribute that to you, Edey, you taught me how to think and act with indirect resistance. Like the time Leofric's priest pressured me to seek divine intervention for fertility, so I sought help from the witches of Brom Legge?" She grinned. "The priest changed his tune and said he'd rather a barren Christian countess in his flock than a fecund heathen."

Edgiva looked almost wistful. "I think Leofric would have loved a child with you, for all that," she said.

Godiva uncomfortably waved this away. "He has no need of more offspring, they'd only fight among themselves, and anyhow, I do not trust myself to do it well. Besides, that's not the point— the point is being able to find the solution hiding in the problem, and I learned that from you."

Edgiva shook her head. "I will take no responsibility," she said, "for having formed you. You are *sui generis*. Although if you were to have a child and Leofric had any sense, he would send it to be raised at Leominster Abbey."

"Very well," said Godiva cheerfully. "I found you an excellent teacher; surely a child of my womb would flourish likewise. But do you really want more Godivas?"

Edgiva, with a soft grin, again put her arm around Godiva's shoulder and pulled her toward her. "Thank you," she said in her deep maternal voice, "for never being dull as almost everybody else is."

Later in the hall, Godiva was settling onto Leofric's cot, when she noticed Sweyn Godwinson. The glow from the fire pit illuminated one side of his face and body. Enjoying what a pleasant view it was, she thought of Edgiva's flustered state.

And then she thought of something else.

Edgiva and Sweyn were both headed directly north from here tomorrow. They would surely caravan. By custom, in fact, Edgiva would likely stop in Hereford overnight before continuing on the last leg of her journey to Leominster Abbey. Suddenly that trip seemed, to Godiva, fraught with . . . opportunity. She could not part ways with her friend if she did not first satisfy herself that Edgiva would be safe.

Or if not safe, at least in capable hands.

That Edgiva was smitten with Sweyn, Godiva knew. She was almost as sure of Sweyn's affections . . . but not quite. Nor was she confident about his nature. Yes, he was gallant to an abbess publicly at Council, but at home, away from oversight, he had gratuitously tested Leofric's borders. He was young, as yet unsettled in his character. If he were too wayward for Edgiva, Godiva must find a way to protect her from him. Perhaps invent a reason to send one of Leofric's housecarls along with Edgiva's retinue.

But she could not tell Leofric the reason; could not say, even in jest, even in confession: "What if Sweyn Godwinson should ravish Edgiva?" Eternally leery of all things Godwin, Leofric would not let that go.

All she wished for at this moment was to lie against her husband and put her hands under his loosened leather jerkin to feel the particular warmth of his skin and the familiar fuzz of his chest hair. But she had to assess Sweyn's character first, or she would not be able to rest easy.

"I am going out," she said brusquely to Leofric. (To speak so indifferently to each other in public was their custom. It gave her greater purchase with other men, if they did not perceive how madly fond she was of her husband.)

Sweyn, as a member of his father's entourage, slept in the hall. But he was exiting now, a long leather cloak wrapped around him. Pulling on the green wool mantle she had laid over her side of the cot for warmth, she followed him into the dark courtyard toward the stables. The delicate crescent of moon had not yet risen, but the sky was grand with dazzling, subtle starlight. It would be a cold dawn later, for those in tents.

"My lord earl," she said gently into the darkness as she was fastening the brooch. The handsome body stopped, stayed unmoving for a moment, and then he pivoted in his tracks to see her. "Ah," he said. "Good evening, lady."

"Where are you off to? An evening assignation?"

He chuckled briefly. "Do you never tire of being a provocatress?" he asked. "But no, I am going for a drink in the stables with your stepson and some other thanes. After a day of putting up with men of my own rank, I am in desperate need of something . . ."

"A bit less rank?" she offered.

He smiled. "You are deft of words."

"I am deft of tongue," she corrected, promisingly. "Shall I prove it?" And she grinned at him.

He laughed a boisterous baritone laugh. "One day, some man will tire of your playing with him, and you'll regret it," he said.

"What exactly will I regret?" she asked, as if daring him. She walked closer to him until they were nearly touching. "What might 'some man' do to me? Exactly?"

He sobered and took half a step away from her. "You are my neighbor's wife and also, I hope, a friend, and I would never abuse your forwardness. But I cannot speak for other men——"

"A moment there," she interrupted, taking that same half step forward to remain nearly up against him. "Mean you to say that you never would mistreat me because we are friends, or because it is not in your nature to take advantage of any woman's frailty?" She leaned in toward him. She could feel the warmth of his breath in the cool night. She seldom allowed herself this kind of proximity; usually it was just a touch or a passing closeness. His scent was different from Leofric's. That distracted her.

"It is every man's nature to take advantage of a woman's frailty," Sweyn said, as if she should have already known this— which she did. "But most of us are able to resist the impulse when required."

"And you are able to?"

"I have not ravished you, have I?"

"Well, it would not be ravishment, of course," she said with an artificially flustered laugh. "It would be seduction."

He chuckled knowingly. "No, it would not. For all your teasing, you would never willingly let any man but Leofric lay hold of you. Which is admirable, of course—I do not say it as a criticism." He mirrored her own teasing smile. "Only a lament."

"Very gallant of you," she said. "Although somewhat under-informed."

"I beg your pardon?"

She wished there were more lights around them, that they might read each other better. So much was easily miscommunicated in grey half-light. "I assumed you knew the whole truth," she said. "About myself and Leofric."

He gave her what she took, in the darkness, to be an amused look. "I believe I do, lady," he said. "You counterfeit in public to have no particular affinity for him, and then you twist other men around your finger by dangling unspoken, unspeakable offers before them. Offers you will never act on. Your cunning little secret is that you are entirely devoted to your husband."

"There is more to it than that," she said. "Perhaps I was expecting too much, to think you had grasped it all."

He held up a hand to silence her. A pause. Then he very deliberately took one large step back, away from her. "Stay there," he said. "Continue."

She wished he had not done that. "I am devoted to Leofric, in that I act always with his interests at heart. But there is a considerable age difference between us; we have different appetites, he already has an heir, and he trusts me to keep my heart in check."

A silence.

"Meaning?" Sweyn demanded.

"To further confound everyone around us—and to accommodate my surplus of appetite—I do, in fact, take the occasional lover." How she wished she could see his face more clearly.

Another silence. "I do not believe you," Sweyn said flatly into the chill darkness.

"Why not?" she asked, arch. "Is your ego so wounded that I have not chosen you already?"

"I am not wounded, and I do not believe you," Sweyn said.

"I am barren," she whispered. "Not that I was desperate for motherhood anyhow, in this world where someone else nurses the babe and someone else yet raises it. Where is the motherhood in that? No wonder the likes of Queen Emma became such a heartless and conniving monster. My very womb rebelled against it early. So you see, there is not the slightest danger of embarrassment to Leofric, and he knows I would never make a fool of myself."

"Barren women have no appetites," said Sweyn, crossing his arms.

"That is not true, as I would be delighted to demonstrate," she retorted, almost fiercely.

He released a short, nervous bark of a laugh. "I do not know why you are doing this, Godiva, you have already played me for all I'm worth this Council—"

"That's true, I have," she said. "So I need not play you now. Nor am I so desperate or besotted that I have come to throw myself at your feet and beg you to ride me."

"My lady—" Sweyn said, and took an even larger step back away from Godiva, his arms clutching against his chest as if he would break his own ribs.

"I am simply inviting you to enjoy yourself with me, if you are so inclined." She reached toward her brooch and began to unclasp the cold metal.

He twisted his upper body so that he scanned the courtyard from one side to the other without turning his head. "What, *now*?"

"I leave tomorrow morning between Prime and Terce for Coventry. It would be challenging to arrange a tryst from such a distance." The brooch unclasped, she held the mantle closed at her right shoulder with her left hand.

Sweyn closed his eyes and shook his head briefly. "This is most unexpected."

"If you are not interested, please give me the courtesy of declining swiftly, as this evening is my only opportunity for a dalliance, and if I must settle for somebody else, I would like to get on with it."

He shook his head in slow, broad arcs. "I still do not believe you," he said.

"I do not really care if you believe me or not," she said. "All that matters is whether or not you are willing, and you do not seem to be, so Godspeed to you." She turned to head back toward the hall door.

"Wait a moment," Sweyn said, and taking a step, grabbed her arm and pulled her back to him.

If ever in her life she felt the impulse to throw away her virtue, it was that moment. Both of them were looking at his hand on her arm; both of them knew how easily he could have overpowered her. She gave him an inviting smile.

"That's more like it," she said. She was trembling slightly, only in part from the night air. He took the trembling to mean sincerity.

"You would do this?" he whispered.

"You would not?" she whispered back. "How many times have you imagined taking me, since you first came to your earldom?"

"As many times as you *wished* me to imagine it," he said.

"Do you always do as I wish?"

"I am learning not to," he said, and released her arm.

"All right then," she said, releasing the mantle. It slid to the ground sinuously in a pool around her ankle boots, and at once the cold crept up her fluted sleeves. She took his hand. "Do as *you* wish." She pressed his palm against her rib cage. It was deliciously alarming; no man but Leofric had ever been so near to her before by her will.

But he pulled his hand away, as if she had scalded it. "My lady, stop that," he said. "I see what you are doing now. It is unkind."

"What is unkind?"

Although they were alone in the darkness, he lowered his voice to less than a whisper; the air hardly moved as his lips shaped the words: "You are mocking my . . . impotence. Or perhaps"—and here his voice returned to normal—"you are testing me. Which is commendable of you, however oddly you are going about it."

"I am not mocking you," she said quickly. "I would never do that. I am offering you an alternative, because I'm fond of you. If you want to have me for an hour and call me Edgiva, I will not judge you for it."

He did not bother to deny the name.

"That would make it worse."

"Then use me to forget about her for an hour."

"It would not work."

"You insult me."

"I do not mean to. But I know my heart in this."

"I do not require your heart," she said. "You may save your heart for Edey."

There was a silence, and it was too dim for her to read his face. She wished she had not said that, for it would be a terribly awkward matter getting away from him if he took her offer. And she wished she had not doffed her mantle—the chill was moving through her clothes.

"I think you are testing me. If not, then I am testing myself. So I say no. All my capacity for passion is invested in her. The world's most cunning prostitute would not stir me."

"You sound like a moon-drunk girl!" Godiva said. Approvingly. But then, sternly: "Does that mean her virtue is at risk if she is near you? You resist the temptation I offer because you want her, and I approve of that, but tempted by the chance to take her . . . ?" She let it hang in the air.

"What a ridiculous thing to ask me; of course I am going to tell her dearest friend that I would guard her virtue with my life." He chuckled.

"I can arrange an assignation," Godiva whispered impulsively.

He gasped slightly; she could not see him clearly but could nearly feel the heat rise to his face. "You *are* testing me," he replied.

"I can arrange an assignation," she repeated slowly.

He took in a slow, pained breath and let it out with a slow, pained sigh. "What a little tormentor you are!"

"Will you meet with her alone?"

"I . . . of course not!" he said. "By Olaf's bones, that would be disastrous. I can hardly *speak* in her presence."

"You would not need to speak," Godiva said.

"Now I know you're testing me, and this is nonsense," he said. "Edgiva would not do that, even if she wished to, so you are offering me something I'd have to take by force, and I would not do that to a woman I find so excellent in all regards. This is an unfortunate flaring of desire that has no future and I must simply ride it out—"

"So to speak."

"The abbess does not deserve to be spoken of in such a manner," Sweyn said, very cross.

That convinced her. She stood on tiptoe, kissed his cheek, and then gave it a mothering pat. He was worthy of Edey.

"And there she is, at it *again*," said Edward's tenor nasality from behind her. "Mind your wench, Mercia. If you so readily cede that which the Holy Church has given you, you should not be surprised if other possessions slip out of your grasp as well."

She turned quickly to see her husband, illuminated by a torch at the doorjamb, standing in the door, wearing only his shirt with his mantle wrapped around him, looking something between amused and embarrassed; the king, in bed-robes, was disappearing back into the darkened hall.

Godiva immediately knelt, grabbed her mantle, and with the awkwardness of chilled limbs, began to wrap it around herself. Sweyn took one very large step sideways.

"By Odin's wounds, your wife's intentions toward me were entirely decorous," Sweyn said. Godiva had never seen him nearly so demure. "She was only testing my devotion to another."

"I know what she was doing," Leofric said drily. "The problem, wife, is that *you* do not know what you have done."

Part 2

CHAPTER 7

Hereford

Sweyn had planned to hunt with the king the next morning, as many of the earls were doing—Great Councils always met near the best hunting grounds. But upon hearing the abbess required an escort, he gave regrets to the king and his huntsman and ordered his housecarls to prepare for departure at dawn, when the stone cathedral's bells tolled Prime. So Edgiva rode pillion behind a lay brother, in a convoy with Sweyn and his housecarls, as far as Hereford.

It was a rough day's ride, over hilly terrain, in raw weather, with no spring flowers worth the notice to liven the road. Truly, Edgiva was glad of the hard pace they kept because it would make casual conversation impossible. She spent the morning with gloved hands clenching the grips, head bowed, praying to St. Pelagia for protection from sexual defilement. Sweyn gave her no reason for it; it was her own heart's pounding that alarmed her.

She had assumed—as Godiva teased her often—that she

had been born without the urge to mate, or even to crave that manner of attention. It was such joy and yet such agony to spot him out of the corner of her eye as they rode. He looked so maddeningly handsome in his fawn-colored leather gear and cloak, on his mare—even that he rode a mare, she could hear Godiva japing filthily and gleefully about this, and her cheeks reddened and she had to consciously control her breathing.

He made it worse—although he did not mean to—when after the brief break for a midday meal near a flowering pussy willow, as they were walking the horses for a stretch, he reined his mount up alongside the one she rode on and struck up a conversation with her. He was so obviously eager to entertain her; she became embarrassed for him, that everyone in the riding party could surely read his interest. He was an overeager pup, with more energy than the rest of the travelers combined. Had his horse gone lame, she thought, he could easily have carried the creature home and arrived undiminished in his vigor.

He invited her to stay on an extra day in Hereford to make pilgrimage to St. Ethelbert's tomb at the cathedral. She said she would consider it gladly, as she had desired anyhow to visit with the brothers of St. Guthlac's.

"You will be amazed how holy our Hereford is," Sweyn promised, wide-eyed with desire to impress. "We have an *enormous* number of relics."

"I know your roster," said Edgiva with a maternal smile. "I hope it will not crush your pride to learn that little Leominster boasts far more. We have Earl Leofric chiefly to thank for that."

They spoke of the arranged and so far fruitless marriage that had made them legal kin: Sweyn's sister Edith to Edgiva's uncle Edward.

"I was never fond of Edith," Sweyn confessed. "And she was never fond of me. I am the most expansive sibling, and she the most implosive. I am Jupiter to her Saturn." He grinned at her. "Do you prefer I not make pagan references, Mother?"

"Of course not. The stars and planets were here, and worshiped and studied, long before Our Lord was born. A newer wisdom need not defame an older one."

"Sounds like the sort of thing Bishop Lyfing would say," Sweyn said, approvingly.

Edgiva smiled. "I take that as a compliment."

Sweyn then began to boast to her of his excellent treatment of Hereford's serfs and slaves. This had been her fervent cause at the Great Council some eighteen months earlier; she was surprised he remembered, as he had not seemed so very interested himself back then. He was only telling her now because he wanted her approval, surely.

He had it. Merely by existing, by having that smile, that voice, those eyes. She was appalled at herself for this. With the exception of her dearest childhood friend—whose behavior she forgave in her heart over and over and over again—Edgiva was exacting in her appraisal of people. Especially of men. Let a man prove his character through actions, not words, and he earned her regard. It should not be the case that he win it with a grin. Grins did not deserve regard. Grins were just grins.

She adored his grin.

She abruptly turned the talk to the heregeld, and whether Godiva was likely to convince enough lords to actually sign their mark to a petition.

"Godiva, I believe, can convince near anyone of near anything," said Sweyn. "I speak as one of her perennial victims."

"You have a weakness for a pretty face," said Edgiva, not daring to look at him. She supposed her face was not unattractive, but she had never, until this week, cared much about that. Nor about her undelicate hands or unmusical voice.

"It is not just her pretty face," Sweyn said. "She is the most disarming person I have ever met. Even when she approaches me with that look of purpose in her eye, and I steel myself for it, determined to ignore her charm, somehow within two bird-songs she has wrested something from me I was not prepared to give—and I do not begrudge her for it. In fact, I feel pleased with myself for having pleased her. I do not understand how she does that, but she does it very well. She is Leofric's most potent weapon.",

Edgiva felt a strange tightness in her gut, an alien sensation she supposed must be jealousy, although she would much sooner have attributed it to riding in this chill. To be jealous of anyone was a sin; of one's dearest friend, a worse one. She clutched the support bar of the pillion harder and wished as she bobbed along that she could will the feeling in her gut away.

"I enjoy Godiva's cheerful subverting of men's scheming," she said. "I do not admit that to her, but I see the games of intrigue the lords and bishops do play, and I do not like them. I do not like the duplicity. What she does is no worse, and ofttimes, much better. There is generally beneficence to her scheming. She would never plot to hurt anyone or undermine them. However much she meddles, it is always with a happy intention."

"Excellently put, Mother."

"But sometimes I do fret for her," Edgiva continued. "Sometimes Godiva believes she is merely lighting a little candle somewhere when really she is heaving oil upon a bonfire. I am so grateful for her taking up my cause against the heregeld, but I am aware it is a complex matter, and Godiva is not at her best with complexity of any kind."

Sweyn laughed. "True enough, that. And Edward seems not to like her. Were she any woman but Leofric's, I hate to think what he would scheme to do to her."

Edgiva winced then. "Edward troubles me," she admitted quietly. "Kinsman though he be."

"He is better than Harthacnut," said Sweyn.

"That saying has sustained Edward on the throne for three years now," said Edgiva. "Soon he will need more praise than simply being better than Harthacnut."

They changed to fresh horses at a posting station and set off at a hard trot; the ceasing of conversation made Edgiva no less aware of what a beautiful color of light brown Sweyn's hair was, or how well his short cloak sat pushed back over his shoulders, or how dashingly his eyebrows swept up at the edges, or how obedient his mare was under him. Sometimes she was dizzy.

They had left very early, and reached Hereford by nightfall, as it began to drizzle. An outrider had been sent ahead, and food— not quite a supper—was waiting in the hall. Sweyn's bower contained a small guest chamber adjacent to his own sleeping quarters. Most visitors were quartered in the hall, but when Godwin or the king came through, Sweyn took this smaller room and yielded his own to his superior. His chamberlain offered Edgiva the smaller room and she accepted it, both gratefully and warily. Alone for a few moments, she offered God a psalm and St. Christopher a prayer of thanks for safe arrival. Then, as a reassuring ritual more than an act of faith, she rapidly recited nine *Pater Nostrums*. She finished with a plea to the Great Mother for inner calm, as the women of the forests had taught her in her herbal foragings. It was no skin off St. Christopher's nose to share the gratitude; was Gaia not also *Terra Mater* to St. Christopher?

A serving girl called Aisly brought her a basin of water and a stiff, dry towel. With weary gratitude, she washed herself before dressing again for dinner. Over her tunic she refastened her still-dusty scapular, belt, wimple, and veil. All of it was dark and drab; for the first time in her life, Edgiva wished she had something pretty to draw attention to her face. How Godiva would cackle to know that! . . . And how she would then have lovingly helped Edgiva to indulge the vanity.

"I will confess this all when I am home," she promised herself softly. From the packet of medicinal herbs she always carried with her she pulled out a small leather-bound codex, her only private possession, and looked around the room for a quill and ink. She could not find one, so she spoke to the book instead of writing in it. "I will do penance and I will cleanse it from my soul. And I promise," she added with a wince, "to be more compassionate when others come to me bewailing this condition of the liver. I have never understood their complaints as I do now. Thank you, Mother Mary, for visiting upon me this atrocious experience. I understand now why I have been subjected to it."

Because Earl Sweyn had been gone for days—and because he returned with an esteemed religious lady as his guest—there was a festive air to supper, however drab the oysters were that had been carted in barrels up from Gloucester. The vegetables and bread were mushy from being reheated several times whenever the porter thought the earl was arriving. But the seasonings were splendid compared to the dull fare of the abbey, or even of the king's kitchen. The table was decorated with primrose and sweet violet blossoms and painted eggs taken from a growing pile resting in straw near the entrance to the kitchens.

She was seated beside him, as the honored guest. Throughout the meal, she was distracted by his presence. She wished that he were not so handsome, that his voice were not so resonant, that his shoulders were not quite so broad. She began to resent him for it. Halfway through the meal, he rose to circulate among his reeves and servants, to greet them after his absence. Her whole right side felt colder and somehow lonely when he was no longer near her, and she felt far too happy when he returned, even though he did not acknowledge her. She tried to turn her mind from noticing him at all and recited the *Pater Nostrum* in silence to regain her composure. Over and over again she did it, until she was successful; Sweyn moved away again at one point and she did not even notice. *There, you see?* she told herself. *'Tis nothing. I am well.*

On the Road

The earl and lady of Mercia, and the earl's son Alfgar, reached holy Evesham that evening as a light rain began. The abbot of St. Mary's graciously received them after Compline services were done.

They had ridden on good horses at a moderate pace that was too hard for idle chatter. But still Leofric seemed more taciturn than usual. In the small, low-ceilinged room where the couple would sleep that night, as they were rinsing the road dust off their faces, Leofric did not look at her, and responded to attempts at conversation with indistinct, disinterested grunts. She stretched her limbs gracefully but broadly, directly in his line of sight, lunging from one knee to the other to relieve the tension of a day in the saddle. Leofric always, *always*, watched her when she did this, enjoying the flash of ankle she revealed. This time he ignored her. Was he upset with her for testing Sweyn? For prompting those other lords to support Edgiva's charter?

"What have you done with my husband?" Godiva asked him finally, standing straight and removing her travel veil.

He was taken aback. "What?"

"I am in possession of one husband, who, while not known for expansive lightheartedness, is still a commendable partner for conversation and even the odd bit of banter. Whoever you are, you have taken possession of his body and I demand to know where you have put the rest of him."

Leofric attempted, wanly, to smile. "He is off worrying about things," he said. "And he did not want you to worry with him."

"But I always worry with him. I am extremely good at lightening his load."

"Perhaps this time you *are* his load."

She frowned as she unpinned her wimple. "Oh, I see what this is about, then. Too much flirtation, is it? Even though it was to advance a good cause that surely you support?"

"Not too much by my estimation. Too much by the king's."

"Yes, he had quite the chance of encountering me at moments that looked much naughtier than they were. Poor frightened Aldred—"

"God's wounds, it was not *chance*, Godiva," Leofric said. "Last evening he assigned two servants to tail you and to report back to him whenever you were in a conversation with any man, even in a public place. I almost believe he wanted me to notice." He gave her a tight-lipped grimace. "He knows you worked your charms on all the thanes you wrested vows from for the petition. You are quite out of the favor of His Majesty. Which means I might be also. At a time when he is looking for excuses to bare his claws. So as good a cause as it may be, in the name of Woden, leave the heregeld problem to Edgiva."

Hereford

After the ordeal of dinner, Edgiva had written her daily entry into her codex, undressed down to her shift, and was about to release Aisly when there was a rap on the door between Sweyn's chambers and the one she was to sleep in. Aisly opened it to reveal the earl, absent his usual short cloak.

Even in the dim lantern light, Sweyn looked uncomfortable. It was not a mood that suited him. His boundless energy seemed trapped in his feet, and so as he spoke he rocked back and forth as if on a boat.

"Forgive me if it is forward to come to Mother's chambers this late," he said, not looking at her. Of course it was forward; it was far more than forward. With a sense of panic, Edgiva gestured to Aisly for her dark wool mantle, which the girl tossed to her; Edgiva hurriedly placed it round her shoulders and pulled it closed. Sweyn noticed none of this, staring at the floor, seeking some excuse to stay. "I have some thoughts on how I may help you oversee Godiva's attempts to champion your petition, and make certain she does not endanger herself. As we both have matters attending us tomorrow, this seemed the only time to speak them . . . Would you like to hear them?"

Aisly looked at Edgiva.

"Let him come," Edgiva said, badly affecting disinterest.

Once through the doorway, Sweyn seemed to want to move toward her, but became rooted to the spot, his energy still shifting back and forth from foot to foot although neither left the ground now. The earl and the abbess stared at each other stupidly, without speaking. His large frame made the small room smaller. The aroma of his sweat mingled with a spicy scent on his clothes and made her wonderfully dizzy.

Finally Edgiva managed to splutter, insipidly, just for the sake of something being said, "I believe we will be triumphant in this cause, for surely it is God's will for the realm."

"Then we should celebrate the coming of God's will. Let us do so over wine."

She stared at him, every part of her going taut except her face, which went red. She realized her mouth was hanging open. She closed it, and tried to look away from him, but couldn't. He himself looked slightly terrified.

"Excuse me, milord," said Aisly, "I'll just get some from the cellar, if you like."

"Do not leave us alone!" Edgiva said, more intensely than she meant to. At least looking at the girl meant looking away from Sweyn. "It . . ." She tried to sound lighthearted, and instead sounded brittle. "It would be indecorous."

"Why?" Sweyn demanded with a nervous laugh. "Is there a

risk you might be something other than a chaste observer of your holy vows?"

Edgiva blushed so intensely she felt her scalp tingle. "You pretend to chastise me, sir, but actually you are asking that question with too much hope."

Sweyn laughed a little, and she found she could hardly breathe. "You must not accuse your noble host of improper intentions," he said, with forced playfulness.

"I hope my host *is* noble," Edgiva shot back, feeling desperate.

There was an awkward pause. Aisly cleared her throat to remind them she was in the room. Sweyn caught her eye and then gestured out the door with his thumb.

When he did that, Edgiva felt her knees weaken and a strange feeling surge through her legs and stomach. "Mother," the servant said, curtsying, without quite meeting her eyes. It almost sounded like an apology.

Edgiva's ears were ringing and she felt light-headed. She tried to speak and could not even whisper. She tried to cross herself and was unable to move her arms. She could not look at Aisly; she could not look at Sweyn either. She heard the girl leave. She heard the door close, aware it was now only herself and Sweyn in the very small room. She could feel his eyes on her and was terrified of looking at him. She was dizzy.

"My lady Abbess," he said, sobering, and walked closer to her. The closer he came, the dizzier she felt. "I do not pretend to understand this."

"You feel it too?" she asked. She was thrilled. She was relieved. She was terrified.

"I do not think there is a soul in Hereford who has seen the two of us in the same room without noticing."

"Although I am a decade your senior, you are a man of the world and are no doubt familiar with this feeling," she said. "While I have never—"

"I have felt desire before, but nothing near to this," he corrected, and reached out to take her hand. She made a strange sound without meaning to and sat down hard on the thick sleeping mat. Her hand released the mantle, which fell off her shoulders and pooled around her on the bedding. Sweyn knelt down beside the mat. She was disappointed he had not sat on it with her. She looked at him, looked at the empty spot beside her on the bedding, and looked at him again. He smiled, and chuckled apologetically. "I dare not sit beside you," he said. "If I did, I cannot promise to control myself."

"Would it hurt?" she asked, and then turned even redder hearing herself ask the question. Of course it would hurt—Godiva had told her all about that, years back. Despite her vows of chastity, it was a detail she had never quite forgotten.

The pressure of his hand gripped hers a little harder and he made a small sound in his throat. "You are a virgin?" She nodded, terrified to meet his gaze. "Then yes, it would hurt." A pause. "But only the first time."

She made a feeble attempt to pull her hand out of his. Sweyn's grip tightened, and Edgiva's heart leapt with pleasure. "This must be the devil's work," she pressed on. She tried to remember the prayer to St. Mary of Edessa against sexual temptation, but she could not. Instead she found herself thinking of the pennyroyal tincture against conception. She tried to remove her hand again, but he squeezed it even tighter. As she'd hoped he would.

"Not the devil," he said softly. "You are too pure for the devil to have a grip on you."

"You would rob me of that purity," she said, looking away, cringing at how badly she wanted to be robbed.

"I swear I would never rob you," he said, and rose up on his knees so that he was nearer to her. She felt fluttering sensations low in her stomach, the nearer he got. "I would only substitute your virgin purity with something equally . . . significant."

A long pause as she looked into the darkened corner of the room, and he kneeled upright as near to her as he could balance. She could feel his breath against the skin of her bare neck. She could smell the leather of his jerkin. She had never been so distressed and happy.

"What do you want?" he asked after a long moment.

"I want you to sit next to me on the bed," she whispered.

"I have warned you—"

"Sit next to me on the bed," she repeated, more certain.

Another nervous chuckle from him—it struck her as an apology to God—and he released her hand, rose from his knees, and then settled beside her on the sleeping mat. He was trembling even more than she was. She offered him her hand again. He stared at it for a long moment, then took it, but only to place it in her own lap.

Once his hand was in her lap, it remained there.

An hour later, there was blood on the sheets, and Edgiva was in thrall to Sweyn Godwinson.

CHAPTER 8

Coventry

It was a relief to reach Coventry, as small and crude as the town and their lodgings were. They would stay here through Easter before beginning their spring circuit of Leofric's lands. Traveling was never pleasant, but Godiva preferred circuiting to what they had just concluded. It was more bearable to travel with a full retinue, with creature comforts and temporalities brought along by their own people, who knew their routines and preferences. The housecarls, although good men and devoted to Leofric, were not much interested in keeping a lady comfortable. Her groom was the most sympathetic man among them, and he was not conversational. It had been a dull, unpleasant journey, with weather raw and damp throughout. She felt chilled to the sinews, despite her excellent beaver-lined riding cloak. On their way to Gloucester they had been light at heart and Leofric had been chatty; on this return journey, despite the rousing presence of Leofric's son, Alfgar, they seemed to travel under a cloud of gloom. She had no patience for gloom, but it won the battle, and despite Alfgar's friendly conversation, she was as heavy-hearted as her husband when finally they reached home.

"Home" at Coventry was barely that. There had been nothing but a dismal hamlet here until three years ago, when work had begun on the monastery. They had poured their largesse into that, and artisans and craftsmen (as well as farmers and shepherds who elected to become artisans, for the lure of lucre) had collected around the gates of the religious enclave, or around the gates of their simple manor. Small houses, with low walls and heavy thatch roofs, now lined the route from manor to monastery, a distance of a couple of arrow shots at best. Halfway along the route, the road opened briefly into a market square. Paths wide enough for a cart went off of this main path, leading to the river or the pond, to the gristmill and the fulling mill, to a separate livestock market in what might be called the outer skirts of the town, if only there were anything to count as inner skirts.

The soil was not bad here, although the villages a mile or more away had loamier earth and yielded better crops. The families immediately around Coventry who were not craftsmen raised sheep or pigs or sometimes cattle. The settlement had developed briskly in the past three years, but still it was small, and at night, between village, manor, and monastery, not eightscore souls whispered evening prayers before head was laid on pillow.

The manor itself was modest. There was one central building—a hall, with a chamber at one end for Leofric and Godiva to sleep in, and another beside that where all the officers of the house organized their days and passed their nights. Godiva intended to build a separate sleeping hall, of course, but for now all labor was dedicated to the monastery. The manor staff all slept in hall, as did the housecarls; the cook and his assistants slept in the kitchens just beside the manor; and the grooms slept in the stables with the huntsman and the reeves, except in winter when all of them came into the hall, sometimes bringing the horses and dogs with them, although not when their lady was present, as she did not fancy the smell of horse dung first thing in the morning.

The steward, the dish-thane and the chamberlain, the huntsman and the chief groom, had none of them left Coventry. They'd been alerted by an outrider, and Godiva was grateful to see her attendant, young Merewyn, among those waiting to receive her.

Their first full day back would be taken entirely with unpacking and resettling, and relocating the crudely dyed and decorated eggs that had been placed in unexpected places as homecoming gifts—upon their pillows, in their chamber pots, hanging from their clothing pegs on colored thread.

Also this day they would be sending Alfgar north to his own estates after some morning hours of mead and rapport around the hearth. He and his stepmother Godiva loved each other like puppies from the same litter. Their cheerful banter on matters trivial and topical managed finally to lift Leofric's spirits from the gloom of the ride.

Alfgar had in mind a love match for himself, the daughter of a Northumbrian thane. Leofric professed not to approve, but Godiva advised him cheekily on what to say, what not to say, what to do, and most of all what not to do, to win a woman's heart.

"Did the lady's techniques work well for you, Father?" Alfgar asked.

"The lady is still married to me after a dozen years," Leofric replied. "I must be doing *something* well."

"I only keep him because I am so fond of his son," Godiva said conspiringly. "Whom I hope will return to Coventry for Easter?"

"Alas, honored mother, no," Alfgar said with a regretful smile. "My would-be lady's father has allowed that I might celebrate the day with them, and I must leap at the chance to ingratiate myself."

"I thought Northumbrians were pagan," Leofric said laconically.

"That's no reason not to celebrate Easter," said Alfgar. "Anyhow, it isn't true. Well, not entirely. Not when the archbishop's dining with them."

"Ah, these thankless sons." Godiva sighed to Leofric, gesturing toward her stepson, who was nearly her own age. "Show them a pretty face and they will throw over their own mother!" She swatted his knee. "Go with our gladdest blessing, even if your father will not say so."

The second day, after a breakfast of watery porridge, the couple went to the monastery to see the progress there, for the weather was good and all the workmen were about. Godiva was proud of this monastery, the first project she had helped to fund from the ground up. Or nearly the ground up: the actual foundations were already in place from a nunnery that had stood here, beside Coffa's Tree, until King Canute razed it a quarter century ago.

Coffa's Tree, for which Coventry was named, was a massive oak just beyond the monastery walls. The hundredcourt assembled there, as did most festivals—Maying dances, harvest suppers for the town. Nobody knew who Coffa was, but they were grateful for his tree.

As they walked back toward the manor, they could see only the top of the spreading tree, leaves just budding. Godiva liked the way the cut of her new light-on-dark-blue tunics moved against her figure when she walked briskly or when the breeze blew across her. She felt almost girlish as she moved through town.

As they reached the market, a rugged-looking man about her age approached them, bowing every second step, as if he were nervous of offending them with his presence.

They both stopped, and the retinue stopped with them.

"My lord," said the fellow, and "my lady," also, bowing low.

"Are not you Avery?" Godiva asked. "You are the tithing man for this region?"

"Yes, my lady, and a farmer," he said, bowing again. "We are many of us growers, on the south side of the town." He seemed about to speak, then hesitated.

"What would you with us?" Godiva asked. "Do not be afraid to ask." She offered her hand.

He kissed it and then glanced nervously behind. Godiva followed his look and saw that between two of the homes just off the square, at least a dozen equally burly fellows huddled together, watching.

"We have had several bad years, my lady, as you know—"

"I do," said Godiva gently. "Our own stores are low, and our grain comes mostly from you. It is widespread in these parts. Do you ask for an abatement in your food-rent?"

He looked flustered. "We would always be grateful for that, my lady, but that is not why I approach you. We—the farmers—are hoping you might do us the honor of reciting the Land Ceremony Charm for us, this being the fierce month and Hreda seeming particularly fierce this year."

"But the weather has been mild," Leofric observed.

Avery bowed again, specifically to the earl. "Yes, my lord, but there has been no rain for such a while. Seeds will not sprout without water, my lord." And back to Godiva. "'Tis an imposition, I know, and we can perform it on our own selves, and the priest at the monastery has already said we may bring the turf there, but it would be such an honor to us if you lead the ceremony."

Godiva smiled. She glanced at Leofric for approval; he seemed passively amused. "My little heathen," he crooned drily. "Whatever will our Lyfing say?"

"That he hopes I paid enough attention to him to learn his lines by rote," she retorted. Then, more gravely, she turned back to the farmer.

"It is my honor," she assured him. "And, I think, my duty. Shall we wait for the Equinox or do you wish it sooner?"

"The Equinox, my lady, is a propitious time, according to the priest," said Avery. "It is a very holy week. Annunciation is the very next day, as Easter is the eve of April Kalends."

Godiva shrugged agreeably. "Very well. I shall tell our steward to expect someone to collect me . . . after Nocturne, isn't it? The night of the Equinox, then. As Pisces yields to Aries. Shall you come, love?" she asked Leofric.

He smiled wanly. "I suppose I should keep an eye on you, make sure you do not get frisky with the peasants."

Leominster

Edgiva, upon returning home to Leominster on a grey, damp, windless afternoon, had gone straight into her chamber without even thanking the groom with whom she rode or greeting Audry, her acolyte, or Maire, her prioress. Her face was almost green and etched into a scowl—an expression nobody in Leominster could ever remember upon her face.

"Please leave me alone," was all she would say when Audry asked to see her. "Unless you send me word of Bishop Lyfing's health."

Ignoring the display of intricately decorated eggs gracing her pillow, she sank to the floor and rested her head against the leg of her bed, wishing she were dead. She heard the bells toll for None service. Maire would attend on her behalf. She could not bring herself to offer God a psalm for her safety.

She must tell no one at Leominster what had happened. She needed to confess it—desperately, as nothing she had ever needed before—but there was not one priest in all this double house whom she could rely on for absolute secrecy. Only Lyfing—quiet, wise, and imperturbable, with endless compassion for human frailty—had her trust, and he was days away, and possibly still ailing. She was afraid even to consign her sin to print in her private codex, where she reported everything that happened to her and every unfortunate thought or emotion she ever harbored, to keep herself accountable. She most certainly could not write it, even anonymously, into the chapter house's prayer book.

She most especially could not tell Audry. She was Audry's mentor in the healing arts; the girl was gifted, and it was important that she stay at her studies. But she was also rigid and judgmental, and she would not survive the shock of learning how unsanctified her idol had become.

But Edgiva was not a liar. Besides being opposed to duplicity on principle, she had learned in childhood antics with Godiva that she was entirely incompetent at it. When she was tall enough to look out the side windows of the church, she made an oath that she would always tell the truth and never deceive anyone. So her soul was in a doubly perilous state now, and she could conceive no way to salvage it without worrying poor Lyfing. Her distress far outweighed any pleasure she might take in memories of last night with Sweyn. Already by the morning she knew it never should have happened; she was alarmed by his bounding enthusiasm to show affection to her in public and had quietly informed him they were absolutely never to be alone again in each other's presence. He had been crushed; the charming fool would have propositioned marriage if he'd had another go with her. Godiva had been right about . . . oh, dear. Godiva. She wished Godiva knew, so that *somebody* knew until she could confess to Lyfing. She could trust Godiva with such a secret. Godiva's strengths, however dubious, included the art of concealment.

A sense of happiness was trying to work its way to her attention, snaking up from her gut in ticklish waves, but she refused it, would not nourish it, waited for it to die of starvation.

Until that happened, she could speak to nobody. It was one thing to keep a secret, she decided, another thing to lie. One was a tactic, and one a sin. But to go about the abbey now, in the state that she was in, would be worse than merely secretive, 'twould be deceitful—she would be counterfeiting to be a good person, worthy of shepherding them, when she was not. She would have to somehow keep alone until she could expiate her sin. But that meant, to start with, confessing to a priest, and there was nobody here she could tell.

She summoned vellum and a quill, and wrote to Bishop Lyfing. She trusted him, and she knew he would forgive her and provide a proper penance. It would be a heavy penance, that much she knew. Knowing that—knowing exactly how salvation awaited her—she was able with a calmer mind and heart to open her door and return to her position. She still kept a secret, and she did not like that, but she knew it would soon no longer be a lie, and that gave her the courage to perform her duties.

How confounding that something so joyful and meaningful, something that in no way competed with any part of her that belonged to God, should be such a heinous sin.

CHAPTER 9

Coventry

G odiva had never actively participated in a Land Ceremony, but for the past few years, she had been Bishop Lyfing's guest to observe the custom in the estates outside the burgh gates of Worcester. She supposed the peasants did it every year, but when the growing season was bad—as had been the case, alarmingly, for years upon years now—the farmers believed that a person of high status, and especially a churchman, added gravity and power to the ritual.

The night of the Equinox, she wore layers of wool to bed, and told Merewyn to expect the steward in the dead of night. She found she could not sleep, and was already awake and dressed in every green-dyed garment she had with her in Coventry when the steward arrived. She chose green for fertility. Silk undertunic and green hose, woolen tunic girdled with a green-beaded belt and lots of gold embroidery, then an overtunic of green leather;

then a cloth-of-gold veil to add a touch of majesty. She wished she had a mirror-glass. She felt bulky under all those layers but hoped she looked at least a little elegant for the farmers.

When the summons came, Leofric almost stayed asleep, but her excitement finally roused him. He pulled his heaviest woolen tunic over his shirt, belted it, put a looser leather tunic over that, and then took the waiting cloak from the sleepy-eyed chamberlain. A lantern and a rush light together lit their way into the hall, out of the hall, through the courtyard to the gate, where they were met by Avery and the dozen or so farmers they had seen before. There was much bowing and expressions of gratitude, which Leofric waved away gruffly.

They walked all together in the darkness. The day had been sunny, then clouds had rolled in from the west in time to trap the solar gain, so it was not as frigid as Godiva had feared. They reached the market square, and then, turning off one of the paths, they traveled around behind the monastery to Coffa's Tree. It made sense, thought Godiva, that they would gather here.

The farmers, with their wives and children and aging parents, had spent all night, and likely the day before, in preparation for this moment. A trestle table had been set out under the tree, dim-lit with lanterns. A plough waited beside the table, harnessed to a sleepy-looking ox. As if an elaborate dinner feast were to be assembled, the table was lined with neat, small piles of fist-size objects, each of which Avery showed her, to demonstrate how ably they had prepared.

"Here is the earth," he said, pointing to four small pieces of sod. These had come, she knew, from the four corners of the farmland that was about to be blessed. Beside the turf were four jugs—"holy water, honey, oil, and all the milks," recited Avery.

"All the milks" meant milk from each kind of livestock, or at least the sheep and cow. She wondered if one could milk a sow, and then decided it was too early in the morning to worry about it.

Avery now walked her down the table, showing her chunks taken out of different trees, to represent each kind of tree but oak, which was exempt; the aspen, unlike the ash, birch, hawthorn, and other shards of wood, was neatly cut and fastened to make a cross. Next along the table was the most unruly pile, a heap of stems of every known plant on the property to be blessed, from what was grown to what was gathered. These included wilting daffodils, primroses, celandines, violets, and hazel flowers.

"It is well done," she said, sensing his desire to please her. He smiled with satisfaction, and led her back to the head of the table.

Four weary girls each picked up one piece of turf and turned it upside down in their hands. Avery was about to coax Godiva, but she politely brushed him away, remembering this part of the ceremony from when Lyfing had led it.

She took the smallest jug, which held the holy water, and put her hand into it. As Avery held the lantern close, and all the farmers and their families craned to see, Godiva carefully dripped three drops of holy water on each piece of turf, and over each piece she recited, "Grow and multiply, and make the earth replete with harvest. *Pater Nostrum . . .*" The congregation joined her for the rest of the prayer.

That was her first role in the ritual, and she felt a thrill, even for that small gesture. The farmers and their wives gathered into aprons and sacks all of the flora on the table, as a few of the men carefully picked up the jugs of milk, honey, and oil, and led by the girls holding the pieces of sod, the entire group moved toward the stone walls of the monastery, where a waiting monk silently let them in through the narrow post-door. Inside the compound, they herded themselves into the church.

At this point, Bishop Lyfing would typically have taken on his more conventional priestly role to sing four masses over the turf (still upside down, so that the damp muck would not spoil the altar). With the local mass-priest performing this, Godiva struggled to stay awake in the chill dark. Finally the priest—whose name she ought to know, and did, when she was more alert—placed a token of the four saints upon the arms of the aspen cross. He picked up the sod, and lay each piece upon an arm of this cross. The congregation stirred themselves again and all of a voice they chanted *"Crescite"* over and over, before segueing again to the *Pater Nostrum*.

And now again Godiva had a role to play. This one she did not know well enough, and Avery stepped up to her, kissed her hand with his dry lips, gestured her to face east, and held up a piece of battered vellum and a lantern with enough light for her to read the charm:

"I stand facing eastward, for I've favors to beg," she began, chanting in a monotone as she remembered Lyfing chanting. Her chest resonated with the depth of her tone, but her voice was nothing near as sonorous as his. She wished she sounded more like Edgiva, at least. "I ask the great and glorious Lord, I ask heaven's holy guardians, I ask the earth below and the heaven above, and the holy, righteous Mother Mary, and the hallowed halls of Valhalla, that I might be worthy, by God's grace, of fulfilling this charm, and cause the crops to start growing. With my faith, may I make the surface of the earth beautiful with bounty."

At a gesture from Avery, she turned around her own right shoulder in a circle three times, and then lay herself upon the cold stone before the altar with her arms outstretched so that her body formed a cross. At this point, the priest began to recite in Latin—which meant nothing to any of the congregants—the Litany and then the Sanctus, then the Benedicite and the Magnificat, and by now her body was shivering from the cold radiating from the stones, even through the silk and wool and leather, and despite her best intentions, she was less concerned about the harvest than about sensation returning to the tip of her nose.

Finally she heard the congregation begin to recite, yet again, the *Pater Nostrum,* and gratefully she joined her voice with theirs. She wondered if Edgiva participated in such a ritual at Leominster, or if it fell only to the priests and monks.

Leofric, involving himself for the first time, helped her to her feet and wrapped his own cloak round her; hers was chilled through and he could see the misery on her face. He gave her a paternal smile of approval as the priest commended the pieces of sod to Christ and the holy virgin and the holy rood, and to the honor and benefit of Earl Leofric and his subjects.

Then the priest and the people and the earl and his lady moved all together back out to Coffa's Tree, where it was much colder than it had been hours earlier. By now it was dawn and turning very quickly into full morning.

Avery gently gestured for Godiva to stand behind the plough and take the reins, and again he held up a battered piece of parchment; there was enough light from impending sunrise that she could read this.

"Earth-Mother, may the Almighty Eternal Lord grant you thriving, growing fields, that increase and strengthen, with tall stems and good crops, the broad barley and the wheat. May God Eternal and all his saints in heaven grant that the crops of this land be protected from all our foes, from all the ills of the world, from drought, from sorcery. May God who created this world assure that there be no man nor woman so skilled of tongue that they are able to undo this spell I set."

Avery smacked the ox on the rump and clicked his tongue at it; the animal began to pull the plough. Godiva, remembering the closing verse from watching Lyfing, shouted out, "Mother Earth, mother of men, we greet you! And pray you may grow all our crops in God's protecting arms, filling your fields for the health of mankind."

Avery nodded, took control of the plough from her, drove the ox a few more paces, and then stopped to turn his attention back to the ritual.

A woman stepped forward with a loaf of bread and two small jugs. She placed the loaf of bread in the furrow the countess had just ploughed, and over it poured milk from one of the jugs and holy water from the other. To Godiva's surprise, the words that completed the charm rose up in her as if she had known them since childhood:

"Oh, you field, full of food for us, brightly seeding, you shall be blessed. May the god who created this soil bless us with the gift of its fertility, so that each grain shall bloom into corn. Grow in the name of the Father, and blessed be."

Two hours later she was finally warm and dry, and best of all, inside her own chamber; she felt both fulfilled and depleted, elated and withdrawn.

"A beautiful ceremony," she said to Leofric. He was nursing her. He had ordered a fire-warmed shift be ready when they arrived home; he had taken off her chilled clothes and pulled the warm ones over her head, kissing her collarbone and breasts and belly as he did so. Then there were warmed blankets that he had wrapped around her like swaddling clothes, and he kissed her forehead and rubbed her chilled fingers between his large warm palms. He was proud of her, she could tell, although he would not say so. "If mass felt more like that, I would be far more enthusiastic about going every morning. Easter Sunday shall be such a come-down after a dawn like this!"

Leofric allowed himself a small smile. "I think Lyfing would be quite delighted to hear he has such an apt pupil. Although let us not mention it to any other bishop. I was surprised how much of that litany you knew."

"So was I," she said. "Although I am grateful I was not expected to know the priest's parts; I have forgotten much of my Latin. Leofric, do let's write Lyfing and tell him. Perhaps if he is well enough he could join us here for Easter. Think what *that* would do for the spirit of the villagers and farmers! And we could talk to him about Edgiva's—"

"Lyfing is not a young man, Godiva, and his health is diminishing. Let us not burden him with extra duties when he can hardly carry out the ones he has now."

Godiva gave him a look. "You should at least speak to *him,* of all men, about the heregeld, how to best resist it. Let us see if he can come to Easter, or perhaps we can join him in Worcester if he is not well enough to travel. Let's write to him tomorrow so we may sort it out in time."

"As the lady of the fields wishes," said Leofric, with a troubled smile.

Now he would have nightmares about the razing of Worcester, she knew. She should not have mentioned it. "When the king gives an order, you must obey it," she said.

"Do not make that argument," he said warningly. "That is no excuse for what happened. It has not always been that way. The Great Council had been very powerful under Harold and Canute. Harthacnut's rule was tyranny and we should have resisted him. All three of us. If we had all three refused to attack the town—"

"He would have had all three of you assassinated, Leofric; he was that kind of man. Edward is no saint, but thank heavens, he is not the despot that his brother was."

"Amen," said Leofric. He gave her a tired smile and rested a hand on her swaddled leg. "Yes, let us write to Lyfing tomorrow. It would do my heart good to have an actual friend in residence. Write Alfgar, too, and see if you can make him change his mind about his Easter plans."

"Of course I shan't. Let him try his hand with this lady-friend, Leofric. I like the look in his eye when he speaks of her. A pity Edgiva is too far away to send for in time, though," said Godiva.

"Perhaps she can go to Hereford and celebrate with Sweyn," Leofric suggested drily.

Leominster

She had celebrated Matins for as long as she had memory, and loved how it seemed authentically to sanctify the start of the day. Yet now, in the aftermath of her great sin, it felt an alien artifice, and she seemed to view herself as from a great distance, sleep-walking through her duties and responsibilities as she herself hovered, waiting for a response from Bishop Lyfing to her plea for audience. Somehow she forced herself to rise to consciousness, and remain there, when at each Matins bells, Audry would enter her room with a candle, tap her feet, and reverentially chant, "Lord, ope my lips." Without any expression Edgiva would fling down her blanket, climb out of bed in her long-sleeved shift, her stockings, and her undecorated girdle; fasten on her scapular, her cowl, her dark wimple and veil, pulling the veil down to meet her eyebrows; tie on her crucifix.

Some Edgiva-looking stranger gave each morning's circator a lantern to wave in the face of those weak-willed nuns whose attention drifted dreamward during Lauds and Prime; some other creature, whom the sisters all called Mother, led the meeting in the chapter house after morning mass, read aloud in her deep mellifluous voice the day's chapter of the Rule, prayed for the dead, announced the saints' days, listened with the others to the confessions of their sisters, determined fair punishment, even— although rarely—lashed penitents, and then salved them herself in the infirmary. The soul "Edgiva" was but a distant consciousness watching some other spirit fill her body, move her limbs and jaw and vocal cords, as she washed her hands outside the refectory before each meal, washed her sisters' feet at weekly Maundy, raised her voice in chant and prayer at Terce and Sext and None and Vespers and Compline and wrote her daily observations in her private prayer book and then finally returned to the little room with the little bed, too small for two people to thrash around in, as this stranger's body she now watched had thrashed around with the Earl of Hereford.

She would sleep and dream of thrashing, and rise some few hours later with Audry tapping her awake for Matins to begin it all again.

. And somehow also, nearly daily, she would take reports from the lay brothers, of how the ploughing progressed, and the clearing of fields, and the diverting of the stream near the fishpond; she would check the stores of the shrift-corn and check the state of the baking and the mead; she would meet with the cellarer and the infirmarian and the gardener; she would make a circuit of the workshops, and meet with the prior from the monks' side to make sure all was well there. She would check the soundness of the water clocks, and see the time-candles were in good supply. She would herself receive patients at the infirmary, victims of abusive kin or farming accidents or age or illness or weather or goblins or elves or unhappy ancestors; she would treat them not only with bleeding (since the moon was waning), with tinctures and poultices, but also with charms to fend off evil spirits. She would visit the west side of the cloister, where the white-veiled novices were being schooled, some wide-eyed, some sullen, all more innocent than she; then to the north side, her favorite place in all the compound, perhaps in all the world: the famed scriptorium of Leominster Abbey.

Each nun bent dutifully with inks, quills, and other tools over her parchment, each sequestered in a shallow, low-ceilinged nook with a table-board, each nook illuminated by a window to let in God's light. There was a similar, smaller scriptorium on the men's side, but—perhaps for the novelty of it—it was the copies made by the sisters that fetched the highest sums for the abbey. The most recent had been bought by Sweyn of Hereford. His strong, broad hands might be unclasping it even now, pressing open the vellum pages. No, she must not think that way, especially not in here, the room most sacred to her heart.

The scratching of quill on vellum was as soothing to her as a mother's heartbeat to a babe, and it was here, and only here, that she almost felt she was, indeed, Mother Edgiva, Abbess of Leominster, despite her transgressions. She knew each pen scratch, could sometimes almost tell which letter was being formed by the rhythm of the scratches, which ink was being used by the scent of it.

No monastic house was allowed its own style. She formally instructed each of her calligraphers, nuns and monks alike, to follow the model of the scribe Eadui Basan—the thick lines and enormous capital letters resting on patterns of warmly tinted background colors. Privately, however, if she saw that any scrivener had a gift, and wished to indulge in animals or mythic figures or horological symbols, she allowed it and even encouraged them. The illuminations had little enough to do with the matter they illuminated anyhow; truly, they were just an opportunity to add beauty to the world.

Also, she had always felt, there was nothing sinful in having the opportunity to resist pridefulness, and how could one learn to resist a sin but to be tempted by it first? A talented botanist, she herself was admired among scribes throughout England for having perfected a certain blue ink from the juice of larkspur petals mixed with alum. *That is who I am.* Not some wanton whore. Not even Godiva—so reckless and absent of all modesty— not even *Godiva* had ever behaved as shamefully as Edgiva.

Every time a messenger approached she would send a novice rushing to see if he was from Bishop Lyfing; she needed Lyfing to come to her, or for him to summon her to him. She could think of almost nothing else. At one time she had moved among her charges daily, hourly, by the minute, spirited yet self-contained, outspoken but soft-spoken, a calm bundle of energy. Now she was distracted, distant, sometimes confused. She was supposed to represent the presence of the Virgin Mary. Something had gone terribly wrong.

Approximately weekly, usually Saturdays, she received a letter from some superior in the Church, instructing her or reminding her of the newest proscriptions that would touch upon her position or her charges. She would at once reply, carefully but firmly, protesting the erosion of her rights and duties, pointing out, as she did every week, that forbidding sisters from touching holy books was difficult when they were themselves the ones who *wrote* the holy books. But so it goes in Rome now, came the tart Lateran replies, and howsoever Rome evolves, so must the rest of Christendom follow suit—and especially in England, where finally at last there was a good continental and wholly Christian king to help repair the laxity of a semiheathen past.

Sundays, she led the ceremony to sprinkle holy water on all the buildings in the compound, although reports from Rome warned her that new theology suggested only monks should do that. Weekly, usually Mondays, she would counsel Audry through her confusion: the young sister never understood why penance was not a part of healing, since clearly ill health was a punishment or trial from God. No, Edgiva would say patiently, that is not so, although in fact the great religious minds of Rome were beginning to consider that.

She watched herself, and she watched Audry watching her with increasing concern and curiosity, and all the time she fought to keep her thoughts away from Hereford and focused on the gold band on her finger that wedded her to Christ. She needed the calm and understanding Lyfing to help her to renew her vows.

Coventry

On the feast of the Assumption, Leofric and Godiva wrote to Bishop Lyfing, inviting him to join them for Easter, and briefly, proudly recapitulating Godiva's role in the Land Ceremony. Godiva, cheered at the possibility of the bishop's presence, estimated the size of his entourage and informed the cook and steward to prepare extra food and cots.

But the following morning, Godiva returned from a visit to the monastery, enjoying how the drying breeze buffeted her blue silk outfit . . . to find Leofric sitting at his chair, staring into the hearth-pit with sorrowful eyes. The steward and the other hall servants moved quietly around the edges of the room, afraid of disturbing his trance.

Somehow she knew before he even said the words that Bishop Lyfing was no longer with the living. She took a stool and placed it close to Leofric's chair, sat on it, and rested her head sadly on his lap, breathing in his scent for comfort.

He handed her an unsealed scroll; she unrolled it and began to read, as Leofric said, "It is a disrespectful way to tell us. Disrespectful to Lyfing, I mean. As if he were an afterthought."

> *King Edward sends friendly greetings to Earl Godwin*
> *and Earl Leofric and Earl Sweyn and Mother Edgiva*
> *and all the thanes in Worcestershire and Hereford-*
> *shire and Warwickshire and Gloucestershire. I inform*

you that, upon the passing of the inimitable Lyfing,
I have granted to the abbot Aldred the bishopric of
Worcester, with sake and soll, toll and team, within
borough and without, as fully and completely in all
things as ever any of his predecessors possessed it.

Sixty-odd miles to the west of Coventry, Mother Edgiva was receiving the same news. She wrote with trembling hands into her private diary and felt more alone than ever in the world. There was nobody upon whose knee she could rest her head. The news brought with it far greater dismay than her saddened sisters ever could begin to know.

CHAPTER 10

Holy Week was always a blur to Godiva. She and Leofric conventionally hosted somebody of prominence wherever they were, and always invited the housecarls and the manor population, including servants, to feast with them. This year there would be no guest, but there was still to be a feast—the largest feast Coventry manor had yet tried to provide. It rained most of the week, which was a blessing for the crops, if not for anybody's mood. The cook was testy, and everyone supplying any kind of foodstuff was rightfully afraid of him.

There was some anxiety underlying these preparations, because the stores were low. Godiva knew this, and knew things were worse for the villagers and farmers—that was why she had been asked to perform the Land Ceremony spell.

"Perhaps we should feed everyone," she said to Leofric. "The village, the monastery, all of them."

"Must they all receive new clothes?" he asked in a lugubrious voice. "I haven't many castoffs with me; I brought only enough from Brom Legge to cover the regulars."

"All will get eggs," said Godiva. "I'll hire that young Edwyn from Baginton to decorate the rest of them; they will understand the gesture." Eggs and milk were forbidden during Lent, but one could not tell hens and cows that. By Easter, when the prohibitions were lifted, any given household had a mass of boiled eggs and plenty of cheese ripening; these were the main ingredients in half the dishes of the Easter feast. It was a custom borrowed from the Continent to dye the eggs and decorate them festively, leaving them all over the house to add some color to what was otherwise the blandest forty days of the entire year.

The local hundredcourt met the day of each full moon at Coffa's Tree, where the men (this time of year) would carelessly tread upon the daffodils and celandines. The earl had gone to oversee the hundredcourt on the first day of Holy Week, and had been rained on. Godiva took an hour away from her endless whirl of chores: "I'll dry you off . . . and then I'll dampen you again," she offered, closing her arms around his waist beneath his cloak.

He pressed her hard against him, and she let the worrisome duties of the week fade away. Just for an hour.

The shire-courts of Worcester and Warwick were both to meet at Easter, but Leofric requested a deferment out of respect for Lyfing's death. He bemoaned to Godiva how dull the Worcester court proceedings would be now, without the bishop as company. "I'll give you something entertaining to look forward to," she said. "Step into our chamber and I shall give you a sample of it now," and again they found an hour to escape the cacophony of being earl and countess.

They approached the holiest of holy periods, the Triduum—the Tedium, Godiva called it secretly—feeling stretched beyond their means to feed the household, and excessively weary of the odor of boiling eggs. The so-called feast of Maundy Thursday represented Christ's last supper about as much as a dandelion resembled an oak. There was nothing but fish stew, withered winter greens, and baggy-looking root vegetables. This was not God's fault, of course, but the natural cycle of the year. There was precious little around to eat, Lent or no Lent—at least Lent gave Hunger the illusion of accomplishment.

Good Friday found Godiva in the monastery, creeping toward the cross on bended knees, an occasion for which she donned her nearly monastic dark wool dress. This was more to protect her brighter tunics from the dirt than to appear demure and holy, but she was fond of her monks at St. Mary's and liked to please them too. God knew her soul, her sins and charities, no matter how she dressed. (For that reason, Edgiva's aggressively drab nun's habit had always seemed to Godiva an empty gesture, bordering even on an inverted kind of vanity.)

Late morning of Holy Saturday, finally, it was dry again and even sunny. Every member of the manor household rushed about fulfilling their particular chores for the greatest and most joyful day of the year. A young man on a palfrey appeared on the southern road. He wore the king's livery, and Leofric, seeing this from the door of the manor, groaned quietly to himself.

This messenger informed them that His Majesty King Edward had decided to honor them with his presence for the Easter feast, and would be arriving in Coventry by nightfall. With his retinue. Of approximately ten housecarls, his chaplain, and his groom, but not his wife.

This meant that in addition to preparing the Easter festivities, the household now had also to turn its attention toward preparing for an unexpected royal visit. Leofric was fuming most of the day, but Godiva managed to keep in fairly good temper as they rushed to prepare their home for him. Their chamberlain outfitted their room for His Majesty and turned the manor office beside it into a bedroom for the earl and his lady, while the steward and other household officers would sleep on bedrolls on the hall floor with the king's retinue. Likewise the horses had to be moved about in the stables to make room for His Majesty's equine train.

"Why is he coming?" Leofric muttered to himself in her hearing each of the three moments their paths crossed during the day, which meant he was probably muttering it to himself constantly, even when she wasn't there.

"He is clumsily flexing his royal muscle," Godiva said reassuringly, the third time, when they encountered each other by the kitchen screens. "Do you remember at Council, he was forever making noise about wanting to demonstrate his independent power? Even Aldred commented, and Aldred never comments on anything. So here's his go at it. Inconveniencing an earl, just because he can. He thinks if he can force us to be gracious over dinner, he has somehow belittled you for his own aggrandizement."

"He will certainly be belittling my stores," said Leofric grumpily. "We've hardly anything to feed him."

Godiva shook her head. "We'll not give him the satisfaction of knowing that. This must be handled with Edgiva's trick of indirect resistance. He is coming for a feast, and thinks he will break us by demanding that? We will throw him such a feast he'll think our means are limitless. He will be cowed, and move on to bully someone else. 'Tis a petty show of power, that is all. He lacks imagination, and thank God for it."

Having a moment to spare in the late afternoon, Godiva went into the wardrobe of the room she would be yielding to Edward overnight, and pulled from it the most flattering double-tunic she had with her. Her favorite girdle was in Brom Legge, but she had here the one with green glass beads, and the veil with gold thread woven into the scarlet silk. As she was adding an unnecessary Byzantine-style garnet brooch to her outer tunic at the neck, Leofric walked in. He stopped abruptly and eyed her up and down.

She smiled, expecting a compliment. The brooch had been a gift from him.

"Godiva, that is a dreadful idea," he said sternly. "Put on your most modest clothes."

"Why?" she demanded.

"Whatever the reason that man is coming here, I know he does not like to see you dazzling, and you are dazzling in that outfit."

"I will not dress to please him," she said, and reached for her rosary, to hang it from her girdle. "He was put onto the throne to return this kingdom from tyranny to lawful rule, and there is to my knowledge no law against my dressing festively. I will remind

him that the earl he is trying to prove himself superior to has by
far the superior wife."

"You will provoke him," Leofric said.

"Provoke him to do what?" Godiva scoffed.

They received His Majesty in the hall at sundown, with all
the necessary formal obsequities and rituals of greeting. They
thanked him for the lavish gifts of clothing he brought them both.
But there was no ease between them. From the way Edward
looked at her raiment, Godiva felt a stone in her gut and realized
Leofric had been right. After a moment, however, she decided
she was glad to have dressed this way, and determined to dress
even more vibrantly tomorrow.

When asked the reason for his arrival, the king declared
that he had heard from Lyfing, and now Aldred, such marvelous things about the development of the monastery here, and
he wanted to be present for its first full Easter services. He was
especially glad to have arrived in time for the Tenebrae service.

After midnight, the whole of the manor proceeded down the
town's street to join the villagers, lay brothers, and monks within
the monastery's church. It was the first time since the Land Ceremony that Godiva had been here for religious observances.

The inverted V of the hearse candelabrum sat upon the altar,
every candle lit, sending terrifically spooky shadows against all
the walls. Godiva, Leofric, and Edward sat on a cushioned bench
up at the front, Edward shrinking somewhat away from Leofric,
and Godiva grateful that her husband was between them. Most
everyone else stood behind them, shifting about throughout the
service.

The monks and the priest recited Psalms, and Lamentations, and sections of Jeremiah, all in Latin and therefore unintelligible to almost everybody in the small, crowded church. Godiva, remembering Latin well enough, still could not keep her mind upon it, and she shivered in the dark, shifting frequently from one buttock to the other, occasionally worrying Leofric's gloved fingers with her own, just to feel something of his touch.

At certain points during the service, one candle was extinguished, and then another, until deep in the recesses of nocturnal hours, there remained only the top light on the candelabrum. The priest reciting Lamentations, assisted by tonsured brothers, lifted the candelabrum off the altar and lowered it behind the altar, throwing the church into almost total darkness.

A loud crash, and Godiva jumped—as she did every year. Behind her, villagers and servants yelped in startlement. She knew this was just a trick—monks breaking crockery against the church walls while others rattled metal sticks—but still she liked the drama of it. Finally something interesting was happening inside a church: the symbolic re-creation of the earthquakes following Christ's death.

If only his resurrection were so engaging, she thought, then crossed herself guiltily.

A few hours of fitful sleep back at the manor was allowed then. Then a hurried return to the church, where Easter services themselves began shortly before dawn and went on for approximately ten months, to judge by how empty the countess's stomach felt. This was the most exalted and most joyful of all days within the Church calendar, but the Land Ceremony had been so much more meaningful to her that it was hard to pay attention now. At almost every reference to the risen Lord, she had to squelch the urge to whisper "We already took care of that last week by Coffa's Tree."

Once they were released from services, the earl, his wife, and the king and his retinue walked the still-muddy length of Coventry back to the manor, followed by the population of the town and monastery. In a coordinated convocation of every person who owed allegiance to either Leofric or Godiva, or both, Godiva had orchestrated a merry gathering in which scores were fed and given decorated eggs, and dozens were given gifts of new clothes from herself and her husband. Daffodils and catkins were woven into hawthorn branches to decorate the tables. Edward would not catch them throwing a paltry feast.

Honestly, though, she was so exhausted from the week of preparation, she was too bleary-eyed now to enjoy or even notice most of the festivities. Mostly she was glad all those painted eggs would no longer be underfoot everywhere. What she had conjured would have been quite an accomplishment, even if she had not had to rearrange the household at the last moment to accommodate King Edward's abrupt arrival. Given that added burden on their time and resources, Godiva considered her household's achievement nearly miraculous; if the ornate silver necklace she was donating to a statue of Mary at the monastery had been rendered into coin, she would have strewn it freely around the room for her own people to collect. They needed it more than Mother Mary did.

The earl in leather, his lady in silk, the king in fur, and his retinue in wool had put on smiling faces throughout the tour of the town, and continued so throughout the feast; the commoners were ecstatic to be in the presence of His Majesty, which for most of them would happen only this one time in their whole lives. Even the brothers from the monastery were awed at the honor of sharing a meal with His Majesty. The nobles smiled and beamed with tired beneficence to the housecarls and the well-dressed local thanes, the cheese maker, the beadle, the beekeeper, the shepherd and oxherd and goatherd and cowherd and hayward, the barnman and woodward and sowers and grooms.

But His Majesty and his hosts were warm as frost to each other, as they exchanged and received toasts in their intricately decorated green-glass wine cups, a recent gift from Alfgar. Godiva found herself counting to one hundred and then backward again to one, and then forward to one hundred and then backward again to one, to try to keep her patience as she waited for the feast to be over. Beside her, Leofric ate his lamb in cream sauce and boiled eggs, and quail and boiled quail eggs, and spring greens garnished with boiled eggs, without once smiling or even looking up from his food. *Why is Edward here?* She could hear his thoughts grinding over and over like a groaning gristmill. She wished she could remind Leofric of the answer: *Merely to prove he has the right.*

Finally, at last, after hours, when the sun was slanting westward behind a wash of stubborn clouds, the feast ended, the final benedictions were bestowed, and those who did not reside in the manor house were gently expelled from it, carrying baskets of decorated boiled eggs.

Now at last they would be relatively private with the king and hear from his own lips his excuse for his presence.

They set Leofric's high-backed chair on the south side of the fire for him. Godiva ordered the steward to bring oil lamps on stands and an extra cushion for His Majesty's feet near the fire.

Edward watched her, his blue eyes glittery below greying brows, his chin resting on one gloved hand, saying nothing. When the pillow arrived, she asked permission to place it; he nodded, still watching her intensely as she knelt gracefully and lifted each of his booted feet, then resettled each on the cushion. Smiling as if this was the greatest of privileges, she settled on the stool beside him. She was dressed entirely in bright blue and rose, with gold embroidery on everything to catch the light. Certain outfits, she knew, made her look beautiful, but in this one, she looked pretty, with an air of innocence.

"Your Majesty," she said. "We have been honored by your visit on such a joyful day."

"It is a very comfortable cushion," Edward said, no longer looking at her. To Leofric, he said, "I have come to speak to you about Coventry."

After the slightest pause, Leofric said, "Very well," and waited for His Majesty to elucidate.

"It appears to be a small but very promising town."

"Yes, it is," said Leofric. "Godiva knows this well. Lady, would you sing praises of the town for His Majesty?" As if sharing a private jest, he added drily to the king, "She is very fond of Coventry."

"It is ever my pleasure to trumpet our strengths. Where we sit now," the lady recited, "is almost the exact center of the kingdom."

"This I know already," said Edward, and then added, to Leofric: "The town farthest from any invader, no matter where they land."

Leofric deliberately turned to his wife. "An accurate assessment, Godiva?"

"Yes," the countess said serenely. "But let us assume there will be no more invaders, Your Majesty. Let us assume the kingdom will thrive and trade will expand. When that happens, Coventry will grow to be a lively trading hub, precisely for its location. It is on the trade route for both iron and salt. The soil nearby, as you must have noticed as you rode here, is loamy, and the land directly around the town has been reclaimed for grazing—we are able to support tremendous herds of livestock. The wool production in the immediate area must be measured, for surely it excels any other hundred in England. There is a natural abundance of forest game; there are springs and streams abounding, and wells are easy to dig. The town will be healthy and self-sustaining. It is remarkable to me that there have been no larger settlements here since Canute destroyed the nunnery."

"I find that remarkable as well," said Edward, speaking only to Leofric, as if Leofric were the one speaking to him. "When first I heard about the hamlet, it surprised me that there was not already a well-established manor here."

"We are working on that," Godiva said pleasantly, as if he were not ignoring her. "And of course, with the blessing of Leofric's purse, the monastery shall blossom, so this shall be not only a spiritual city, but a center of learning as well."

"Yes, I had the same thought," said Edward—to Leofric. "Nothing encourages stable industry like the founding of a minster."

"They have the means here to outshine even Leominster Abbey," said Leofric, putting a proud hand on Godiva's veiled

shoulder. "I think before my life is out, Coventry shall rival Winchester."

"I think so too," said Edward. "That is why I want it."

There was a silence.

"Pardon, sire?" said Leofric.

"I have come," said Edward, "to take possession of the town
of Coventry."

CHAPTER 11

W ould Your Majesty," Godiva asked, "care to explain by what rights he feels entitled to Coventry?"

"Given the facts your harlot wife has just laid out so boastfully," Edward said to Leofric, turning his shoulder slightly away from Godiva, "if ever a town is destined for historical and strategic value, 'tis this one. Therefore it should be held by the crown. I require it for my own estates."

After the word *harlot,* the veins on Leofric's neck suddenly stood out, but he returned Edward's look calmly, as if nothing troubled him, and for several heartbeats said nothing. And then: "Are you, then, sire, requesting me to offer you Coventry?"

"I am informing you that you will give it to me."

Leofric, furious, looked almost amused. "Are you indeed?"

"Indeed," said Edward without amusement. "Mother Edgiva is agitating for me to repeal the heregeld. If I do that, I must do it carefully. I have determined that each of the great earls shall yield me a concession, something that attenuates my loss of revenue from the heregeld and further, gives me more security, not less. Once that has been accomplished to my satisfaction, I shall repeal the heregeld."

"That is an outrageous concession," said Leofric quietly. Godiva began to worry about those veins on his neck. They were purple, and nearly casting shadows.

"Each of you shall make a concession to me, and I shall make a concession to the kingdom. If I repeal the heregeld simply because you demand it of me, then my power is diminished by repealing it. This way, it is not."

"You would claim a township from every earl in England?"

"Only the three of you. And you know why."

"How will you maintain your hold over these conceded places when you have wrested them from Leofric and the others?" Godiva asked politely.

"This is a matter between your husband and myself," said Edward dismissively.

"How will you maintain your hold over these conceded places when you have wrested them from myself and the others?" Leofric demanded, not so politely as Godiva had.

"As your lady wife proposed back in Gloucester," Edward said. "In lieu of a mercenary army paid for by the heregeld, I shall be supported by my lords' own men. By the *fyrd*. As it was in the days before the violence. All of our interests shall be interwoven, and mutual aid of ruler and ruled shall be renewed."

Leofric considered this. "Being policed by foreign mercenaries is no way for a people to feel secure. But let me understand you: this goal is only attainable if each earl provides you something to your advantage."

"That is correct."

"And you have determined that in all Mercia, even more than Chester or Brom Legge, the town of greatest advantage to you, the town I am to *provide* you with, is Coventry."

"Yes."

Leofric looked at Godiva. She looked back at him. "I am sorry to inform Your Majesty that shall not pass. I cannot give you Coventry."

Edward frowned. "Why?"

"Because it is not his to give, Your Majesty," Godiva said sharply. "It is mine."

Edward looked between the two of them. Leofric shrugged in a pretense of apology.

"But he is your lord," Edward said to Godiva with a hint of exasperation, chastising her.

"He is my husband," she clarified. "In marrying him, I gave up none of my position or estates. Coventry was mine by inheritance, and mine alone it will remain until my death, or until I will it to another. Your claiming Coventry would not constitute a concession on Leofric's part. Only mine."

Edward received this information and mentally masticated it.

"Very well," he said, after a moment. "As you are the one so wantonly agitating against the heregeld, *you* shall yield up Coventry to me."

"What?" said husband and wife together.

Edward took a moment to consider his new angle of attack, then nodded with satisfaction.

"As a show of good faith. To show you understand that when one makes demands, one pays a price for their fulfillment."

Leofric lowered his eyes, letting Godiva know he would not stop her, whatever she said next.

She was suddenly so flustered she could hardly breathe. She was used to taking others by surprise; she was certainly not used to being confronted, as the king had done twice now. She opened her mouth and found no words. She closed her mouth again. She wished she could freeze time, flee to Leominster, and ask Edgiva's guidance. What might the abbess do, if she were here? Edgiva's method was always to find the solution hidden in the problem. There was no solution hidden in a king's turning tyrant.

Speak through me, sister, she prayed silently. Then she opened her mouth and let words flow out.

"Your Majesty displays an uncharacteristic lack of wisdom," she heard herself say. Leofric winced.

"Do I?" Edward asked.

Edgiva. Be Edgiva. Her hands were clammy. She was sweating in her rosy silk. "It would set an alarming precedent. It is unfortunate enough that you expect a hamlet from each of the great earls, but if you start taking estates from everyone, you will be perceived as worse than your accursed brother, whose shadow you are already struggling to diminish."

Leofric gave her a warning look. But she knew it was the sort of look Edgiva would have disregarded, so she did too.

"I would not be taking estates away from everyone," said Edward. "You are right, that is the manner of thing Harthacnut would have done. But I am taking estates only from those very few who pose a threat to me."

Godiva was amazed. "Am I a threat?"

Edward gave her an annoyed look. "You are capable of stirring my lords to discontent, so yes, you are."

Edgiva will be so impressed, she thought. She smiled despite herself.

"I would not be so pleased, Countess. I can take the town by force, of course, but that will be very ugly, so I advise you to yield it up to me freely. Then, once the three earls also yield up certain estates, I will remove the heregeld. But let us begin with the lady's contribution to the effort—"

"No, Your Majesty, if you will excuse me," said Leofric. "That is an unjust imposition upon my wife. It was Mother Edgiva, not Godiva, who started this."

Godiva began to protest, but Leofric put a large, heavy hand on her knee, and she stopped.

"My reverend niece has opinions I am not fond of," said Edward, "but she is not the threat to me your lady wife is."

I'm more threatening than Edey, she thought, amazed.

"The abbess," continued Edward, "does not go about *seducing* recruits to her cause—"

"In the name of all saints, Your Majesty must not speak of my lady in that manner while you are under our roof."

Edward ignored Leofric and gazed upon the heavily jeweled countess. She stared back defiantly. "If you do not feel compelled to forfeit a tiny hamlet in order to repeal a heinous tax that burdens the entire kingdom," Edward warned her, "perhaps you need to be reminded how heinous a burden that tax is. To remind you, I shall levy it against Coventry, and only Coventry, immediately, if you do not comply."

Leofric shifted with impatience on his stool. Now it was Godiva who silenced him with a hand upon the knee. "That is wrong," she said, and stood up, radiating her sudden rousing awareness that she was capable of causing Edward such worry. She was the secular Edgiva, a fearless woman of power. "As odious a tax as it is, at least it is national, and therefore odious right across the map."

"There are always pockets of the population who are exempted or favored when the tax is levied," countered Edward. "For example, I favor the Church by assessing estates worth one hundred hides at a single hide. Today, here, I levy the tax and then favor everyone in England with a complete exemption, except the residents of Coventry."

Godiva felt her face turn red with fury.

"And of course," he went on, brightening, "the Coventrians shall have to take up the slack for all those who are exempted." He was pleased with his unexpected discovery of an endgame for a different game of chess. "So rather than two shillings per hide, the hide-rate would become . . . have you a hundredman to do the math? I confess such vast sums defeat me."

The difference between fury at a man one fears, and fury at a man one frightens, struck Godiva. "If you took," Godiva hissed, "the value of every object in the town, every coin, every plate, every dog, every head of livestock, every building, every acre of soil, and everything growing in that soil, there would not be enough to meet your demand."

"Then," said Edward happily, "I suppose *you* shall have to pay the difference for them."

Godiva blinked in disbelief at the direction this conversation was going. "I do not have the means," she said. "And I am sure you know that."

"That is a problem," said the king in his grating, nasal voice. Then, brightening: "Now here's a thought. Were Coventry mine, I would exempt the people—my people—from the heregeld."

"You will not have Coventry," she said.

"Then you must somehow pay the heregeld," said King Edward. "Would you like to borrow from the royal coffers?"

"I will pay it for her, sire," Leofric said loudly, discomfort in his tone. "Given your intention in coming here was to take something of tremendous value from me, be content that you have succeeded."

"Leofric," she objected, still glorious with rage, "You should not have to—"

Edward was now ignoring Leofric as steadfastly as he'd ignored Godiva earlier. "You," he hissed at Godiva, dropping the leonine pretense of pleasantries, "are wanton of spirit, and unsuited to rule a place destined to become one of the greatest cities and trading centers in all of England. There is a monastery here. What kind of reputation will you give it, if you flounce about my kingdom behaving like a harlot?"

The earl said angrily, "She will give it the reputation of a thriving town, and a pious place of worship, and an ably administrated estate. If you do not know that the lady of Mercia is, before all else, renowned for her piety and—"

"Piety?" Edward sniggered.

"I was raised in Leominster Abbey," Godiva said, as if this proved something. "I am constantly providing jewelry and money and relics to Leominster, and St. Mary's, and a number of others—"

"That does not prove your character," Edward retorted. "That only proves you can purchase a good report *about* your character."

"True," Godiva agreed. "But irrelevant. My means are different from yours, and you may not like them, but they do not defame me. I have never done anything to cause shame or distress to my husband, or my people, or my own soul."

"I am glad to hear it," said Edward. "In that case, surely you will find a way to protect your people from the heregeld."

"I will pay it," Leofric said.

"No," Godiva said to Leofric. "You will not. I will not let him use me or mine as a tool to control you. This is between the king and the people of Coventry, for whom I am responsible."

"As your husband was responsible for the people of Worcester?" Edward said in a cool voice.

Leofric looked ill, and even crossed himself. "Godiva, I will pay the tax. Let this matter go."

She ignored Leofric and turned on her stool so that she was facing Edward directly. "You risk becoming odious," she warned.

"No, I do not. I am not threatening to destroy the place. On the contrary, I want to protect it—by putting it under my dominion. Give me the town."

"No," she said.

"Then pay the tax," he said.

"No," she said.

"Godiva—" Leofric said, sounding unusually anxious.

"*No*," she repeated.

She was radiant; she was in a rhetorical ecstasy like Edgiva's but unshackled from the demureness of a nun's habit. Her cheeks glowed the rose of her tunics. "I will not give you the town, and I will not pay your outrageous abuse of the tax. You were brought—*brought*—to the throne to end the age of tyrants, and to serve the law as we serve you. If you do not treat me as your loyal subject, then why should I treat you as my lord? That reciprocity underlies every stable reign in history. If I give you what you demand now, you will come out of it far worse than I. I will lose a hamlet; you will lose the trust of everyone you rule."

"Godiva," Leofric muttered warningly. She ignored him.

"My answer, Your Majesty, for the good of your own rule, is: no. Go home to Winchester and your wife's bed."

"Your mind never strays from fornication, it seems," Edward said crossly.

"Try," she advised, ignoring his cut, "to give us a future king, one to the manner born and raised. Rule your people so wisely that when your son comes to the throne, he will have had the most unexciting maturation of any king of the last century. Do not waste your time playing petty games with minor nobility. Because it is nothing but a game, Your Majesty. What will you do if the tax is not paid? My villagers will not murder your tax collector, they will simply disregard him, and then what? Will you harry Coventry as your brother harried Worcester? Or will you send your collectors into people's homes to take food from their children's mouths? Does that make you a better king than your despised brother?"

Leofric stood in agitation. "Godiva, stop speaking in this manner. Your Majesty, I beg you to disregard her, she is—"

"She is giving me an excellent chance to prove I am not my brother," Edward said, amused. "Shut up and let her speak."

Leofric gave his wife a look and sat down. Godiva, pausing long enough to think, was suddenly aware that her heart was beating very fast and her breath had become far too shallow. She herself could not quite believe she had just said all that. She stared at Edward, feeling wide-eyed and still defiant, but confused by his smug smile as he regarded her.

"You may sit," he said after a moment.

She sat. She hoped he had something in mind to say, because she suddenly could not form any coherent thoughts.

"Thank you," said Edward, "for giving me a chance to demonstrate what I am made of. Of course I will punish you for refusing to pay the heregeld—"

"I will pay it for her," Leofric said, almost desperately. Edward made a dismissive gesture, as if the earl were a bug. "Harthacnut harried Worcester because the townsmen killed his men, but this is not what people remember. People remember only that Harthacnut burned the town down when its people refused to pay the tax. To prove I am not like Harthacnut, I need only find a very different kind of punishment to exact for a similar resistance, to show that I am made of different stuff. You tell me you are taking the town's burdens on your head? That you protect and represent the town? That in a sense you *are* the town."

"Yes, I am," she said, her voice suddenly sounding small to her. Edgiva now seemed very, very far away. Dimly she heard the bells down at the monastery tolling Vespers, and for perhaps the first time in her life, she lamented that she would not be at the service. She crossed herself.

"Excellent. So we are agreed that you shall be punished if you displease me, but I am not Harthacnut, so I will not *destroy* you to make an example of you." He gave her a subtle, triumphant smile. "I will merely humiliate you." And to Leofric in a confiding, reassuring tone: "You see, she is in no bodily danger at all." He turned his attention back to Godiva. "If a subject is defiant of His Majesty," said His Majesty, "the subject must be held to account. There is a certain cost in failing to be biddable. I do not wish to harm you, but it is a necessary ritual between ruler and ruled. You do that with your own subjects when they challenge you, and you can expect no less for yourself."

"Of course," she said, attempting to sound calm. She tried

to imagine describing this conversation later to Edgiva. Edgiva would admire her. That thought alone kept her from falling apart now. "Tell me what my humiliation will be if I fail to be a dutiful subject."

Edward stared at her a long moment then. An endlessly long moment.

She was expecting him to take all her jewelry, or confine her to a nunnery for a year. She thought, with sudden terror, that he might condemn her to a trial by ordeal.

That is not at all what happened.

"You," he said, leaning forward, blue eyes bright, "who are so fond of trying to bend the will of others with the charm of your body. You shall take that impious impulse to its logical conclusion. Drown yourself in your own impropriety. Expose yourself to the world. Literally. Bare yourself. Walk naked, in public, through Coventry."

"*What?*" Leofric said in a furious voice.

Godiva laughed from fear for the first time in her life.

Edward nodded, satisfied with his pronouncement. "On your hands and knees," he decided. "Crawl. Be as lowly as the earth itself. Beg forgiveness for your offense."

Godiva was speechless.

Her husband was not. "That too much resembles a religious penance," Leofric said quickly. "Let her do that, and the arch-bishops will fall on you like a cathedral toppling. You may as well presume to excommunicate her. I recommend another tack."

Edward frowned and sat back hard against the chair boards. Earl and countess waited, watching. His Majesty's face shifted slightly, sly, and suddenly Godiva felt cold.

"Thank you for your guidance," the king said to the earl. "It is an excellent point. It is too Christian—the humility of hands and knees—so she shall not crawl through the streets of the town."

"Thank you, sire," she said, with genuine relief.

"You shall rather ride naked on a horse to do it. That better reveals your own bestial nature. Bareback on a naked horse, as naked as its rider."

"Your Majesty," Leofric said, sounding as if he might vomit. "I will pay the tax, there is no need—"

"On May Day," Edward continued, increasingly delighted. "Yes, on the Kalends of May, when lechery comes most to light. Do nothing to hide your shame. Ride through the streets and let your people look upon you and know their lady is a harlot." He nodded, with an air of polite satisfaction. "I will give you time to reconsider your defiance, but this is the price I exact from you if you refuse to heed me. I am not Harthacnut; I am not a barbaric violent foreigner. I am more politic than that. Thank you again, Countess, for giving me a chance to demonstrate it. Compared to what my predecessor did to tax offenders, my behavior will seem saintly. So. To review. I will receive from you the town, or money, or your abject humiliation." He smiled at her beatifically. "You may choose which one to render to your king."

CHAPTER 12

Leominster

S he was early enough along that a simple brew of certain herbs would accomplish it. But they were low in stock in the abbey dispensary—enough for one heavy dosing only. There were new supplies drying to dull-hued crispness from the rafters of the workshop. But Audry would notice the depletion, and she could not lie to her own acolyte about where the stores had gone. Also, the side effects would not be pleasant—and Audry would recognize those side effects.

She would have to take Audry into her confidence.

No, she could not do that. For so many reasons. Her own distress would distress Audry, for one thing, but that was not her main concern. Audry believed Edgiva to be impeccably incapable of error or duplicity. Edgiva took no pride in that; in fact she found the responsibility of it quietly burdensome. She had often wondered how Audry would respond the day Edgiva inevitably toppled from the pedestal. If this was the event to do it, the result might be catastrophe. Better Audry hear Mother curse, or fall asleep in Lauds, or mutter heretically when Rome sent ever more laws that disempowered nuns. Let it not be wanton sluttishness.

Nobody here could ever know.

She was still mired in that uncomfortable moral swamp between the tactic of keeping secrets and the sin of lying.

But at least she had the means to make the problem disappear.

There were scattered huts in the fields around Leominster. Herders had built them to have shelter while moving their flocks. Some were still in fields, some now in woodland, where the sheep had not cared for the taste of the grass and so the shepherds had allowed the cleared land to revert to wood. These had become, as well, squatters' homes for herbalists and mystics, some of them entirely Christian, most of them not; some were the occasional lairs of robber bands, usually Welsh. But there were a number that were—so small and derelict—left empty most of the time. Here lovers sometimes met clandestinely; sometimes, rarely, a sister or a brother from the abbey would receive a message in a dream that they were to subject themselves to nature's forces for a period of a day or a week or longer, and meditate within a hut.

Edgiva decided she would take the herbs, a skin of water, a brewing pot, and means to light a fire, and sequester herself in such a hut for three days. She could spend time foraging for early-spring herbs that the dispensary needed, so that her absence from the abbey was not entirely selfish.

She departed one cool, sunny morning after Prime. She left through the gatehouse, exchanging blessings with the lay brother who guarded it. She walked through the eastern half of the small village, turned north, then bore east again, and without fear or fanfare wandered into the excellent grazing lands that surrounded Leominster for miles. Shocks of violets and daffodils peppered the ground with purple and yellow; the hazel and primroses and pussy willows offered their flowers as well. She made a note to herself to come back and harvest the celandine roots within the month.

The first mud-walled shack she encountered, some two miles away, was harboring a shepherd family, moving their flocks; the next two, just a few hundred paces apart, each hosted frightening-looking fellows in them, passed out drunk; the fourth, protected from view by a screen of witch hazel, contained a handful of naked people all entwined. Spring brought out every imaginable strain of lechery, Edgiva thought, glad that she was not the one who would eventually be hearing their confessions. She kept walking, hearing the bells of the abbey fading behind her at each service. By noon she had found an empty hut, on the edge of a glade of young oaks, still dormant, and hawthorn, whose tips were budding green. She laid her meager supplies outside the opening, beside a patch of violets; she wanted to stay in the sun for a while.

She lit a fire outside the hut. She poured water from the skin into the pot, and levered the pot over the fire on a branch. When the water was hot, she added the herbs. The delicately dusky scent of the dried herbs—half air, half earth—transformed into something syrupy and green, as the passivity of earth and air yielded to the active energy of fire and water.

When the decoction was full brewed, she removed it from the flames and set it on the dirt. As it steeped and then cooled enough to drink, she prepared what she needed for the aftermath: a bundle of clean rags outside the hut and a comfortable sleeping-sack with an extra blanket inside it, with more rags in ready reach; the rest of the water; a bag of dried apples. She knew this brew would ruin her appetite, but she would have to eat something.

When the pot had cooled enough for her to hold it, she sat cross-legged on her cloak by the dying fire, picked up the pot, and stared into the murky liquid. She said a few prayers for comfort. She thought for a moment about Sweyn, and what life might be like if, under different circumstances, there was some way that she could keep this child. She already suspected it was a boy, which made no difference to her but would probably have pleased him. She apologized to the spirit hovering near her that was waiting for the moment, months from now, when it could inhabit what was, as yet, not human. She promised it that there were many more babes due for birth. It would find a vessel soon.

She crossed herself, raised the pot to her lips, and felt the heat of the iron radiantly warm the inside of her mouth. She breathed in the acrid smell of the brew.

And then she set it down on the ground beside her.

It was an attack of nerves, that was all. She was not used to taking her own medicine—she was rarely in need of healing—and so she was nervous about the side effects, because she knew they'd be uncomfortable. That was all.

There was a rustle in the woods behind her. A mousy, dark-haired woman from the village, the blacksmith's wife—in a dull, ill-fitting tunic, torn stockings, no girdle—hesitatingly emerged from the scrub-oak glade. She was in tears. And when she saw Mother Edgiva, she looked frightened. She stopped short, was briefly rigid, and then turned, as if she would flee into the underbrush again.

"It's all right," Edgiva called to her in a gentle voice. "I know why you're sobbing."

And suddenly, she did know.

The woman looked even more frightened, even more rigid. But Edgiva, almost trancelike, held out her hand in a welcoming gesture, and slowly the weeping woman moved toward her.

"I fought him off, I swear I did, Mother," she said. She was cringing with fear, her shoulders hunched up to her ears and forward almost to her breastbone. "But he's a lot stronger than me. Always has been, since we were wee. Mother used a shovel to get him off me. I know t'aint natural, but I swear I ne'er provoked him."

"I believe you," Edgiva said with almost eerie serenity.

"But my husband, he dinna believe me, he says if there be child—"

"There will not be," Edgiva said. "Here. I have prepared this for you. Drink it."

CHAPTER 13

Coventry

Having been raised in Leominster Abbey, Godiva had exqui-
site penmanship, and she herself wrote to the new Bishop
of Worcester. She did not much care to have anyone else, not
even her most discreet scribe, know the substance of it.

Your Eminence, she wrote, the quill casting a long shadow
over the parchment as Leofric paced behind her in broody agitation. He was nursing his second glass of mead. The monastery
bells distantly tolled Compline.

*I write to express my great pleasure that you have been raised
to your new position as Bishop of Worcester following the sad
passing of our esteemed Bishop Lyfing.*

"I cannot conceive you would contemplate this," Leofric said
for the seventh time that hour.

*The Bishop placed great faith in you and I am confident you
will honor his memory now that you wear the mantle.*

She paused and read this aloud, wondering how obsequious she would need to be.

"If you must pursue this, go and speak to him in person."

"There is no time for that. The lambing will begin soon." She dipped the pen into the well again and then wrote, saying the words aloud as she penned them,

"I seek your guidance on a remarkable matter that has been set before me this afternoon by His Majesty. As you may recall I am assisting my esteemed friend, Abbess Edgiva of Leominster, in a protestation of the heregeld. His Majesty graced us with an unexpected visit to my estate of Coventry to celebrate Easter with us."

"You sound like a self-important gossip."

She raised her head and pivoted it elegantly to look over the scarlet veil draping her right shoulder. She gave him a sultry look. "No. I do not," she said. "*You* sound like a curmudgeonly fishwife." She returned her attention to the letter. After sketching out Edward's ultimatum, she came then to her point:

"Your Eminence, I am prepared to make this ride, at the king's pleasure, if it will protect my people from His Majesty's machinations."

"It won't," Leofric said brusquely, and drained the cup.

"But I hesitate to commit to this ordeal unless the Church condones it. It strikes me as a very heathenish act to perform on a day still tinged with heathenish associations. Do you believe His Majesty means to endanger the immortal part of me, or merely to blemish my reputation? I do not oppose a blemished reputation if it saves my people from hardship. But as good a shepherdess as I try to be, I must not risk my soul for them. Your

Eminence, you are the only man whose advice on this I trust. I beg you write to me, or summon me to Worcester to speak in greater depth. I am deeply grateful for your consideration. Leofric and I intend to come to Worcester soon, to make an offering at the Cathedral in celebration of your ascension—"

"No we do not," said Leofric, reading over her shoulder. "If you wish to court Aldred's favor, you are free to do so, but do not speak for me. I do not trust that little piglet of a man. He appears to me a cipher."

"Lyfing's sandals are hard to fill," she said in a pacifying tone. Squinting in the lamplight, she waved a hand over the ink to speed its drying. It was foolish of her to have worn her favorite blue tunic while writing, but she had not spilled a drop.

"He was trying to fill Lyfing's sandals three years before Lyfing had vacated them," Leofric clarified.

"Lyfing was ill," she reminded him. "He requested Aldred's assistance, and Aldred has never overstepped his bounds. Indeed, I have found it a challenge to coax him to even *approach* his bounds."

"Let us see if that remains true, now that he is himself bishop," said Leofric. He sat heavily on their bed. "I still cannot conceive that you would consider this."

She stood and turned to face him. "What else should I have done?" she asked.

"You should have let me pay the tax," he said.

"The manner in which he would levy it makes him a tyrant."

Leofric snorted and ran his finger along the elaborate gilded decoration on the glass he held. "It is naive to think this kingdom is ready for anything except a tyrant. Sweyn Godwinson was right: the king requires a whiff of despotism." A grimace. "This, however, is much more than a whiff."

"I think he is sincerely grateful for an opportunity to demonstrate he is not like Harthacnut," she argued.

"He is grateful for this opportunity to ruin you."

"That is not how I see it at all," Godiva said reassuringly. "He and I would be staging a morality play for the rest of the kingdom. If one does *this thing*, the king will do *that thing. That thing* is not pleasant, but it is not despicable."

"I find it very despicable."

"Razing a town is despicable. Making somebody ride naked on a horse is quite an improvement over razing a town."

"Razing the town was punishment for the townsmen committing *murder*."

"Forcing an earl to raze a town over which he is liege—that is despicable."

Having no response to that, he slumped back on the bed. Godiva loved the somber dignity of his carriage, even slumping, even aging now. His was the most dignified slump in all of Albion. She bit her lower lip to contain a grin, knowing how out of place he'd find it.

"He would not ruin me," she said. "I would survive it."

"Would you?" Leofric said, almost under his breath. He patted the empty mug with his left hand, and his rings struck the sides with tenor raps.

"I have ridden a horse bareback. I do not think the removal of a few layers of skirt is going to destroy me," she said.

"Your physical well-being is not a concern; I know you for a strong rider," Leofric said impatiently. "He is a shrewd man,

Edward. He knows how you work. Once you are associated with such an act, you will never have the same freedom to tease and coax any man who is not an idiot."

"I can make most men idiots," she said, trying still to make light of it.

He gave her a look and sat up straighter. "It is one thing to believe oneself the special object of a lovely woman's interest— even if you know you are but one item in her large collection of special objects. But, Godiva, if you do this thing, you shall have such a reputation on your shoulders, no man will allow himself to exchange three words with you. Either they shall think you truly wanton, which is Edward's intention, and avoid you for their own reputations . . . or else they will be too proper and polite to you, lest they remind you of your shame. Either way, you would lose your power." He shrugged in resignation. "I would love you no less, but it would be a shame." He gave her an almost fatherly smile. "You have been a very useful coquette, all these years."

"I'll teach Edey how to flirt, and she may take over the practice from me," she said. "Of course her loyalty will first be with Sweyn, but I am sure that if she learns anything of value . . ."

He laughed with tired exasperation. "Will you stop that?"

"You saw how she looked at him—"

"You look at him that way too, Godiva, but I have never for one moment worried I would lose my bride to him. If I do not fret about that, I am sure the Lord frets even less."

She tucked her chin down, tipped her head to the side, and gave him a knowing look. "You do not fret at all?" she challenged. "Not even for the moment between an inhale and an exhale? Ever?"

He gave her a grim grin. "No," he said. "I do not. If I did, I would not trust you with a priest, let alone a man like Sweyn."

"What does that mean, 'a man like Sweyn'? Does he have a reputation for roughness with ladies? If he does, I must protect Edgiva from him."

His eyes narrowed with wry amusement. "First, you need not protect Edgiva from anyone, Godiva. The Church does that. The walls around the abbey do that. Propriety does that. Second, to answer your question, I do not mean Sweyn has a reputation, beyond being a bit dangerously fetching for a bachelor with lots of land and power. Godwin should get him married off at once so that he stops being a temptation to all the married ladies."

"If he is a temptation to us now, why would he be any less a temptation when he's married?"

"Because until he's married, he might tempt some married women to arrange to become widows," Leofric said.

She grinned. "I shall have the cook poison your soup."

He moved back to the bed, sat on it, and patted the space beside it. "Put that quill down and come here, my little scribbler."

"I have not finished the letter yet."

"Do not finish it, Godiva. Do not send it. Do not even contemplate this."

"I must," she argued.

"I will pay the heregeld for you," he said. "It is not your doing that Edward has placed this burden on you. He thought he would be placing it on me. In a sense, it is my fault that you are in this position, so let me resolve it for you. Let me resolve it for *me*. I have already suffered through one heregeld revolt; do not make me suffer through a second."

She placed the quill down carefully on a piece of scrap vellum next to the letter. She moved to sit beside him on the bed. "Admit it, Leofric," she said in a soft voice, giving him her most inviting smile. "You would love to see me riding naked on a bareback horse. You want to watch. You want to see my bare thighs squeeze tight against the horse's hide, so you—ha!"

He had grabbed her round her girdled waist, lifted her up, and tossed her into the middle of the bed. "You are such a vixen!" he said, with a huff of frustrated bass laughter, twisting until his body stretched over hers. She loved the feeling of his weight on her.

"'Tis true, though, isn't it?" she crooned to the bed's canopy, running her fingers through his hair.

"That is beside the point, Godiva."

She raised her head to grin at him. "So I am right. You long to pull me naked off the horse and take me right on the grass with the sunlight illuminating all our—"

"Stop that." He laughed, raising his hips away from her when she wriggled. Then, sobering: "It does not matter what your husband would find provocative in private. It matters only what seems prudent in public, and you know that, so stop preening."

"How could it look ill?" she asked. "I am obeying the will of the king in order to protect my people from unfair taxation."

He pulled himself off of her, and off the bed, and then stared down at her, still aroused despite his irritation. "My wife rides naked through the streets of one of her villages. By the blood of all the saints, how could anyone take that amiss? There is no risk whatsoever of unfortunate rumors springing from that. It would occur to nobody, ever, to wonder if you had gone mad, or taken up with pagans, or become a prostitute. No, clearly, everyone who hears of it will think, *Oh, yes, Godiva, that modest, retiring lady of Mercia—she is goodness, humility, and purity embodied, look what a model subject and ruler she is being, both at once."*

"I do not care what they think—"

"I care," said Leofric. "You are not the wife of some minor thane. You are married to one of the three great earls. As a result of such a ride, there might be only two great earls remaining."

"Nonsense," she said. "As long as the Church is not opposed to it. In fact, I wager the bishop would be willing to go on record praising me for my humility."

"Humiliation is not humility," said Leofric impatiently. "I think perhaps both you and King Edward have forgotten that." He walked away from the bed, pacing with long strides and rubbing his hair askew at the temple, as he always did when he was agitated. "Come along, love, if you insist upon writing this, finish it and send it out at daybreak. If Edward has set something in motion, let us at least be finished with it as soon as possible."

She rose from the bed.

"But promise me," he said, as she settled on her stool, "that if Aldred advises you against this, for whatever reason, you will refuse to make the ride? And allow me to pay the heregeld for you?"

She paused a moment, looking into her lap. "But you do not like Aldred. Why would you have me make a decision based on the counsel of a man you do not trust?"

"We give more to the Church than anybody else. Godwin is not known for generosity or piety, Siward is half pagan, and nobody else has near our means. Regardless of what I think of the man's strength of character, he will look after us because that is a way of looking after himself and his interests. If he advises against it, there is a very good reason for it. So." He pointed to the letter. "Finish writing that immediately. What is taking you so long?"

CHAPTER 14

There was a letter in the chapter house at Leominster, writ a generation earlier from one anonymous nun to another. Godiva and Edey had memorized this together in their girlhood; it was the text they used to practice penmanship in private, away from the novice mistress, who made them always write out the Holy Writ.

Every person distrustful of her own counsel, it read, *seeks a devoted friend in whom she has such faith that she lays down before her the secrets of her heart. Nothing is sweeter than having someone with whom one can converse as with oneself, who will treat our grief as their own, and so comfort us, sympathize with us, and counsel and uplift us with their wisdom.*

Coventry

The messenger Godiva sent to Bishop Aldred was a lad named Piers. He was the cook's son, a nervous boy but good with animals; the groom had taken him on, for he was as calm with horses as he was jittery with people. He left for Worcester the morning after Easter, and they did not see him for a fortnight, although Worcester was just two days' ride away. By then Godiva and Leofric had decided to delay their circuit until after May Day, no matter the outcome.

When Piers returned, as the bells tolled Sext and the midday meal was completed, he was sent straight to the kitchens, not only to be fed but also to calm his anxious parents. His mother rubbed his face clean with her dirty apron, fed him her own dinner, kissed him hard on the forehead, and then sent him into the hall, where Godiva and Leofric waited by Leofric's chair. Godiva wore two tunics, green over blue—the colors, she thought, would soothe the boy and help him to speak calmly. Around them, the daily buzz of manor business continued, but all of the servants and housecarls gave them wide berth.

Bishop Aldred's reply was strange. Nothing had been written. He'd had Piers memorize a speech to recite upon return to Coventry, and gave no excuse for detaining Piers for so long.

It often fell out that Godiva was in Coventry without Leofric, and Piers was unused to the earl's presence. Now, Piers bowed continually to Leofric until the earl asked him if he were suffering a stomach spasm, a question the boy looked too frightened to answer.

"His Eminence Bishop Aldred of Worcester bids you welcome and the blessing of the Christ on your head and wants me to explain to you that he has destroyed the message that you sent him lest it fall into the hands of King Edward's spies and likewise he is giving you a spoken response and not a written one lest I the messenger be overtaken likewise and have his response ripped away from me likewise by Edward's spies."

"A surfeit of *likewise*s there," Leofric said. Piers looked worried.

"I am only saying what I was told to say," he said. "Please dinna whip me."

The earl frowned. "Of course I will not whip you," he said. "That would distract you from delivering the rest of the message. Out with it."

The boy blinked nervously, three times, and then decided that looking at Godiva and ignoring Leofric would best steady his nerves. "His Eminence says there will be no bad reaper cushions if you do what His Majesty says."

"Those pesky reaper cushions," muttered Leofric somberly.

"That is not helping him, darling," Godiva said.

Piers glanced between them unsurely, then presumed it was safe to continue. "The worst is you might have to perform some small penance after, if your personal confessor says so. But His Eminence says you are a good lady for accepting the humiliation to protect your people." He stopped, with an unselfconscious nod of his head to reassure himself he'd finished. He bowed.

"Is that all?" Leofric said, after a moment.

Piers stared at him and bowed again. "Should there be more? I am sure I have not forgot anything." And then, looking down almost cross-eyed, he began rapidly to repeat to himself the whole of his speech. They waited patiently, and then the boy raised his head, bowing. "Yes, my lord. That is all."

Leofric gave his wife a look of droll displeasure, and then

dismissed Piers, who bowed twice before darting out of the hall back toward the kitchens.

"Well, there you are," Godiva said with no little satisfaction, radiating certainty.

"There I am what?" Leofric demanded. "There I am proven correct in my suspicions?"

"No, proven incorrect! Aldred condoned it, and with sound reason. It is not as if we are sacrificing an ox to Thor in church."

Leofric frowned. "It is suspicious that he did not consign his opinion to ink."

"He explained why."

"Yes. But, of course, there is a reason equally compelling to avoid writing, and it does not speak well of him."

"What is that?"

Leofric looked at her knowingly. She shrugged, bemused. "You are usually shrewder about these things, Godiva. He does not want any evidence that he encouraged you to do it."

"Why not?"

"Because if you do it, and then another bishop—someone more established, more powerful, more respected—condemns it afterward, you cannot wave Aldred's letter about and use it as defense. He does not want to be held accountable for his counsel. He is a coward. He should not be bishop, he should be left alone to pray in a cave somewhere, like the hermetic monk he is."

"Leofric. If he were determined to leave no trace of his counsel, he'd have sent his own man to give us the message. To assure that nobody else would be able to gainsay him."

The earl shook his head. "That is the precise detail," he said to the roof beams, "that suggests his fearfulness. If we call him to your defense at a Great Council, and our only witness is a near-simpleton in our own employ, it will appear that we have forged a story about his counsel. Any messenger of ours will naturally be biased."

"But a messenger of his own would cover for him—"

"Are you certain?" He turned his gaze to meet hers. "He has just become bishop. Lyfing casts a long shadow, and I am sure there is some settling of dust yet in the Bishop's Palace. In Aldred's position, I myself would not trust anyone, at present, and I am not the fearful, fretful fellow that he is. He is not loved enough to be confident of his own messenger's discretion. So he used our messenger instead."

She frowned. "This assessment comes from your dislike of the man."

"My dislike of the man comes from my assessment of him," Leofric countered. He grimaced briefly, then reached out for her hands with both of his. He squeezed them gently. "I will not condemn you for doing something you believe in, but I insist you ask another prelate's opinion on this matter before you go any further with it."

"Who?" she asked.

"Somebody who will go on record with their counsel." He thought a moment. "Perhaps you should go directly to the archbishop."

Godiva made a scornful sound and pulled her hands away from him. "Do you mean Archbishop Edsige, or Nearly-Archbishop Siward? Edsige has been King Edward's lapdog, beside which he is on death's door. Nobody is certain what Siward's role is—as he is only an abbot, I don't see how he could possibly perform adequately as a deputy archbishop when he's surrounded by bishops who certainly feel that they should be in his place. Anyhow, he's creepy, and I have heard he's starving Edsige to death in hopes of taking his place. I would not trust Edsige's judgment and I do not trust Siward's character." She thought. "Perhaps the Archbishop of York instead?"

"Alfric the Buzzard?" Leofric said, alarmed. "He's more reprehensible than all the other churchmen put together! It was he who framed Lyfing for murder—"

Godiva held up her hands in concession. "I spoke without thinking. Of course, I agree with you."

There was a grim silence. With one calloused finger, Leofric traced the Saxon decorations along the edge of his chair, critically, as if he found the workmanship unsatisfactory.

"Lyfing would have been the man." Godiva sighed.

Leofric stopped assessing the furniture to smile nostalgically. "Lyfing would have told you that your actions were pagan, but that there was nothing wrong with that, as long as you truly believed in your purpose."

She nodded. "He was the last of his kind, I think."

A sad pause.

She ran through her mental roster of high-ranking churchmen. Something unsavory was to be said of every one of them.

"But we are thoughtless fools!" Leofric said suddenly, brightening. "There is an abbess you can ask."

Godiva laughed. "She will be biased, surely! She will want me to do it to advance her cause."

"I think if anything she will be against it," he said. "It discomfits her when you parade your femininity about."

She grinned at him. "I think this would be different. I would not be reveling in my femininity, but rather being shamed by it."

"I do not think she would want you to be shamed," said Leofric. "Any more than I do."

"At least she's honest, which is more than we can say of any of the others. Let me think on it. I wonder how things are in Leominster."

With remarkable synchronicity, their steward, Temman, entered the hall, leading a dusty young man in dusty black riding clothes, a large cross sewn across the front of his tunic. "A message from Mother Edgiva of Leominster Abbey," Temman announced, "to the lady Countess of Mercia."

"Ask and it shall be given," the lady Countess of Mercia said with a smile to her husband.

"When *you* ask, it shall be given. Few can say as much. Well, then." Leofric clapped his hands together, grateful to change the course of the conversation. At the sound of his clap, every person in the hall—from the women weaving in the warmest corner to the musician restringing a harp by the door—looked up, at attention. "I am for the monastery to see how the refectory progresses." Everyone but his chief housecarl, Druce, returned to their work. Druce went at once toward the earl's chamber to collect his cloak. "If I see an honest monk or abbot, I'll bring them home to supper, and you may speak to them of your plight."

"It is not a *plight*," she said lightly.

He passed by the dusty Leominster messenger and on into the sunlight, where he paused, awaiting Druce. The messenger bowed to Godiva and handed his folded parchment to the steward, who turned and handed it to her.

"Thank you," she said. "Temman, give this fellow water and something to eat, and let him bathe in the lake if he wishes."

As fond as Edgiva and Godiva were of each other, it was unlike either of them—and especially unlike the abbess—to casually send letters. Besides the lack of leisure time for writing, there was the expense of a messenger; vellum and ink were dear, and in Godiva's case a nuisance to obtain. Edgiva presided over one of the most famed scriptoriums in Britain, where the residents made their own ink and laid in huge supplies of parchment. But Leofric and his wife were in almost constant motion circuiting Mercia, and it was untenable to have anything but the most basic of supplies in small towns like Coventry. The monastery had a decent store, but none that she might filch to exchange letters with a friend.

Also, Leominster Abbey had precious few palfreys, and its village had only plodding farm animals. For Edgiva to send a message by horseback was no small thing. Godiva stared at the parchment with apprehension and thought about her friend.

Edgiva's seal had been designed for her when she was too young to truly fathom its significance. There was a central cross, the top quarters filled with crosiers to signify the abbey, and the bottom two quarters containing doves to signify her bloodline. She was Edward's niece, born in Normandy but brought to England at the age of five as a political hostage in the never-ending stratagems of rulers and would-be rulers. She had been deposited in ancient, tiny Leominster Abbey at about the same time Godiva was (in Godiva's case by well-born, well-intentioned parents who were not sure how best to foster her, given her willfulness). Because of Edgiva's lineage, it had been established early on—by now-dead men whom she had never met—that Edgiva must never leave the abbey, but neither must she be demeaned there by a lifelong lowly rank.

And so, at the age of eight, she had been designated abbess-elect, or deputy abbess, or vice-abbess, or some such title Godiva could never remember, and informed that someday, she would be in charge. She received this very seriously (Edgiva received everything seriously), and Godiva believed it had ruined her already fragile sense of humor.

Ten years later—after Godiva had escaped the abbey to marry the widowed Earl Leofric of Mercia—the reigning abbess passed away. A convocation of Religious Men swooped down upon the abbey and catechized Edgiva nearly to death, then pronounced her ready to assume the mantle of leadership, which was placed upon her following an election by the nuns. Just at that time, the earl and lady of Mercia elected to endow the abbey with an enormous gift of money, gold, and relics—and suddenly it was no mere abbey but a minster, bustling with industry as well as piety and study. Mother Edgiva took this in stride. A dozen years and more had passed since then.

Godiva walked into the cool sunlight, squinting in the sudden glare. She cracked the seal on the letter. In Edgiva's flowing hand were words reminiscent of their childhood scrivening:

> *To you, I lay down the secrets of my heart. I am*
> *fallen. I cannot free myself of his presence, though he*
> *be not by. What I crave and what I fear are become as*

one. I am distrustful of my own counsel, and would
converse with you as with myself. Advise me imme-
diately, before the problem takes on a life of its own,
I beg you. Edey.

Godiva smiled, delighted. Leofric would have told her not to, would have told her it was unsympathetic, but she could feel only satisfaction. Edey was in love! With Sweyn! And Sweyn was in love with Edey! How delightful. And how very convenient, politically, for Leofric.

She called for parchment, quill, ink, and her green mantle. She settled on a bench outside the southern wall, with a board across her lap. It was chilly, but the air was fresh and the sun held promises of warmer days to come. *She craves my advice.* Usually it was the countess writing to the abbess, quoting plaintively the friendship letter. Edgiva wanted Godiva's advice. Had that ever been the case? Ever? Suddenly the countess felt extremely wise and worldly.

She stared at the parchment. What should she say? What counsel did Edgiva really want? Surely she knew Godiva would never say, "Forget him." And yet surely she knew Godiva could not say, "Run off and marry him" (although Godiva desired very much to say that). Did she desire Godiva to come in person? But Godiva could not do that until she had sorted out Edward's demands. On the other hand, had Leofric not just suggested she seek out Edgiva's counsel about submitting to the ride? Surely the two women could advise each other.

She stared at the blank parchment before her until her teeth began to chatter in the cool. She wished she were wearing her warmer stockings. She could not think of a reply. And she could not presume to ask for aid in her own dilemma if she was not helping Edgiva with hers. Although Edgiva's, to be frank, was not a dilemma; it was merely an inconvenience. And a convenient inconvenience, by Godiva's lights.

She took from Edgiva's message that perhaps Sweyn knew. That they had perhaps acknowledged their feelings for each other, and had perhaps agreed to hide them, only now Edgiva found she could not.

Or, perhaps, she meant only that she had managed to keep aloof from him entirely, and now found the burden of perfect secrecy too hard to bear. What then should Godiva say to her?

I should tell her to tell him.

But the abbess could hardly tell the earl in writing, and when were they likely to cross paths again? They lived a dozen miles or more apart and occasion almost never placed them in each other's presence.

There it is, Godiva thought. *That is how I can help.* She sat up straighter, finally dipped the quill into the ink, and wrote clumsily with numbing fingers: *If you want her, you need but go to Leominster for her.*

She rolled the vellum around two chilled fingers, moved the board aside, and went in to call for sealing wax, her warmer mantle, and a glass of hot wine. She sealed the message with her ring—a complicated signet of Leofric's double-headed eagle above, her dragon below. Then she gave the scroll to her fastest messenger. He was a grown man who weighed barely more than a boy, and could travel two dozen miles a day—not in itself too remarkable, but he could continue on at that rate for several days on end.

"This is for Earl Sweyn of Hereford," she informed him. "Find him at Hereford Manor, or if he is on circuit, follow after. Ask him to indulge me in a verbal response."

As she went out again, heading across the yard to the carding shed with her hands cupped around the heated wine, she made a calculation. Sixty-odd miles lay between Sweyn and Coventry; if the messenger had half of today and all of two days after, and did not falter, then Sweyn might get the message the evening of the day after tomorrow. The following day, Sweyn could go to Leominster, and by three days after, she might receive news of what had transpired, either from Hereford or from Leominster. Hopefully something both to Godiva's liking and to Leofric's po-litical benefit.

She was fond of Sweyn, but he had his father's ambition and energy. Possibly his ruthlessness as well. He had recently made an alliance with Gruffydd of Gwynedd, the brutal Welsh chief-tain who had killed Leofric's brother Edwin in a gratuitous in-cursion into Mercia seven years earlier. The best way to contain the Welshman was to have sway over his chief ally. That was plain enough, and Leofric would agree with her.

Having recently taken two of the three Welsh kingdoms by usurpation, Gruffydd also wanted the third, the southernmost one. He had convinced Sweyn—and indeed, King Edward—this would be in England's interest, as the current prince of the south-ern kingdom was raiding the marches even more often and more violently than Gruffydd raided them himself. When Leofric had learned last year about Sweyn's pact with Gruffydd, he had spent a day raging about the rashness of the young, the rashness of the Godwins, and therefore the impossible rashness of Godwin's sons. That Edward had blessed the Hereford-Gwynedd pact had only made him rage more.

Sweyn as their neighbor could become increasingly dangerous with time, unless there was a mitigating factor—such as his marrying Godiva's closest friend. The Church would go into seizure about that, but every churchman Godiva could think of was either corrupt, untried, or dying. With the value of nuns eroding as it was, there would be little time to fret about an absent abbess—indeed, given how formidable a woman Edgiva was, the Church might be glad to be rid of her. Edgiva had organized and stewarded the abbey so magnificently that even the most ordinary of sisters might step in to replace her without the place going to ruin, so—decided Godiva—there was no harm done there. Now that Edward was married, and (one assumed) in the process of getting an heir, his niece's potential offspring would pose no dynastic threat or complication.

Clearly, Sweyn and Edgiva marrying would engender far more good than ill. It would engender no ill at all, in fact, just some temporary upset with the Church, but nothing compared to most of the other upset the Church was already dealing with. Most of which it brought upon itself.

Satisfied with the reasoning, Godiva turned her attention from policy, which was tiresome, to choosing dye colors for the spring shearing, which was pleasantly distracting. She had in mind a new overtunic for next Christmas, and now was the time to ensure that the red she was after would be rich enough. But the dye required cockles from the coast, and so she elected not to have it made in Coventry. She settled instead on a simple blue that could be made from local berries.

She forgot entirely about actually responding to Edgiva in the process.

It was only that evening at supper that she was reminded, when she saw the Leominster messenger dining with the lower servants. She told the steward to invite the fellow to stay the night in hall, and then depart for Leominster in the morning with a verbal message: *"Trust me."*

CHAPTER 15

I t was only after she'd sent the messenger off that she realized she had complicated her own circumstances: she required Edgiva's counsel regarding the ride before committing herself to it, but she must now delay the asking until she knew Edgiva's own evolving circumstances.

As soon as she received any news, she would herself ride to Leominster—or Hereford, or wherever Edgiva was—and seek her advice. There was nothing else to be done until then. If Edgiva of all people told her she was foolish, that she should pay the tax with Leofric's help, she would pay it and wait for another opportunity to protest the heregeld.

The next morning, she began counting the days. As she took communion at mass, as she visited the monastery in her lovely layers of blue tunics that moved so flatteringly when she walked, as she discussed with Avery how the ploughing and sowing were progressing, as she helped to card and spin wool and oversee the improvements on the fulling mill, as she and Leofric received reports from their estates around Mercia and sent orders and requests in response, her mind stayed triply bent on Edgiva, Sweyn, and Edward's demands. Leofric asked nothing of her plans, which most likely meant that he hoped she had abandoned them. She knew he'd sent a messenger to Brom Legge, where his coffers were, no doubt to alert his chamberlain of a huge— perhaps impoverishing—expense. It was uncomfortable, not to be in counsel with him. But there was no seeing eye to eye on this without Edgiva's mediation, so until they had it, it was best that they each keep their own minds.

Two more days of dry but cloudy weather gone by—her green tunic, and then the lovely blue ones again—and their runner had surely reached Hereford. A third day (pink silk—from her Easter costume, as she had run out of new arrangements of rai- ments) and Sweyn was certainly to Leominster, given how im- pulsive a youth he was. Godiva was giddy with anticipation all that day. Something so joyfully momentous made her problem with Edward seem quite transient. It was very difficult to keep anything from Leofric, but given that they were already avoiding discussing the ride, she swore herself to secrecy regarding Sweyn and Edgiva. When it all came out—assuming it came out well— then she could preen to Leofric that she had been the shepherd- ess; if it did not come out well, she would escape his rebuke. And in the meantime, she did not want him to worry. He had enough to worry about already.

Assuming no complications, two evenings from now, or three at most, she might receive some word, from either Leominster or Hereford, and then she would know where to seek out Edgiva for advice.

She went to mass, she breakfasted with Leofric, she sent for jewelers and goldsmiths to display their wares for purchase for the monastery; she combed out her long pale hair and gritted her teeth when the comb found snarls; she wrote to Alfgar, asking how his Easter had been, and if they should expect to hear news of a betrothal soon; she watched the dyes she had chosen being tested; she received a summary of the manor's stores; she heard reports of the wood storage, the granaries, the mill, the flocks; she sent alms to the outlying chapels and promised to visit them all before departing Coventry. The weather continued strangely—ever cloudy but never damp, no rain but no sun, chilling without being cold, even as spring flowers and leaf buds promised spring.

She helped to card wool, and to spin wool, and more wool and more wool and more wool. She helped repair the rollers at the bottom of the looms with her own delicate hands, which could reach into crevices the serving women's couldn't. She expected to hear something, surely, by the sun's first night in Taurus. No word. She knew she must be patient. She was not good at being patient. Expecting something by Sunday evening was, in fact, evidence of her impatience. Although given how quickly Kalendis Maia was approaching, her urgency felt justified. She wished now she had written to ask Edgiva's advice after all. Edgiva was a wise and gracious woman; she would surely have given counsel, even if her own life was amok.

Monday morning, in the layers of blue that were her new favorite, while in the gilded wooden chapel for Terce-mass, Godiva heard the mark-bells from the west announcing a traveler, and she was joyful with hope.

But when they exited the building, the porter came for Leofric, not for her. The excitement in her upper belly sank to frustration in her lower belly.

The air was damper, but still no rain had come—there had been none since Holy Week. As the bells down at the monastery tolled Sext, and she was reviewing the herbs in the kitchen garden with the cook's wife, the horses in the stable neighed together plaintively, as they often did when another horse approached. She felt shivers of anxious delight in her stomach, butterflies of expectation. As soon as she had finished the list of new herbs to be added to the garden, she fairly skipped across the courtyard to see who was at the gate.

It was no messenger from Sweyn, or even from Edgiva. The livery was loud and boastful: a golden cross on white, a bird nestled in each quarter, a fifth perched atop it. King Edward had sent a messenger to query her.

May Day was only ten days away, and His Majesty was growing impatient for her answer.

Leofric had heard the horses too. He joined her, and they received His Majesty's messenger in the hall. Leofric sat in his chair by the fire pit; Godiva sat on a stool at his knee.

The messenger was pompous. Worse, he had a Norman accent, which made his pomposity all the more pompous. They found it hard to be polite to him.

"I have not yet determined my course of action," she said as airily as she could, when they had begun the official audience. "I require more time to determine what is best for Coventry."

"His Majesty requires a response immediately," said Pomposity Embodied. "I must depart from hence at once with your answer, in order that I may return to him with it and he may then begin his journey hither in time to be present on May Day."

"Who uses words like *hence* and *hither* in common conversation?" Leofric scoffed.

"There is nothing common about any discourse concerning His Majesty," the messenger said loftily.

Leofric opened his mouth to retort, but Godiva put a hand gently on his arm and asked the fellow, "Will His Majesty arrive on the Kalends of May regardless?"

"Indeed he will. He wills it that he arrive knowing what to expect—either that you yield the town, or pay the tax, or that, in the event that you refuse to do either, that you acknowledge your state of rebellion and surrender yourself to his demands by—"

"I know what he has required of me, thank you," she said tersely.

"But who else knows?" Leofric said. To the messenger: "Tell me what you know of his intended punishment for her."

There was no blush, or sneered lip, or anything in between, on the man's face; only mild confusion. "In lieu of corporal torture, His Majesty will demand of the lady a punishment of the spirit, which the two of them have already discussed in private."

Leofric relaxed a little. "That is all? No details?"

The man shook his head. "Not one. He took great pains to create the phrase, as he is a most gentle and considerate—"

"Thank you, stop talking now," said Leofric. The messenger looked as if he'd been slapped. Leofric turned to his wife. "So. Edward is not discussing it."

"A good thing," she said.

"Yes, unless it is a bad thing." *How very Leofrician,* thought Godiva at that. "Perhaps it means the king assumes you will yield and give him either property or money. But perhaps it means he is holding the arrangement secret so that he may divulge it publicly at a moment of benefit to him."

Godiva sighed with exasperated impatience and spoke to the

messenger: "I am not prepared to give an answer yet, so I will deliver my answer in person on the first of May."

The messenger blinked. "But I must *bring* your answer to His Majesty."

She shrugged. "Well, then, you must wait until I am prepared to give you one. We are quite full to capacity here at the manor, but I am sure you should be able to find lodgings in the village, or perhaps at the monastery, although I am not sure any of the roofs are complete yet on the guest wing, and I hear we may have rain tonight. Godspeed." She stood up and began to walk away from them; she could feel herself trembling with rage. Even her knees were shaking.

Behind her, Leofric said to the fellow, in a tone of mock camaraderie: "I would help you if I could, but there is just no controlling these Saxon women."

She walked toward the hall door, needing air. She noticed the strewing herbs had lost their savor over the winter and a cool mustiness was starting to take over. She would have to discuss that with Temman.

Outside, she inhaled deeply of the sharp April breeze, willing the cool of it to quiet her blood. She wished she had asked for a mantle—these tunics were all thin silk, and the damp went right through them. She stood there, lost a moment, acutely aware of her own body under the draping silk as goose bumps rose up all over it.

A moment later, she felt Leofric approach her from behind. He draped her beaver-lined green mantle over her shoulders, then pressed his chest against her back, encircling his arms around her. "I sent the scoundrel off," he said into her veil.

"Thank you."

"I am glad you did not commit yourself. Please, Godiva, do not do it."

"I suppose you think I *want* to do it," she said, tensing. "I suppose you think I *relish* the idea of *exhibiting* myself."

"Not to a herd of common villagers, of course not," Leofric said, squeezing her.

"Not to *anyone*," she protested.

"I've sent for money," he said. "It will be here by the first of May."

She nodded, pursing her lips. "You should not pay him."

"Nor should you by abject humiliation."

She said nothing.

"The entire town is not worth a fraction of the tax he's levied," Leofric said, carefully studying her. "Its accumulated worth over the course of your life is less than what he is demanding now."

She gave him an alarmed look. "You are suggesting I give up the town. To a tyrant? To spare myself a horseback ride?"

He closed his eyes and shook his head, frustrated. "The way you always paint a problem simpler than it really is . . ." He let it trail off. Then: "It is a husbandly instinct I cannot ignore. I do not ever like to see you exposed. Come inside now; if the gods have compassion it will start raining any moment."

She pulled her arms tight against herself to shrink from his touch. "I do not *expose* myself. I have used my wiles on enough men to understand the power of concealment. What is exposed loses its power; what is covered remains a mystery and thus alluring."

"I fail to see how that is an argument for making the ride."

"Edward is forcing me to display how literally vulnerable I must make myself at his commandment."

"Yes, he is. What about that makes you want to do it?"

"I do not want to do it!" she protested. "But I would sooner do it than lose the town. If I must choose between being bereft of my dignity for half an hour, or a potent source of revenue for a lifetime, it is an easy choice."

"Those are not the only choices, Godiva," he said, again tightening his grip on her.

"I will not be ransomed. We will not let him use the wife's dilemma to extort money from the husband."

Leofric blinked, as if hearing something that surprised him. Then his expression, usually calm even in his irritation, suddenly grew very hard. He turned her around so that they were looking at each other, his arms still hooped about her.

"How could we not see this?" he said. "Extorting money is nothing compared to what he really wants. He wants to cuckold me, without laying a hand on my wife."

"What?"

"He wants control of your body above my objections . . . how could we not have grasped that the moment he said it?"

"Leofric—"

"You are a means to an end. You are nothing but an instrument for punishing me. Not just taking money from me. Actually shaming me, and so undermining me."

"Oh," Godiva said, considering.

"To all the landed women of the kingdom, Edward is warning: see what I can do to you. And to all the lords, he is warning too: see what I can do to your wives. Is that not worse than simply paying an unfair tax?"

"I . . ." She shook her head, confused now. "I cannot believe that is it. The Great Council will not allow such a perverse use of power."

"You are assuming he cares about the Council. Harthacnut did not care."

"He does not want to be like Harthacnut. That is why he demands I ride naked rather than demanding you burn down Coventry."

"So my forced submission is not compelled by violence, but it is forced submission all the same."

She grimaced and looked down. Her goose bumps were subsiding, and she liked him for that, even though she still felt disposed to argue with him. "But it is also a forced submission if you pay the heregeld. If every choice is a forced submission, should I not make the choice I most believe in? A choice that will not beggar us for decades?"

Leofric made a noise, half grunt, half sigh, and brooding, he looked into the distance. Thinking.

"There is still the matter of the Church's response," he warned.

"The Church's response," she echoed, with an ironic sigh. "Towering over all of us, over everything, recklessly meting out punishment and blessing, and eternal damnation to the wayward."

"That is no small thing," said Leofric. "And Edward intends that your behavior offend the Church."

"The Church is quite selective about what offends it," Godiva insisted. "Just look at the Land Ceremony, or Rogationtide. Such things are not in the Bible, they stink of heathenism, and yet the Church does not denounce them."

"But God himself is invoked in those hybrid convocations,"

Leofric objected. "A naked woman riding bareback on a horse on Kalendis Maia is doing nothing in concert with God's will."

"On the other hand, how could there be anything nefarious about it?" Godiva retorted. "I am performing no ritual, invoking no charms. I am simply riding. On my own horse. On my own estate. The temporary absence of clothing means nothing. Surely, it means nothing."

"Unless somebody wants to claim it means something."

She groaned with aggravation. "I need Edgiva's counsel," she said. "And clearly I can wait no longer. I shall ride to Leominster straightaway."

His arms stiffened around her. "No," he said. "You will not." It was spoken not as his desire, but as a statement of fact.

"As if you could stop me," she said casually. "I will take an escort, of course." She was surprised by the expression on his face. "But why do you say that?"

"The Welsh chieftains are warring with each other, and Sweyn Godwinson has gone into Wales to fight beside Gruffydd of Gwynedd," he said. "I received word just this morning, before Edward's sycophant arrived."

Godiva felt a surge, almost physical, of dread.

"Where is the fighting?" she asked hoarsely.

"Beyond Offa's Dyke, I know nothing more. Sweyn sent a brief statement to the three earls, and the king. I know nothing of how close to the border the fighting has moved."

"Oh, heaven," Godiva said, feeling ill.

"There may be reprisals on Sweyn's estates or those near him. The abbey is not safe."

This was why she had not heard about their rendezvous: there had not been one. Sweyn, off warring in Wales, had not even received her message.

Why, then, had her runner not returned yet? Had he gone on, into an unknown battlefield, to find Sweyn? He was a dutiful man, but . . .

"Godiva?" said Leofric. "Your mind has wandered."

"Yes, sorry," she said. "If Sweyn is in Wales—he is her lord protector—and he is not there to protect her, and we are the abbey's patrons, so we must go at once to guard Edgiva."

"She is guarded well enough by virtue of being *in* the abbey. It is *around* the abbey that would not be safe."

"I must go to her. I *require* her advice, and I am running out of time."

"Godiva—"

"Based on Bishop Aldred's counsel, I *will* make the ride. If you want to dissuade me, Edey is your best hope. So you had better let me go to her."

He knew her stubbornness well enough, and that his own stubbornness could not sway it. She saw his jaw clench; he closed his eyes and grimaced. "*Woman,*" he growled in frustration.

"Women, actually," she said in mock apology.

Part 3

CHAPTER 16

On the Road

She took five housecarls. Including Druce. Armed to the eyebrows, all of them. She promised that if she heard any word of fighting, she would return at once to Coventry, or at worst, divert to Bromyard. Godiva wore the dress—the costume, really, as she thought of it—that she saved for visits to the abbey: a long shapeless tunic of dark blue, with a matching veil and wimple. She refused to lay aside her jewelry, especially her heavy necklaces . . . but for Edgiva's sake, she dressed nearly as demurely as if she were a nun herself.

They set out next morning after mass, leaving the flowering gorse of the northern heath behind them.

Their journey took them along a path linking small villages and smaller hamlets. The weather continued queerly, cloudy but no rainfall, as if the weather gods were mocking all the farmers. Godiva rode astride, but behind her saddle was a pillion pad for respite. This was at Leofric's insistence, which only made her determined not to require respite. From Coventry to Meriden to Solihull to Alvechurch to Bromsgrove to Droitwich they walked and trotted and sometimes, briefly, cantered, and on the second night, they approached Worcester.

The town was beautiful, strangely fresh for one so large— but five years rebuilt since the heregeld razing. The cathedral of St. Mary was still sooty from the fires, but the wattle-and-daub houses were redolent with clean thatch—surely nowhere else in England boasted such a large collection of newly thatched roofs together, in a town that housed more than a thousand souls.

Were Lyfing alive, Godiva would have been his guest at the Bishop's Palace, but she was riding incognita and did not even pay respects to Aldred. Instead her party lodged in a town home maintained by one of Leofric's thanes.

In the morning they went on to Bromyard, moving at a leisurely pace and arriving in time to rest that night. Godiva liked Bromyard. It was a market town for the surrounding villages, in an area excellent for growing hops. As a result, the town was famous for its ale. The lady of Mercia was accustomed to drinking mead, as the Earl of Mercia kept his cellars stocked with little else. "Life it bitter enough already," he often said, "without adding bitters to it."

But Godiva liked variety and made sure to sample all the local wares, and, of course, she treated the housecarls to them too.

They all awoke the next morning groggier than usual.

But they managed to get the horses geared up and were on the road by sunup, moving slowly. In the late morning, as the bells tolled the end of Terce-mass, they approached the bounds of Leominster, waiting for them on a slight rise in the middle of a wide and fertile plain.

It was a suddenly brilliant day. The air was dryer than it had been, and the breeze was strong out of the west, bringing smells and sounds of civilization and river life before they saw anything but pasture and woods, catkins and wild daffodils.

The village of Leominster was much older than Coventry hamlet, but not much larger. Both had bloomed around monastic communities, and Leominster was a model for what Godiva hoped Coventry would become. It was primitive compared to Worcester or Hereford—but much less primitive than what passed for villages west of here, where there was no civilization to speak of, just the Welsh.

They skirted the earthen defenses of the abbey and walked their mounts through the village, to where the abbey gate faced westward. Despite Leofric's misgivings, there were no signs of recent strife, and there was no fear on the faces of the villagers who watched their approach. There was, at worst, some curiosity, for these people's earl was Sweyn of Hereford, and Godiva's escorts wore the livery of Mercia.

There were hardly streets to speak of, just neatly arranged low buildings clustered around an open market space where pigs were languidly scavenging for food. A path led briefly eastward, to a gate in a wooden palisade. This palisade buried itself in either direction into the earthworks surrounding Leominster Abbey.

From outside, the abbey appeared a motley assortment of small roofs clustered nervously around a church. This church, with its Saxon strip-work and semipagan adornments at the gables, was the most stable sanctum the local folk would ever know. Godiva mused upon the pagan decorations and thought that to have carved any one of them upon a church was surely a more suspect act than riding naked on a horse.

Leominster was a double house: nuns and monks worshiped and lived in segregated communities, side by side, both halves presided over by an abbess, not an abbot. The congregants lived separately yet together in an area some four hundred paces to a side, couched by the growing village. There was a remarkable absence of unwanted babes, which Godiva always believed had mostly to do with Edgiva's compassionate aptness with abortifacient herbs.

The riding party was greeted by a porter and let in through the gate; they dismounted in a small outer courtyard.

From here, three smaller gates allowed entrance: to the nuns' portion of the abbey; to the monks'; to the stables. Lay brothers came to take their horses, and Godiva told her men to wait in this outer court. The porter sent for an escort, and soon a white-veiled girl of no more than a dozen years appeared and bowed shyly.

"Bless me, Mother—my lady," she corrected herself, pinking.

It was not Godiva's place to bless anyone, but the girl knew no other ritual of greeting, so Godiva smiled gently and returned, *"Benedicite."*

The girl led her in promenade up the narrow avenue toward the church. An unpleasant feeling filled Godiva's belly as memories of her childhood here washed over her.

There were wooden sheds to either side of the walk, in which novices mixed ink or scraped and stretched parchment;

larger sheds were workshops for drying and preparing medicinal herbs—this was a specialty of Edgiva's. All of the smells, mingling together, filled the very pores of her soul, wrenched memory from every muscle. True it was, one could hardly encounter a more accomplished group of women in Britain. Although they were sequestered from the tawdry distractions of the modern world of 1046, they knew poetry, history, grammar, and Latin. But her gorge rose at the remembrance of the strict schooling she had survived. If her parents had considered her too wayward and willful for regular fosterage, she thought now, their attempts to make her pliant as witch hazel had miscarried.

"Mother has been told of your arrival," the girl informed Godiva primly as they walked toward the sisters' cloister. She was trying not to stare at a countess, especially a countess wearing great jeweled chains of gold.

"I remember being your age, being here," Godiva said, smiling to put her at ease. "Where are you from?"

The girl blushed and turned her head away. "I do not know," she murmured.

An oblate. A different kind of castaway. "Well, it makes no matter," Godiva said gently. "You are lucky to be here."

The girl nodded, with a hint of a smile. "I know that, milady, I am daily grateful for it."

She meant it. Godiva had not, at her age. Coming from a world of privilege, knowing she was bound to return to that world, she had always found this place confining and unfriendly. She'd sought out rebellion, from sheer resentment. Only Edgiva had kept her from going mad. Sometimes, in retrospect, it amazed her that Edgiva had put up with her at all.

They crossed behind the west end of the church, through the

cloister garden where young sisters weeded, short black veils
fitted under their white ones. Then into the refectory, badly lit
by rush light. The trestle tables were collapsed up against the
wall, and young sisters were sweeping the worn wood floor.
This building was much older than Coventry's manor hall, and
smelled, eternally, of boiled vegetables.

Sister Audry, Edgiva's student in the healing arts and most
ardent devotee, approached. "Greetings, Countess," she said
sternly in a near-whisper with a small, undecorated bow. The
quiet: that was another thing Godiva remembered of this place.
Nobody ever spoke except at service in church, or during lessons,
or in a whisper.

With a gesture, Audry released the novice, who disappeared
silently back out into the breezy sunlight.

Audry was a slip of a thing, wound tightly around a spiritual
core of belief in damnation and the evil of the supernatural.
Ironically, her adoration of Edgiva was based on the work they
shared as healers—a skill Edgiva herself had learned from the
wise women living outside the village bounds, who claimed they
took their lore from fairies, elves, and water spirits.

"*Benedicite,* Audry," Godiva said, suddenly awkward. Audry's
look was disapproving, despite the countess's demure garb. The
young sister was jealous of the affection Edgiva had for anyone
else, meaning Godiva was innately offensive to her. And now
she glared at the jeweled chains. And, in truth, Godiva's "habit"
had demure silk embroidery at the cuffs and hem, and several
ribbons—demure ones, of course—hanging from her veil and
falling nearly to the ground. And that veil did not cover her forehead, or even her hairline. And her fingernails were filed deli-

cately to rounded points. So all in all, she admitted to herself, Audry's disapproval was not unwarranted.

"Mother says you are here on a visit of great delicacy that requires privacy, so she will see you alone."

Godiva blinked. "How does she know?" she asked in amazement, in a normal voice.

Audry made a shushing gesture. "Mother is wise," she said accusingly, as if Godiva's question implied she was not. As if her answer were an actual answer.

"Shall I see her in her closet," Godiva whispered, "or will she come down to the chapter house?"

"She requests you in her room. We will set up the guest bed above the dormitory for you; we did not know when to expect your arrival." There was a hidden rebuke in that.

"I will share Mother's quarters if that makes less work," Godiva said lightly. Audry looked annoyed but said nothing.

Godiva went outside again, blinking in the sudden brightness. She went up the wooden dormitory stairs to Edgiva's tiny room. The abbess was the only resident of the abbey to have a private chamber, although there were two rooms beside it set aside for noble visitors, and a separate chamber off the infirmary for patients with contagious illness.

Her room contained just a simple bed with wool curtains around it for warmth. There was a chest, some pegs on which her habit hung, and a stool. A large crucifix adorned one wall, but otherwise the room was plain. Godiva had heard—and remembered, from her time here—that most religious authorities lived luxuriously upon the backs of all their minions. Even some sisters dressed flamboyantly, and kept proscribed personal decorations around their dormitory beds to remind them of the luxury of their secular lives.

It was against Edgiva's character to do so. Privately, Godiva believed Edey kept herself so austerely as atonement for a secret lack of real faith, although she could not prove that, for Edgiva was an impeccable abbess. Every donation made to the abbey had its assigned place in her accounting, but none of it ever went for her comfort. She had two habits, and one of them had been an Easter gift from Godiva; it had the tiniest bit of gold embroidery at the hems, so Edgiva never wore it.

Now Godiva opened the door and stepped inside. "Edey?" she said softly. The parchment had been taken from the window, and the shutters were thrown open; the window faced southeast and sunlight flooded the room. "How did you know to expect me?"

Edgiva sat on her bed, her arms wrapped tightly around her shoulders, as if she were trying not to panic. Her wimple and veil were off, and her dark hair fell almost to the bed. She leapt up when she saw her friend, ran to her, and threw her arms around her in such a tight embrace that Godiva was momentarily shocked to stillness. She had never seen Edgiva in such a state.

"Thank the saints you've come at last," the abbess said. "I have been waiting for your arrival every day. Why only 'trust me'? What was I to take from that?"

That was the message Godiva had given the Leominster messenger; the message would have made sense if Sweyn had followed hard on its heels to claim her, but of course he never had.

"There should have been more to it, I am heartily sorry the rest has not arrived yet. In truth, Edgiva, I came here to ask for your assistance in a sticky matter that has come up between myself and the king. I have refused to pay the heregeld on behalf

of Coventry, and he has demanded satisfaction of me that I hesitate to—"

"Damn the heregeld," Edgiva said, which confounded Godiva.
"Did you not understand the import of my message?" She lowered her voice to a fierce whisper, with a nervous glance out of
the window. *"I am carrying Sweyn's child."*

CHAPTER 17

G odiva was speechless. Then she had an impulse to laugh from nerves, but repressed it. Instead she crossed herself.

"No, I did not gather that from your message," she said awkwardly.

Edgiva collapsed again onto the bed. "And I was afraid I was too obvious."

Godiva collected herself enough to sit beside the abbess and attempt to play the wise maternal role. She was not much experienced at that, besides which her mind was racing wildly now. "Are you certain?" she asked.

Edgiva gave her friend a look. "*Yes*," she said. "I am the nurse for every expectant mother and would-be mother for a day's ride in all directions; I am very familiar with the symptoms. 'Tis early yet, and I am able to hide most of the signs, but Audry is suspicious of how much peppermint I'm consuming, and she will soon become suspicious of other things."

Godiva was too overwhelmed to think. "Do you . . . what are you going to do about it?"

She took a shaky breath. "I thought perhaps I should get rid of it, and so I tried to. I could not do it. I could not make myself do it. It felt wrong."

"Ah." Godiva still could think of nothing to say.

"But I cannot come to term at the abbey." She gave Godiva a pleading look. "May I come with you to Coventry, or Brom Legge, or wherever you are going, and stay in your protection until I have delivered?"

This was not remotely the direction she had anticipated for this meeting—or for any meeting with Edgiva, ever. Edgiva misread her hesitation and looked distressed. Godiva smiled reassuringly and rested a hand on her friend's forearm.

"Of course you may come with me. But will not that be suspicious? What lie would make such a sojourn seem acceptable?"

Edgiva stiffened. "I will not lie. There are truthful reasons enough for me to come to you." She reached for her small diary beside her bed, and thumbed through the pages, looking for something. "In fact, beyond you. Do you remember I told you in Winchester, there is an unusual yellow flag I have encountered only in powdered form, that I have heard grows in the fens of North Gyrwe, that are best taken when the sun is in Taurus but the moon is waxing in Virgo—"

"And these yellow flags don't grow near Hereford Manor?"

For a moment Edgiva looked confused. "No," she said, and then the meaning of it hit her, and she looked horrified. "Sweyn has no idea of this," she said, closing the codex. "And he must never know. This child will have the blood of both Godwin and the king. It will be a political pawn the moment it draws breath. I know what that is like, and I would not visit that fate on such an innocent."

"Then what would you do with the babe? Surely you don't think *I* should raise it? Would you give it to a cloister?"

"There is time enough to determine that," she said impatiently. "As long as it is raised away from intrigue. Which means Sweyn must not know of it."

"But what if he wants to claim it? What if he wants to claim *you*?" Godiva asked. "You want each other—I am right about that, yes? Did he take you by force?"

"No," she said quickly, and reddened. "But it was sinful of us both. It is a child of sin. I have nobody to confess to and receive penance from to cleanse my soul. I do not trust any confessor with such a secret. Not even my own dear Beor. He is brother to Godwin's confessor, and sometimes I fear they get drunk and discuss matters they must not. And Audry, by the saints, poor child, she believes that I have transformed my own base human nature and become a living saint, and so she believes herself elevated by her nearness to me. I try to dampen that in her, but she cites the *Life of Gregory* and cleaves to it. This would destroy her; she cannot know. And Lyfing's dead, and Aldred is too unknown and weak to trust. So there is no one I can turn to."

"You have me."

"Not that kind of confession, Godiva," Edgiva said dismissively, looking exhausted. "I must receive penance."

"You don't think carrying a child to term in secret and then parting with it is penance enough?" Godiva said without thinking.

"How does that cleanse my soul?" Edgiva demanded.

Godiva stared at her. "How could God be decent if he demands more from you than what you are already going through?"

Edgiva's breath was growing roughly ragged. "I must receive ritual penance from—"

"From who?" Godiva interrupted impatiently. "Those men in Rome? The archbishop? The ones who tell you that after a thousand years, suddenly women must no longer participate in mass, or touch the Holy Writ? How is confessing to one of them better for your soul than confessing to me? I will not tell a soul without your leave."

Edgiva sighed shakily again. Her face contorted, her shoulders shook, and she allowed herself a moment of outright sobbing. Godiva stroked her hair and contemplated the mess of it all.

"Why would you not take him to husband?"

"I am a cloistered woman," she said fiercely, "and my body belongs to God."

"Well, now you have loaned it out without his permission," Godiva pointed out. "Are you telling me, Edgiva, that you would leave here, deliver the babe, and then return here as if nothing had happened? Besides that making you a hypocritical sinner, where does Sweyn fit in? You cannot avoid seeing him again."

"I will never let the two of us be alone again together."

"I am sure you made that vow moments before you found yourself alone with him the first time. Such vows are meaningless. If you are that desperately drawn to each other, then you will find yourself alone again, and this will all repeat. You condemn yourself to great unhappiness. Tell him and see if he will wed you."

The abbess looked horrified. "And what if he does not?" she

spat. "What if he claims the babe is none of his? Or what if he takes the child, but casts me out? Then what becomes of me? I am neither abbess nor wife." Her body convulsed with a sob.

"I promise you that will not happen," Godiva said, putting an arm around Edgiva and rocking her, feeling a sudden surge of motherliness. "If nothing else, Leofric and I will see you installed in some nunnery we patronize."

This did not soothe her. "I am vowed to Leominster by the rule of Benedict; if I go to another abbey I will be even more of a sinner than I am now." A fresh wave of sobs.

"I am certain Sweyn would marry you," Godiva said. "I think that is best. He is just down the road from you; how can you spend your life knowing the father of your child is nearby yet out of reach?"

"That is the price I pay for my sin." She sniffed.

"But you make the child pay a terrible price as well, and it is innocent!" Godiva argued, almost shaking her. "It could be raised an earl's heir on a great estate, while you are consigning it to anonymity, bastardy, and probably poverty for life!"

Edgiva looked taken aback. "I had not thought of that," she said. She got up and began to pace, anxiously fingering her rosary, a bootless effort in such a small room, as she could take no more than four strides in any direction. "This is why I am glad you have come, and why I wish I could get away from here," she said. "I need to think this out in calm and quiet, and I cannot do that here, for here I am completely and entirely preoccupied with all my duties, every day, all day long. When I am not leading the Divine Offices, I am holding chapter meetings, or teaching Audry, or preventing Rheda from undermining Maire's authority, or assuring Maire that Rheda is not trying to undermine her authority . . ."

She stopped pacing, stopped talking, and bit the heel of her hand, staring out the window.

"I long to get away from everyone and everything and think this through. I cannot do that here. I cannot. I hardly had the time to write you the note that I did; there were people clamoring for my attention even as I tried to think of how to phrase my message to you. I wish I could run away into Mercia and have you counsel me when my mind is calm."

"I will," Godiva said.

The abbess bit her lower lip anxiously. "But I am sure Leofric will have strong opinions of this babe, because of its bloodlines."

"I do not believe he would threaten you or an innocent child because of that," the lady of Mercia said. "If anything, I believe he would share my belief that you should marry Sweyn. A hidden bastard is more in danger of becoming a pawn than a known bastard. Secrets are always of interest; if you wed and have the child openly, then whatever scheming might happen will at least happen where you—and Leofric—can each keep an eye on it. Do not worry about Leofric. If I did *not* include him in this counsel, it would be far worse."

Edgiva relaxed a little. "Perhaps, then." Her fingers began worrying the rosary again.

"Anyhow, I truly did come here to ask you back to Coventry with me."

That was not true. But Godiva knew her friend: Edgiva's excuse—going herb hunting—was truthful and yet (as had been drummed into them by the nuns in their youth) a lie by omission. In declining to mention the small detail that she was pregnant by the Earl of Hereford, Edgiva was being deceitful without uttering one deceitful word. Edgiva did not like to be deceitful, ever, about anything. She did not do it well. While lying by omission to her charges, she would fumble from her own self-chastisement. Better Godiva invented an excuse that Edgiva believed completely, so that the abbess did not undo herself.

"I even brought a pillion so you could ride behind me, I was that determined to bring you back."

"Why?"

Without hesitation, Godiva declared: "There is an illness in our court that none of our wisewomen or surgeons can improve, and so I have come to beg the great healer, Edgiva of Leominster, to give assistance. You must come at once."

Edgiva frowned. "I cannot leave here for that reason," she said. "Were I to answer every such summons, I would be eternally traveling. I will send potions, or tinctures, or herbs, and when Audry is old enough I might send her, but for me to go myself—"

"There is a tremendous gift in store for your abbey if you come," Godiva said.

"So you are bribing the abbess to take better care of you than of another who is poorer," Edgiva retorted.

Oh, why must she always be so upright, Godiva thought. *Even now, as an* adulteress, *she insists on trying to remain* upright. "'Tis one of our servants," she said. "One of the lowliest. A serf. A slave. There is some outbreak of a mysterious disease and it affects only the farmers. You come not to save a nobleman with gold, but a whole flock of Christ's beloved. Nobody else can do a thing for them. Please help us, Mother Edgiva." She held out a hand in supplication.

"You are lying to me, Godiva."

For a long moment, they exchanged looks until Godiva broke, and shook her head. "Yes. I am." A shorter pause. "There you are, scolding me again."

"You are trying to deceive me!" Edgiva countered.

"But I do want you to come with me. For my own selfish reasons."

"Those being?"

"I require your advice. Edward has cornered me into an awkward position, and I need a trusted religious woman to guide my actions."

"Why cannot we discuss it here?"

"It is so extremely sensitive, I will not speak of it anywhere but within my own chambers," Godiva said, deciding conveniently at that moment that this was true. "I have come here in person to collect you, because I dare not even send a messenger."

Edgiva frowned again, wary now. "Something so severe surely requires counsel from a bishop, not a mere abbess."

Godiva laughed bitterly. "I sought counsel from Aldred already, but Leofric believes his advice is not reliable. You are the only one whose objective grasp of Church doctrine we can trust."

The abbess smiled bitterly. "That is ironic, given my reputation for relentlessly protesting Church doctrine."

"It will all make sense to you when we are back in Coventry," Godiva promised. Edgiva looked at her unsurely. "Please, Edey. I beg you. It has to do with opposing the heregeld, so in a sense, it is your concern as well as mine."

Edgiva heaved a sigh and rubbed her teary face roughly with her broad palms. "Very well. I shall instruct Audry to pack my travel satchel and Sister Maire to manage in my absence. I confess I am very grateful to receive this summons."

"Shall we arrange a wagon or shall you ride behind me? I am riding astride but my saddle has the pillion."

Edgiva shook her head. "I will take my own horse." She began to put on her veil and wimple. "I do not want to take the abbey's wagon when the spring planting is under way. Besides, I prefer to control my horse myself; the nausea is more abatable that way. There is a mare in the stables. I will take her. What entourage do you travel with?"

"Five men, armed."

"Shall we start at sunup? Surely you would like a rest—"

"I am here on such great urgency, we should go at once. We need only reach Bromyard tonight."

Edgiva thought about it, then nodded. "You and your men need a meal, and dinner is soon served. Let us eat and then be off." She looked around the room with a poignant expression. She picked up the little diary, looped it by its lanyard onto her belt, straightened the simple wooden crucifix that hung on the wall, and, eyes still swollen from weeping, nodded a farewell to the room.

They went outside and down the stairs, where Audry was pacing in agitation. She stopped and looked up as they descended. "I will talk to her, and then to Maire," Edgiva whispered. "Please go to the stables and tell them to prepare my mare, then meet me in the chapter house. Then a meal, and then the road."

They parted at the bottom of the stairs. Audry gave Godiva a suspicious look, as if she'd committed some crime that accounted for the Mother Superior's bloodshot eyes. But Edgiva began to speak with forced cheer to Audry, and Godiva herself hurried toward the outer courtyard.

She was reeling. Her heart was pounding, her stomach was fluttering, a thrill was running up and down her spine, bringing chills between her shoulder blades. She needed guidance from Edgiva about her own dilemma, but how that paled compared to Edgiva's!

She reached the outer courtyard, where her men were playing Nine Men's Morris with a lay brother from the stables. Hurriedly, almost breathless, she instructed the man to saddle the mare for journeying, and then to tell the kitchens to bring food out to her men; she told her men to prepare to ride out this afternoon as far as Bromyard. Then she rushed back into the sisters' compound, trying to think clearly as her mind raced.

Would Leofric not be threatened by this child?

More urgently: would Edward?

There was a rumor—Godwin's surely—that King Edward refused to sleep with his wife, Edith, because he did not wish to make Godwin grandfather to the next ruler of England. Edward hated Godwin. He did not much like Earl Leofric, but he truly despised Earl Godwin.

But if a Godwin grandchild were to suddenly appear in Hereford, with claims of kinship to Edward, that might spur Edward's own impulse to breed. To out-Godwin Godwin, as it were.

. . . If that were even the reason for Edith's lack of fecundity, which Godiva doubted.

She mulled feverishly as she rushed back through the cloister. Leofric had the calmest head of any man she knew; he would counsel Edgiva wisely, much more wisely than she herself could.

He did not trust Sweyn, but he would not speak ill-advisedly to a woman he had such regard for as Edgiva.

She had reached the chapter house.

"Bless me, Mother," she said as she entered the dim room. The chapter house was deceptively well insulated: the moment she closed the door behind her, all the ambient outside noise of breeze and busyness vanished completely. Inside was pure and restful calm.

From the shadows, the murmur of Edgiva's voice rose louder to say *"Benedicite"* in reply, and then returned to the quiet, reassuring murmur. Edgiva was talking to two sisters. One would be Maire, Edgiva's prioress, which meant the other must be Rheda, who was Maire's immediate subordinate.

Edgiva had composed herself remarkably well. She kept her back to the door, so her face was shadowed and the sisters could not see she had been crying. Her voice was low and gentle, but firm. Godiva heard a rapid litany of familiar words— *lambs, sowing, alms, Compline, betony, larkspur, Vespers, St. Winewald's feast, going down the community*—but was too preoccupied to pay attention.

"Shall we to dinner, then?" Edgiva concluded serenely after finishing her lengthy instructions. She sounded as if nothing in the world could have disturbed her. The cluster of women began to exit.

The moment the door opened, the moment light and sound intruded, as they started blinking in the sunlight, they realized the compound was in a sudden disturbance. Voices screamed out in alarm from the direction of the western gate; sisters were running from all directions toward the church, shouting or teary, white faced, red faced, holding up their tunics against tripping, as if the devil ran his fingers down their necks.

"What—" Edgiva began, and stopped in confusion.

Sister Audry came running from the direction of the outer yard, skirts flying about her, veil whipping back, a crow against a field of azure sky. She was crossing herself repeatedly as she ran. "Mother! Mother!" she screamed. "We are under attack! There is an army at our gates, come right from Wales!"

CHAPTER 18

W hat?" Edgiva repeated.

"Leofric warned of this." Godiva shuddered. "Sweyn lately went into Wales to fight with Gwynedd against Deheubarth. Leofric feared the fighting would move beyond Offa's Dyke."

"I cannot believe that in the middle of a battle they would adjourn to come east and sack an abbey," Edgiva said crossly, as if annoyed at the warriors' tactical incompetence. Her calm was remarkable, especially in contrast to the upset over her own fortunes. She took Audry by the shoulder to calm her. "Daughter, go into the church and tell them—"

"They know!" the acolyte yelled as the bells of the squat church tower began to toll.

"The town is undefended, and this is so sudden," Edgiva said, frowning. "Are they already upon us, or merely seen—"

"They're here, they're there, they are outside the gate, they are ready to attack!" the younger sister said, nearly in a tantrum, her right hand convulsively repeating a frenetic perversion of crossing herself. "The townsfolk are already in the church! They came as soon as they heard the horses from the west!"

"I have armed men here," Godiva said, as much to comfort Audry as to inform Edgiva and her prioress. "They can at least protect the gate. For now." There were only five. "How large a force is out there?"

"I don't know!" Audry said, growing more hysterical. Edgiva was stroking her shoulder, trying to calm her. It was not working.

"Audry, listen to me," said Edgiva with gentle firmness. She closed her left hand around Audry's right one to stop the sister's hysterical gesturing. "Check the kitchens for Deaf Adam, and then go to the church. Tell everyone we have an armed guard at the gate and they must wait calmly inside the church until I come to them with news." To Sister Maire, who looked as if she had been charmed into a gaping statue: "Sister, I have deputized you. Go in to the monks and make sure they are all come to the church." She turned to Godiva as the two sisters ran off. "We'll to the gate and speak with your men how best to defend. And we must get a messenger out the back gate, to . . . Hereford is the closest. Sweyn's steward will get word to the king."

"And to Leofric," Godiva said, feeling faint.

"We are safe in here," Edgiva assured her with complete confidence. "The Welsh attacked before and never breached the defenses of the minster. I fear what they will do to the village, though. Come."

There was something invigorating in a danger mitigated by calm reassurance. They clasped hands and ran past the refectory, the cloister, the church, down the walkway lined with workshops, and finally reached the gate. Without hesitating, Edgiva shoved it open and they went through to the small outer court.

The Mercian men were lounging against the wooden wall, looking bored. Druce, the leader, was standing under the porter's roof at the smaller entrance, but his sword was sheathed and he seemed at leisure. They gave the two breathless women quizzical looks.

"Bless me, Mother," said one of the younger ones.

"*Benedicite,*" Edgiva said, on reflex. "Tell us the worst."

The men all looked at each other, amused. "There is no worst, Mother," said Druce. "The porter was wrong to get so distressed. We never thought anyone inside would take him seriously. There's no cause for those bells. It's just Sweyn Godwinson returning from the Welsh wars. He sent most of his army right to Hereford with the prisoners—"

"So they were victorious!" Godiva nearly shouted with relief.

"Of course, milady," said Druce—a Hereford man by birth. "Hereford men are the ones you want if you must fight the Welsh; we know their tactics and we best them at 'em."

Godiva turned to Edgiva, expecting her to share the relief. But Edgiva looked pale as cream.

"Sweyn Godwinson is out there?" she asked in a strained voice.

"Yes, Mother, and asking for you," said Druce. "Wants you to go out to him. Says it's why he's come."

"Mother Mary," said Edgiva and Godiva at the same moment, and then the abbess slumped against Godiva and fainted.

One of the housecarls leapt toward them to take her weight before she hit the ground. "What ails the mother?" he asked.

Godiva felt a wave of a nausea. "I have done this. He's here because I summoned him." She pressed the heels of her hands against her eyes. "My runner must have gone into Wales and found him and given him the message . . . oh, what a mess."

Edgiva stirred, blinked, tried to sit up. "Why is he out there?" she demanded weakly, her low voice barely audible above the din of the alarm bells from the tower.

"Can you stand?" Godiva asked. Edgiva nodded and gently pushed the man away from her. She took Godiva's arm and raised herself up, very pale.

"Farther off, all of you," Godiva said to the housecarls. To Edgiva she whispered, mouth right to her ear, "I promise to explain this, but at this moment you must trust me. Sweyn is out there, he has come to claim you, and that is my fault."

Edgiva gave her a look of confusion mixed with horror. Mostly confusion. Godiva knew that would change as she realized what had been done.

"If you still wish it, I will get you to Coventry. I will tell Sweyn to leave, and I will get you to Coventry. If that is what you wish to do. Tell me."

Edgiva just stared helplessly at Godiva, as if she had awoken from a dream and was still confused about her surroundings.

A pounding on the other side of the gate, louder even than the bells clanging.

"His lordship demands the abbess's presence outside the walls this moment or he will be compelled to break down the gates!" shouted a voice with a Hereford accent from the other side.

Edgiva stared at the gate, suddenly terrified.

"I will manage this," Godiva said, with an increasing level of doubt that she could do so. She gestured to Druce. "Mother is in shock. Do exactly as I say. Her horse is saddled and ours still are as well. Bring them here immediately. Go!"

The men ran through the stable gate.

Cursing her own foolishness, Godiva moved to the porter's entrance. She drew the bolt, walked through, alone, and stood before the walls. She had never felt so vulnerable and exposed.

Sweyn and half a dozen of his housecarls, all heavily armed, in leather armor, on horseback. She saw him open his mouth to call out as she appeared; then he paused in confusion when he realized this was not Edgiva after all.

"Lady Countess?"

"You must leave at once, Sweyn."

The blood was high in him; he was ecstatic, there would be no reasoning with him. "I am here to claim her!" he announced, loud as the alarm bells. "Just as you told me to!"

"Be quiet," Godiva said sternly. "That will not help you now. Get off your horse, come down here to me, and listen."

He frowned. "Why?"

"I must explain to you privately or there will be a terrible outrage."

"What outrage?" he demanded.

"I will not shout it out over the bells. You must not be here now."

"You are the one who told me to come!" he shouted, irritated.

"I know that," she shouted back as the wind whipped her drab skirts around her. "Things are more complicated than I knew. I beg you, go on to Hereford and I vow to you I will explain as soon as I possibly can."

"This is my day of glory!" he shouted, pounding his chest. Oh, no. Was he drunk? "I have triumphed over evil, I have taken prisoners and won fat ransoms, I have secured the borders for my people, I have earned my place in the songs men sing around winter hearths, and by all the saints and Woden's sword, now I come to claim my woman!"

So. He was drunk.

"Claim her in a fortnight," Godiva said. "At the moment she is indisposed."

"I shall not depart without her!" he shouted back, defiantly. "What make you *here* anyhow?"

"I came for her assistance. We have an illness in Coventry and she is the only one with power to cure it. She must come to Coventry with me and then I will send her to you in Hereford after that."

He glared at her. He was not drunk, in fact—not on ale or wine, at least. This was the high raging blood that followed victory in battle; she recognized it from both Leofric and Alfgar. "God's wounds, I have been burning with desire to see her since your messenger arrived yesterday, I have not slept and I have hardly eaten—"

"And how has it affected your drinking?"

"I will bring her to Hereford now, by Woden! Let me have her or I'll scream out to all the monks and sisters what she and I have done together—"

"Oh, heavens, Sweyn, you cannot do that to her," Godiva said, alarmed. "Or to yourself. Carnal knowledge of a nun is as severe a crime as manslaughter."

"Then bring her out here!" he demanded. "Do not tell me to wait, when you're the one told me to come! I would look foolish now, slouching home without my woman, because another woman told me no. I am the lord Earl Sweyn Godwinson of Hereford and I shall not be denied!"

Now she was not at all sure she wanted Edgiva to go with him—ever. She wished the bells would stop clanging, they were high and tinny and the sound was hammering into her skull. "Go home to Hereford, Sweyn," she said. "Return here moderately when you are in your senses and can present your suit as befits you both."

"I am here now, let me have her now," he shouted back. "You are turning this into a battle of wills, lady, and I will not back down to you."

"I have men on the other side of this gate," she warned him. "As many as you have."

His eyes widened. "Are we to make this a battle for an abbess?"

A bad tactic on her part. "Of course not," she said hurriedly. "But they will defend her—and me—if you are ungentle with us. Also"—and here she waved meaningfully at his housecarls—"as much as your men are sworn to you, I cannot think they would willingly raise a violent hand to a countess or an abbess."

The men all looked away. Sweyn and she stared at each other for more than a few moments. She did not bat her eyelashes.

"Go back to Hereford," Godiva said. For the first time ever in their history, she was grimly serious.

"Not without Edgiva."

Behind the gate, in the brief respite between the bell clangs, she heard confused noises. This was getting very messy.

"Listen to me," she said, desperate to make him cooperate. "It is necessary that Edgiva go to Coventry immediately. But I will ride with you to Hereford, and on the road there I will explain to your satisfaction—"

"Nothing will be to my satisfaction until Edgiva is in bed with me!" he roared, the calm exploded.

"That is not going to happen while you are crazed," she snapped. "Lest it be accounted rape. Is it not better that you receive her from some place other than the abbey anyhow? Will there not be less upset if she comes to you from another manor house, rather than your taking her from her own abbey? Think about that, if you are reasonable enough." She gazed at him levelly, without the winsome smile or suggestive eyes that she had ever used before to disarm him. "If you take her from the abbey, you shall be excommunicated and Edward will seize all your lands."

That brought him up short.

He pursed his lips. "You'll go with me to Hereford and explain plainly why I must wait to have her, and then I will collect her in Coventry."

She did not want to ride with him to Hereford, even with Druce beside her; she wanted to simply send him on his way. But she did not trust him to *stay* away.

"I will tell you everything, and then you and I will plan what happens next."

A moment of silence. "Very well," he said at last. He patted his horse's neck. "Hop up here then, let's go."

"I have my own horse, thank you," she said. "On the other side of the gate. Give me a moment and I will fetch it."

"We are galloping to Hereford," he warned.

"You want to kill your horses?"

"The first mile or two. I doubt you can keep up."

"I love a good gallop," she said, and turned back to the porthouse.

Everyone in the yard was mounted, including Edgiva, who looked distinctly green. Within the inner walls, the population

must still be cowering in the church. Godiva wished the bells
would stop, they jangled her nerves. Her shoulders tensed with
every clang.

Edgiva was breathing too hard; she was making herself dizzy
all over again from it. "Can you ride?" Godiva asked her. She
nodded.

"Listen to me," Godiva said to the group. "We will exit this
gate now. Everyone save Druce and me will instantly skirt north
around the abbey and then head east for Bromyard. Travel
slowly, the abbess is not well. After Bromyard, head to Worcester
and wait there at the house where we lodged before. Do not let
anyone know you are in the town. Let Mother Edgiva set the
pace. Druce, you and I will ride with Sweyn to Hereford, and
then turn north for Worcester. We will all meet in Worcester
and then travel on to Coventry together. Let nobody know with
whom you travel."

She eyed Edgiva. They were dressed similarly enough that
Edgiva could have passed as the countess from a distance, except
Godiva's sober tunic had some embroidery on it, Edgiva's veil
was longer, and Godiva had jeweled gold chains around her neck.

Bundling her veil to one side, Godiva pulled the necklaces
off, clanking over her head, and handed them out to her friend.
Edgiva stared at them without taking them. "Put these on. Then
if anyone catches a glimpse, you may pass for a noblewoman
dressed for pilgrimage, and not quite like an abbess sneaking
away from her abbey. Anyone who sees you from a distance with
my men in the Mercian livery will think you're me."

Trembling, Edgiva took the jeweled chains and put them on.
They lay over her veil.

"One of you help her with those before you get to Bromyard," Godiva said. Her neck and shoulders felt strangely light without them. "This way she looks like an abbess trying very ineptly to disguise herself as a noblewoman."

"Why must I disguise myself?" Edgiva asked. She was trembling.

"Because there are so many unforeseen confusions added to this situation that I cannot think straight about it," Godiva said. "And until I can—as Leofric would counsel—the less known by the wide world, the better. I will have to tell Sweyn everything," she added, quieter.

Edgiva went very pale. "No."

"I need give him a reason why he cannot simply take you now."

"Why does he think he could?" she demanded.

Oh dear, thought Godiva. Edgiva did not remember Godiva's self-recrimination from before her faint. "Because I am the one who told him to come here," she said. She did not sound as horrified with herself as she had the first time she'd confessed it. She wished Edgiva could remember the first time she had said it, because that confession, spontaneous, had sincerely struck just the right note, while now, she sounded somehow defiant.

Edgiva's face changed from white to red. "*What?*" she shouted.

"I can explain, but let me get him out of the way first," Godiva said.

Edgiva crossed herself. "Mother Mary," she said, horrified and looking as if she might be sick. "Godiva, you are such a—"

"I know, yes, I know I am," Godiva said, anxious that Sweyn might change his mind if left alone out there too long. "But having interfered, I must mend things now, so unless you have suddenly decided that you want to stay here, let us get out of the gate rather than sitting here and bickering until everyone realizes there is no attack and comes out of the church and wants to know exactly what is going on. Shall we do that? Let's do that. I'll remove Sweyn, and one of the men can lag behind to tell the porter it was all a misunderstanding, Sweyn was merely trying to pay his respects to Mother Edgiva on his way home from defending her borders, he's terribly sorry for scaring everyone, and now we must be off, Godspeed—open the gates!"

The mounted guard closest to the gates nudged his mount over and reached down to unbolt it. The gate was weighted to swing slowly open on its own. Druce followed Godiva out of the gate first, and as they exited they moved to the left. The cluster of men around Edgiva followed them out, then reined sharply to the right, tails toward Sweyn, and urged their horses to trot.

"Edgiva—" Sweyn pined, a moonstruck youth.

"None of that," Godiva said sharply, a knot of worry in her gut. "We go."

"Edgiva!" Sweyn hollered, louder than most men could ever scream. Edgiva, looking over her shoulder at him as they rode away, looked tormented and terrified.

Godiva shouted to her men. "Go north around the abbey and the path will take you back to the Bromyard road." The riding party pushed to a canter and Edgiva faced forward again, as Sweyn screamed out her name.

Godiva reined her horse around to face Sweyn. "Shut up," she said firmly. "Or I will smack you. You promised me a gallop. Let's go!" She closed her riding veil over her face, took the excess length of reins and slapped her horse's rump, turning south as she did it. Behind her she heard Sweyn curse and urge his horse likewise to a run. She sent her thanks to heaven: he would not pursue Edgiva.

At least not now.

They raced the horses until they were sweaty, then reined them to a trot for another quarter mile, and then allowed them their heads. Still ten miles lay ahead to Hereford. The gallop seemed to calm Sweyn's rage; she let him ride in a sulky silence for another couple of miles. She shifted subtly in the saddle, to relax the muscles of her lower back; she had not galloped in a good while.

"Are you ready to listen now?" she asked, when they reined the horses from a trot.

He grimaced, squinted into the sun, and nodded.

"I should never have sent the message," Godiva said. "Not because it wasn't true, but because it wasn't wise. I did not mean you to show up with armed men outside the abbey gates and riotously abduct a woman of the cloth. I did not think I would have to instruct you in that. And I was trying to be discreet."

"What should I have done, then?" he demanded.

"What you should have done does not matter now; you've already botched the should-have thoroughly. First control the damage you have caused. You appeared with armed soldiers at an abbey, terrified its residents, and made a fool of yourself. Even though Edgiva will not lodge a complaint, her prioress will. She will complain to the Bishop of Hereford, and perhaps even to your father. So the very first thing you will do, the moment you dismount at Hereford, is to write to the abbey with your deepest and most shamed regrets, and some plausible excuse for your behavior. Say you were drunk. Say the Welsh chieftain gave you some of those mushrooms as a parting gift and you ate too many of them. If you are chastised—by anyone—you will accept whatever penalty they thrust upon you."

"And what about Edgiva?" he demanded.

Was he not too old for such a childish infatuation? How irritating. She tore her riding veil off her face and welcomed the cooling breeze on her cheeks. "Edgiva is going to Coventry," she said.

"Why?" he demanded. "What's in Coventry? Why is it you may have her, but I must not?"

"I am not planning to seduce her, to start with," Godiva said pertly. "She is going for two reasons. First, I need her there. I have a crisis of my own and I require her counsel, and for reasons I will not explain, I require her counsel in person, there. However, she also needs some time in seclusion, away from her duties, to sort through her own conflicted feelings."

"About me?" Sweyn demanded. Really, Godiva thought, there was no end to it.

"Among other things. Let us use the rest of this ride for you to make your intentions clear to me, that I may share them with her. That will help her to her decision."

"Are you her mother?" he demanded mockingly.

"I am her friend and confidante. She has asked me to help her, and I am honored by the task. So tell me first: what do you want?"

"I want *her*," he said, as if it should be obvious.

"As a mistress? As a wife? Do you wish to run off in the middle of the night together to some foreign clime? Do you intend a clandestine affair that goes on for years while she remains an abbess and you an earl?"

He sighed with aggravation, very nearly a harrumph. "I want

for us to meet and then decide, together, what is right for us. I would not dictate my terms to her."

"Really? You were dictating them to the entire village of Leominster not an hour back."

His young eyes blazed with righteous indignation. "I can cate-chize just as easily as you can, Countess. You are the one told me I should go to get her. Why did you do that, lady? Did you wish me to make an abominable fool of myself and cause a scandal? With the king's niece? That reflects badly on my family and gives Leofric something of a moral advantage in dealing with King Edward, does it not?"

Even in the midst of his accelerated passion, he was not purely impetuous; he could think strategically.

"That is ridiculous," she said.

"Is it? It is meddlesome in precisely the way you, Godiva of Mercia, tend to meddle."

"I only meddle for good," she protested.

"Oh, what I have just described would be very good for Leo-fric, I think."

"If you distrust me, why did you show up there?"

He made an impatient sound. "I had no reason to distrust you until you walked out of the gate and blundered everything."

If she'd had a rock she would have thrown it at his handsome head. "I did not blunder anything—I prevented a far greater blunder. I have saved your reputation, Sweyn, and possibly your office. If you had wrested her from her perch and carried her off under siege, do you know how quickly the wrath of the Church and the crown would come down upon your head? The king's niece. The most respected holy woman in the kingdom! And you some ruffian whelp of Godwin, not two dozen years of age, helping yourself to her? You would lose everything for such an act, with the possible exception of your life. I did not intend you to carry her off, I intended you to woo her."

"I am not well versed in wooing."

"I hear you already managed it nicely once." She reddened and closed her lips. She should not have said that.

He looked at her sharply. "She told you."

"She implied it," Godiva said woodenly. She could not tell him about the child now.

Suddenly the anger and defensiveness faded away. "What did she say?" he demanded eagerly, like the new-minted earl she was used to cajoling. "What did she say about me?"

She burst out with a release of angry laughter. "What a boy you are!" she said. "I was at the abbey not an hour before your absurd approach. I heard no details, I only know that . . ." She tried to make her mind work quicker than her mouth, without appearing to do so. "I only heard there was proof of mutual attraction."

He grinned at that, and looked cocky. "That is true enough," he said heartily. "Several proofs, in fact."

More than you know, she thought.

They rode on in silence. The occasional glance at his face suggested he was thinking—actually thinking, mulling, pondering, considering. She was distracted by the way her veil and mantle sat on her without her necklaces; without the weight of them on her chest, she felt exposed, almost naked. *If that's what the absence of a few necklaces does, imagine how it would feel to ride with* everything *missing,* she thought unhappily. Then she pushed that from her mind. This was far more urgent.

When the horses had their breath back, they trotted them

again for several miles, and when they reined them again to a walk, Sweyn brought his horse beside hers.

"You are wise to have rebuked me," he said, with every bit of the earnestness he had used to defy her before. "Especially given who she is. I do want her at my side, I will marry her if she will have me, but even in the best and happiest of circumstances, that must not happen until Edward has an heir. Otherwise our coupling, especially if she were to have my child, will seem calculatingly ambitious—certainly on my part, and possibly even on hers. I do not care what the churchmen say, but I would not have my peers think suspiciously of her."

Godiva had not expected that, and she was pleased with it. "I confess," she said, "I worried about that myself. I have not told Leofric a thing about this, because he sees the worst in everything and would in this."

"I should have thought of that," said Sweyn. "No matter what happens now, I will make that plain to everyone. For her sake. I would not have scandal touch her—"

"If she leaves the Church to wed you, scandal will more than touch her, it will scorch her."

"Then I would rather, for her safety, that it be a scandal regarding passion and not one in which ambition is suspected. I will not press to marry her until Edward has an heir. Even if we are married sooner, I will swear an oath to Edward not to procreate before he does." Only somebody so young, so fiercely earnest as Sweyn, could say such a thing and sound sincere in it.

"One cannot always control such things," she said.

"Edgiva is an herbalist. I am sure she can control 'such things' more than most women. In fact—" His face lit up with an adolescent sheen again. "If we may not marry, it is entirely possible we could carry on in secret and never be found out for it, as she would be able to cover our tracks completely." He grinned.

"It will not be secret if you show up at her gates and scream for her," Godiva said tersely.

"I will not do so again," he said. "And I will do exactly as you demand to repair matters."

"Then all should be well," she said. "Edgiva might be scolded by the bishop for leaving Leominster to come to Coventry, but nothing so severe as would have happened if she'd gone off with you to Hereford."

"In that case, I am very glad you arrived at the cloister before I did," he said. "And I will manifest my gratitude by handling this matter exactly as you say. Especially if it will make you happy so that you still occasionally flirt with me."

She smiled a little, hoping they had passed through the worst of matters. Her face softened into the expression that was usual for it when she was in the company of handsome men. "Well," she said, "there is still that palisade to be built . . ."

"Ah, the sheep fence!" he said. "Yes, you must come visit me at the border and see how that is going, when all of this bother is settled. Otherwise my minions might accidentally poach your sheep again. Can't have that."

"What a shame Leofric shant be able to come along."

"I shall bring my bride Edgiva to prevent any mischief."

She laughed then, with a glimmer of genuine hope. "I will pray for that," she said.

They approached Hereford. Godiva, having been near no large towns but the newly rebuilt Worcester in a month, was surprised by it.

The outskirts were defined by earth berms and defensive dykes, with wooden trestle-bridges that her horse was skittery to cross. There must have been nearly a thousand souls living within, and the effect was not salubrious: there was filth, noise, and visual chaos; the broad dirt streets wafted odors of feces and urine, rotting vegetables, and general garbage; noisome odors curled her nostrils from the dyers and tanners upwind of them. There were more than a few decomposing animals, especially rats and dogs, along the road, and the smell made her gorge rise.

But within a few streets, something like order and industry began to emerge. There were wells and cesspools, and the roads were in better repair. They skirted a huge square, itself as large as all Coventry, and so crowded with farmers and their animals that wattle enclosures had been erected to keep the nervous live-stock organized. As they moved deeper in, the streets became more regular, the buildings built of better wood and daub and tighter thatch, and more varied in their purposes: here were the cozy shops of the bakers; the smiling brewers and the gri-macing blacksmiths and bone-workers; the clustered, chatter-ing spinners and weavers. People wore bright clothing, in all styles—loose tunics, fitted tunics, extremely fitted tunics; loose gowns, fitted gowns—some of which Godiva eyed with envious approval, feeling weighed down by her dour pilgrim's gear. The noise grew maddeningly loud: peddlers screeching about their wares, unruly children playing loud games in the dirt, chickens hysterically protesting being carried upside down, pigs squeal-ing, dogs barking, and too many souls passing themselves off as minstrels, often competing for attention on the same corner. It was absolute cacophony.

Godiva loved it. *Someday Coventry will be like this,* she thought, and smiled. *And it will be mine.*

As they reached the gates of Hereford Manor, the bells tolled Vespers, and Sweyn invited the countess and Druce to a meal, as he had prevented their dinner and it was close to supper now. They ate briefly—oysters, cold meat and cheese, and bread. Godiva accepted a gold chain from Sweyn, a gift of gratitude for having diverted him from disaster. And then Godiva and Druce set off from the city to get in a few hours' ride toward Worcester before dark.

CHAPTER 19

Worcester

Godiva and Druce had to get through the passes of the Malvern Hills, and Edgiva already had half a day on them. So they rode hard, stopping at a farm finally when the waning moon was all the light left for the road. Godiva was given the farmer's only cot, and they were off again early the next morning. They reached the outskirts of Worcester before sunset.

When they came to their lodging, Edgiva and the rest of the men had not arrived.

This was no cause for alarm, Godiva realized; they were all riding slowly. She calculated that even if Edgiva and the men were to stop for the night somewhere soon, they would no doubt start early again in the morning and reach Worcester by noon. At the latest. Surely.

Druce set up his sleeping roll outside the door of the small closet she would sleep in.

Patience was a virtue Godiva lacked. By noon the next day,

there was no sign of them, and she sent Druce to look out the westward gate of the town. She paced the room in terrible distraction. She wanted to go out, but she wanted to be here, present, the moment they arrived. If it were taking them so long to travel, that must mean Edgiva had dreadful morning sickness, and could not let the men know it. What a miserable experience it must be for her—and they had days ahead of them to ride yet. When Druce came back, Godiva would go to the market and find something to pad her saddle seat, or soften the pillion. Or perhaps they should buy an extra horse and make a palanquin? There was no way to know what best to do until she arrived.

When would she arrive?

Unable to wait any longer, feeling caged in the small room, Godiva decided to venture to the western gate and wait there with Druce. It would mean dragging herself about in this terribly dour nunlike dress and, worse, walking through all the dreck and clamor of the town, but even the smell of rotting meat would be a welcome distraction from the state she was in now. She went down the narrow ladder to the ground floor of the house, told the first servant who approached her that she was going out, and received her mantle from him.

This house was in an outer neighborhood of the newly rebuilt city, just above the Roman walls, north of the stone cathedral dedicated to Christ and St. Mary. Godiva had lost certain track of the days, but believed it was St. Mark's day or perhaps the day after, which would make it Saturday, if she were remembering her calendar correctly. What market would be open on a Saturday? She might meander through this part of town before holding her breath for the thousand-odd strides it would take to reach the western burgh gate by the river.

Pondering the possibilities, she stepped out of the house—and smack into the newly anointed Bishop Aldred of Worcester.

His pudgy Eminence was circuiting his city on foot, under a handheld canopy of white silk with purple decorations in the corner. An entourage of a dozen priests, monks, and robed children surrounded him, but kept a respectful distance from the canopied man in full bishop regalia. A crowd of several dozen followed behind, eyes wide and demeanors solemn, seeing for perhaps the first time the man who had replaced the late, lamented Bishop Lyfing.

Godiva had literally stumbled into him because she had entered the street with her eyes on the uneven step before the house, not looking up. This road was always quiet; it did not occur to her there would be traffic until she caused it to stop.

"Brother Ald— Your Eminence!" she said, flustered, taking a step back and bowing. The canopy carriers paused, their attention on the bishop and each other to stay in formation. The tabour player stopped playing; the boy holding the incense burner stopped swinging it, although the smell of frankincense already filled the narrow street.

Aldred, recognizing her after a heartbeat, looked as flustered as she felt. "Daughter!" he said, and offered his hand. She bowed down to kiss his shining signet ring. For a moment her heart ached; last time she kissed a bishop's ring, it had been Lyfing's. There was nothing bishoplike about this poor man. He seemed no more certain of himself than he had at the Great Council, when he refused to stake out any moral ground regarding the heregeld.

"What an unexpected pleasure and privilege to find you in our town!" He glanced at the solid but undistinguished building she had just exited. "But why are you not staying with us at the Palace, as you always do?"

"I thought you would be at Tavistock," she said, eyebrows slightly higher than their natural position.

"The archbishop felt I must establish my presence here in the cathedral town for a while." *Of course,* thought Godiva—even something as fundamental as his place of residence must be determined by a superior. How would he ever manage as a bishop? He was not capable of deciding anything himself. "But anyhow," he was saying, almost timidly, "yourself and Earl Leofric always stay at the Palace, even when Bishop Lyfing is—was—not in town."

"Of course, but Lyfing was a friend of many years," said Godiva, unusually awkward, hoping that Edgiva did not choose this particular moment to appear on the road. "I would not presume to ensconce myself in your home without your permission."

Aldred frowned. "It is established practice that the earl's family may stay in the Bishop's Palace, no matter who the earl or who the bishop." Another glance at the nondescript household she had just exited. "Is there a reason for your absence? Have we offended you, daughter?"

"Oh, no," she said hurriedly. "This home belongs to Leofric's son Alfgar, and we are awaiting the arrival of his chamberlain's kinswoman, whom I might take into my employ."

Aldred's plump face looked puzzled—almost, Godiva thought, hurt. "Stay with us at the Palace," he insisted. "Tell Alfgar's men to send word to you when the woman arrives. It would be our honor to host you, but more than that, it would be to our shame for you to stay anywhere less deserving while you are in Worcester."

"Of course, Your Eminence," said Godiva, wondering how she would get out of the commitment. "In the meantime, as I have the pleasure of having encountered you unexpectedly, I wonder if we might discuss a certain urgent matter about which we have so far merely exchanged messages?"

Aldred nervously signaled her to quiet. Then he gestured her to join him under the narrow canopy. She took one step to do so. The entourage exchanged glances, wondering what was happening. Few of them would recognize Godiva from her face alone, and she was not dressed like nobility. She did not like being looked at when she was so bland and rumpled. Aldred spoke in a low voice. "I will be happy to speak to you further, daughter, but not here, not in public, not even before my servants. We must speak in absolute privacy."

"Of course," Godiva said, suddenly uncomfortable. Did he fear one of his servants was a spy for King Edward?

"I am very nearly finished with my circuit, and then will have some time before the None service for rest," he said. "Please walk with me to the Palace and we shall have a moment to speak there."

She could think of no excuse that would not sound suspicious.

"It would be my honor," she said, willing enthusiasm where there was none. Aldred signaled, and the procession began again, tabour and swinging incense and all.

Godiva knew sunshine was not good for her complexion, but she still missed the feel of it, under the white silk. She was terribly distracted. What would she do when Edgiva showed up? How could she send word? What would poor Edey think when finally she arrived and found Godiva absent?

But at least Aldred was willing to speak to her in person of the ride. That reassured her mightily. She could pose Leofric's objections and suspicions to him and let him explain or dismiss them, and then she would not require even Edgiva's commentary, which meant she would not have to burden her friend for counsel while Edgiva was in such turmoil. So she smiled and bowed her head, and began to walk alongside him.

Aldred, she learned within minutes, lacked all of Lyfing's public grace and comfort. He was clearly a devout man, but there was an underlying lack of confidence that she could feel, as if it were a breeze creeping along her shoulders. She felt heartily sorry for him; Lyfing's sandals were large to fill, as Leofric had said—or perhaps as she had said to Leofric. As many people had been saying to many other people. Aldred's was not an enviable position. Lyfing had been adored by the people of Worcester, and held in suspicion by his fellow prelates, and so his successor had to win over the former and reassure the latter. Aldred seemed an unlikely candidate to manage either challenge.

"How are you adjusting to your new position, Your Eminence?" she asked.

He nodded, lips grimly pursed together into something that was trying hard not to be a grimace. "It is a holy burden that I gladly undertake," he said. "Every day I am reminded chiefly that I am not Lyfing."

"That is a hard position to be placed in," she said with sincere compassion.

He sighed. "If I may be frank, daughter, I often feel as if I must either attempt to become Lyfing or forswear that goal forever. If the former, I will always fail at it, for nobody could be Lyfing except Lyfing—and so I will be despised, for failing to attain Lyfing-ness. The other option—"

"Is to not even attempt to be like him, and then to be despised for your difference," Godiva said, with a sympathetic nod.

"And I much fear that the archbishop's deputy will try to take advantage of my failings," he amended quietly. "I must not say what I think of him, but he alarms me."

"He alarms me too. His ambition is without bounds. Even Mother Edgiva, who never speaks ill of anyone, distrusts him." She rested her hand gently on his arm; he looked down at it, unused to being touched. Seeing his attention, she squeezed his arm a little with a sisterly affection, then released him and kept talking, still with sympathy. "But for your flock, I think you must give us all a little longer to mourn, and do not take to heart whatever comes your way in these few months. Perhaps by autumn harvest, an adjustment of the spirit will be made, and with the coming of winter surely all your flock will be eager only to see you for what you are, and to embrace you for that. I miss Lyfing, but I will not blame you for not being him."

"If only the rest of my flock were so indulgent, my daughter." He sighed with some bitterness. "I must needs turn water into wine before anyone will take me seriously. If I cannot perform an outright miracle, I must accomplish some extraordinary thing, lay claim or put my mark on something notable, or I shall be quietly mocked by everyone. I lack imagination and ambition to surmount that challenge."

Aldred smiled sadly. He looked a little hapless. Perhaps that explained his ineffective air at the Council. Perhaps he simply did not know how to effect anything.

Perhaps in time, she could show him.

She was getting ahead of herself. Right now it was enough to cajole from him, in person, his committed opinion about the ride that Edward threatened her with. As they continued down the road, which would lead now to the Bishop's Palace, she asked softly, "Not to be a pest, Your Eminence, but if we could meet in private audience as soon as—"

"Of course, my daughter," he said. "As soon as we arrive. And then I hope you will stay for the None service."

She had to get back to the town house as soon as possible, for Edgiva was likely to arrive any moment now—perhaps was there already, and waiting for her, and distressed about her absence.

"I would like that so very much, Your Eminence. Might I ask if we could send one of your party back to the house I was at, to tell my housecarl where I am going? For reasons I must not bore you with, it is essential that I meet the thane's kinswoman as soon as she arrives. I want them to know to send to me, at the Palace."

"Of course," Aldred said, and paused at once. "She is welcome to join you at the Palace, of course."

Godiva smiled and hoped it did not look as counterfeit as it felt on her face. "She longs to pass the time in the house with her family."

He shrugged understandingly.

The moving canopy shuffled and then stopped, and readjusted so that it squarely covered them both. The music stopped again. Aldred summoned a monk to join them under the canopy, and Godiva gave him instructions back to the house, and a message for Druce that she was now a guest of the bishop's, so he was to come alone, without the others, to give her word of their visitor.

Aldred seemed very eager to please her. He was not quite obsequious, not quite sycophantic. But unsure of himself. She was gracious and grateful and tried to put him at his ease. She wanted to take him by the arms, shake him a little, and say: "Stop worrying so much. Trust your instinct. I could sway you to my desires right now, and I should not feel that way about my bishop. I do not want to feel I have the power to shepherd my shepherd."

But she merely continued a banal chatter with him, about the weather and the crops and the need to widen the streets.

When they reached the Palace, Aldred sent Godiva with a lay brother toward his private audience room with the promise he would be there in a moment, as soon as he changed from his street-dusty costume to a cleaner one. She was offered wine and water, both of which she declined. Beside the ecclesiastical throne—this one a small one, not the large formal one of the general receiving hall—there was only a small wooden stool. She did not want the stool and she could not have the throne, so she stood and waited.

And waited.

And waited.

She would query him with every doubt Leofric had raised. She would—sweetly, even lovingly—demand satisfaction, and she would get it from him, she could tell now, because he wanted so badly to be liked. She was very good at scratching that particular itch.

If she did not scratch it, Edward might. Aldred had not seemed to like Edward at the Council, but she might have misread that, and she certainly did not want Edward to lay claim to the affection of anyone she wanted for herself. Worcester was the largest minster in Mercia; Leofric required Worcester's loyalty. She would see to it, over the course of as leisurely an afternoon and evening meal as it took, that Leofric had it. She would charm Aldred to pieces.

Until the moment Edgiva finally arrived, or sent word, and

then she would have to find a graceful way to excuse herself. Running into him had been both a complication and a boon.

She had been waiting, it seemed to her, for rather a long time in this boring little room, which was chilly and underlit. Just as she was beginning to feel uncomfortably confined, the door opened and Aldred entered hurriedly.

Godiva bowed her head, but with an apologetic smile he gestured her not to bother. "My lady, I am so sorry to have kept you waiting for me," he said. "Something has happened and I am afraid I cannot speak with you now after all, I must attend to other business."

"Oh," Godiva said, her fantasy of winning him by bedazzlement instantly dampened. "May . . . I . . . return later and we may speak?"

He averted his gaze. "I would be happy to speak to you, my lady, but I am not sure when I shall be free, now. Perhaps if your ladyship wished to join us this evening for the Compline service, I might be able to speak to you just after? That should not pose a problem if you are staying as our guest."

". . . Certainly," Godiva said, not sure what else to say in the moment. She did not want to stay here—she could not stay here, if Edgiva were at the other house. Hopefully Edgiva had already arrived and was waiting for her. How could she divide her attention, her presence, between the two?

And why was Aldred suddenly unavailable? Was it simply—as she knew Leofric would suggest—that he did not want to be held accountable for speaking to her about her dilemma at all? Hopefully not. Hopefully not.

"Please, Your Eminence, I do not wish to disturb your work," she said, graciously. "I shall repair to Alfgar's house and collect my belongings and bring them back here." *I'm not really going to do that,* she thought as the words came out of her mouth. *What excuse shall I give to explain my absence?* Later. Later. That was for later. She realized her mind was racing, she was so anxious about Edgiva.

"Thank you for understanding, daughter," Aldred said, a note of nervousness in his voice. *Good,* thought Godiva, *you should be nervous about dismissing me. Let me have that much power over you still. I will not abuse the power, but I must know I have it, for Leofric's sake.*

Somehow, with each of them dripping in obsequiousness, Godiva ended up outside the Palace gates, unattended. With a sigh of relief she turned back toward her lodgings and walked with all deliberate speed.

Edgiva still had not arrived.

By sundown Godiva was worried nearly to fits. She had not eaten; Druce, returning for dinner from the western gate, expressed concern. She was tempted to send him back along the road toward Leominster, but to further divide the traveling party was unwise, especially since she herself was now supposed to be in two places at once.

As the church bells were tolling the end of Vespers, at last, there was a rap on the door and the young son of the house announced himself.

"My lady, your men are here, and with them is a fearful-sick woman," he said. "My father thinks she will be wanting wine and ale to fortify her."

She felt a thrill of anxious relief, said a silent prayer of thanks to Saint Christopher, and rushed out to the stable.

Edgiva nearly collapsed from the saddle straight into her embrace. Druce gently lifted her under the shoulders, moved her slack body so that she lay across his arms, and carried her inside and up to the small room. One of the other men brought up a saddlebag laden with herbs—Edgiva never traveled without her medicine bundle.

In the room, Druce laid her gently on the hard cot and left them. The abbess seemed almost comatose. "You are well and safe now, friend," Godiva said to her softly. She removed Edgiva's veil and wimple and ran a hand over her temple; she was very warm. "If you will tell me which of these herbs will best assist you to feel better, I will prepare it for you."

"Nothing for this but mint and nettles," Edgiva murmured, slightly singsong, almost to herself. Her eyes rolled in her head. "Sleep. I must offer God a psalm for my safety and the safety of the babe, and then sleep and sleep and sleep and sleep," and then she was, in fact, asleep.

There was no going to the Bishop's Palace. She would send an excuse come morning. She sat watch over Edgiva that night, in that little room, amazed that they were in such an outrageous position. Godiva did not mind excitement, but Leofric did.

Edgiva's condition would make him dyspeptic.

Edgiva slept very deeply, crying out in nightmares twice. Godiva did not sleep at all.

When the sun rose, Edgiva awoke, looking heartier than the evening before, and declared herself fit to move, provided they travel slowly. Godiva asked for a blanket, and Druce draped it over the saddle to give Edgiva some extra comfort.

Godiva sent the thane's son to Bishop Aldred with a message of regret, claiming an emergency required her to leave at once for Coventry. She was truly sorry not to question him about the ride, but her concern for Edgiva's well-being was too distracting.

They were on the road shortly after Prime. The weather returned to that strange barren cloudiness, dry enough to keep the mud off the roads, even in places where there had been flooding from winter's thaw. Good for travelers, but not, she feared, for farmers. They traveled far more slowly than Godiva had anticipated, and Edgiva seemed too miserable to talk. So despite Godiva's impulse to chatter (as a way to pass the time, if nothing else), they said nothing. They did not talk about Sweyn, or the baby, save for Edgiva's reassuring Godiva it was well, or Godiva's impending humiliation. She could not even remember if she had mentioned any details of that to Edgiva yet.

They were on the road for days. Godiva lost count, in the mind-numbing boredom of it. The pleasing broad swells of countryside grew monotonous. The flowering bullace and mazzard flowers and even the bluebells and cow parsley and pink campions grew monotonous. The unchanging dry clouds above them grew monotonous. The bedrolls seemed harder and damper each night, the campfires smokier, the dried mutton tougher and stringier. Each morning the dew was heavier; the sounds of the men waking and then breaking camp were louder. They bought bread with fragments of coin from the villages along the route, but the quality of that too seemed to worsen with each bite. And through it all, Edgiva felt so ill she was barely conscious—but always it was she who urged them forward, whispering reassuringly to Godiva that this was normal, that the babe was fine. Godiva found herself thanking saints that she herself was barren. And she began at last to appreciate her shapeless, dull garments:

they were comfortable to slouch in, and when she was too tired to care what she looked like, they could not wilt with her as her dazzling outfits did, as these were beyond wilting to start with.

After a couple of days, it was clear the men understood Edgiva's condition. When Godiva sensed they were discussing it among themselves, she waited until Edgiva had gone to once again relieve her stomach in some nearby bushes, and then reined her horse over toward the cluster of them.

"You understand, of course, that the abbess has a stomach bug," she said with a charming, weighty smile.

"'Tis a big bug, my lady," said Druce, "and only going to get bigger." He looked at her, not defiantly, but firmly. She glared and tried to think how best to reply; he read something into her silence and added, "Best to hear that from us, now, when there is no place for gossip to spread, no?"

"Is that a threat?" she demanded, more hotly than she meant to, feeling her stomach clench. "Are you threatening to besmirch Mother's name?"

He reddened. "On the contrary, lady, forgive me—I am asking your guidance on how to prevent such a thing."

"By not mentioning it. To anyone. I can trust you, yes?" She smiled tightly.

"My lady, her ailment will not conveniently abate at the gates of Coventry Manor. People will ask. Will ask us. What should we tell them?"

"Mother has a stomach bug," Godiva repeated.

"Beg your indulgence, but nobody will believe it," he said. "I have control over what I say, but not over what other people choose to believe."

Godiva thought for a long moment. "We will sequester her as

soon as we arrive. Only my personal attendant will ever see her, until she has recovered."

Druce's eyes lit up with alarm. "You'd keep her sequestered for months?"

"This kind of stomach bug only lasts a few weeks," said one of the other men, with the bored knowledge of a veteran.

"That is right," Godiva said with cheerful firmness. "And then she shall recover and nothing further need be said of how plump and rosy she has become. How very obedient of you to understand."

She reined her horse away and back toward Edgiva's mount, which was grazing near the bushes that screened her from them.

It seemed that they were on the road forever. Edgiva remained in a nearly trancelike state of discomfort, speaking only to insist they travel farther, writing tearfully into her codex every evening. Godiva would have deemed her behavior sulking, were it anyone but Edgiva; Edgiva did not, had not once ever in her life, sulked.

So what appeared to be sulking was of force something else, something more meditative and profound. She was sorting through her own confusion. She was not turning to Godiva for advice, which was a disappointment—Godiva had been so eager to actually be of use to her, for a change—but Godiva respected the state she was in. Indeed, she was a little afraid of it.

And finally, on a damp and cloudy—but not rainy—St. Edmund's day, they approached the tiny and contested town of Coventry.

Part 4

CHAPTER 20

Coventry

Leofric had put a lookout on the manor walls, who trumpeted when he saw the riding party. The town—some eightscore including the population of both the manor and the monastery—thronged together in the small, still-grassy market green.

But closer than the green, on the gentle curving rise the hamlet couched in, stood Leofric beside his horse, with several housecarls in attendance, staring toward the west, toward the travelers. When he was in clear view, Godiva's party cantered the last length, as that was easier than trotting for Edgiva.

The veiled sun was behind them, and as they came closer, Godiva saw Leofric freeze for a moment, and then take a stiff step or two toward them, before stopping abruptly. He pointed toward the riding party. The housecarls echoed his movements. They all looked suddenly confused, or agitated. Leofric had not known she would be bringing Edgiva with her; obviously, that explained his change of mood.

No, it did not. There was something more. Somebody shouted, but Godiva could not make out the words. As they approached and drew rein, her gaze was distracted by the population of Coventry swarming, sudden but cautious, around the outlying town buildings, creeping collectively closer to witness their lady's homecoming, anxiously muttering among themselves. When her eye returned to Leofric, she found him staring at Edgiva, his mouth slack with amazement. She had never seen him slack-jawed, and she had never known him to be speechless. He was speechless now.

"Greetings, husband," she said, making herself sound cheerful despite exhaustion. "We have returned safely, and have brought a beloved friend to visit for a while."

The look on his face did not change, but the color of his skin began to darken. His brows began to knit. He was angry—and yet still so shocked he could not speak. The townsfolk's muttering died away.

"The abbess is fatigued from our long journey, and so I request that we dispense with formal homecomings, or at least delay them until later, that she may enter the manor and instantly rest," Godiva said.

He kept staring. The housecarls were staring. The villagers were staring. The monks were staring. The manor servants were staring. Not one person so much as whispered to another.

"You," Leofric finally said, in a husky voice, to Edgiva. "Mother. What make you here?"

"I have come to visit," Edgiva said. She looked as if she might be sick again. "At the invitation and urging of your lady wife. Why look you so amazed at that?" Her voice grew frail, and real fear crept into it. "May I not visit? Am I not welcome here?"

Her voice broke the spell of silence; the villagers and monks and servants—but not the housecarls—all began to whisper to one another, as if on cue, and most of the women in the crowd crossed themselves.

"Silence!" Leofric shouted, without taking his stare from Edgiva.

Silence.

"Husband, what's the matter?"

His eyes still on Edgiva, Leofric informed them: "We have just received notice, over the past day, from the Bishop of Worcester, and the Bishop of Hereford, and Leominster Abbey, and His Majesty. These notices alarmed me, for they had to do with events at Leominster, where I knew my wife had been. I am relieved to see my wife returning safely. But I am confused that she has brought with her Mother Edgiva, who—as half the kingdom has been informed—was forcefully abducted by Sweyn Godwinson to Hereford."

Edgiva now looked as astonished as Leofric had moments earlier.

"Godiva, shall I assume you followed them to Hereford and wrested Edgiva from Sweyn's lascivious grasp? And if so, dare I ask what you did to convince him to let her go?"

"No, no, I . . ." And here Godiva too could not speak for a moment. "She never went to Hereford. She left straight from the abbey gates and headed here to Coventry."

"There were *witnesses*, Godiva," Leofric said, angry, although he kept his voice too contained to be heard by the villagers. "Stop concocting tales; that will not help you now."

"How could there be witnesses? She did not go to Hereford," she insisted. "I will swear that on the Holy Writ. She went straight to Worcester and I met her there, and she has not been out of my sight since."

A confused pause.

"You *met* her there?" he echoed sternly.

"I rode with Sweyn to Hereford to make sure he would not pursue her, and then . . ." Godiva let it trail off. She suddenly felt light-headed and was glad for the warmth of her drab mantle and tunics.

"Mother Mary," said Leofric, sounding pained.

"Who would ever think *I* might be mistaken for an abbess?" Godiva said with a nervous laugh, trying to make light of it. Which was a dreadful mistake. "Is not that the embodiment of irony?"

"Who claims it?" asked Edgiva. She was pale and a sweat had broken out over her face. "Who claims they saw Earl Sweyn abduct me?"

Leofric shook his head. "The witnesses are not named, it is written only that there were both villagers and residents of the abbey, looking over the walls."

"I removed all of my jewelry and gave it to Edgiva," the countess said. "The intention was to keep her from looking like a nun. It did not occur to me that without the jewelry, I myself would look like one." '

Leofric's face reddened with anger. "I should have known you had a hand in this."

"I was trying to *help*," Godiva said. "Sweyn *had* come to take her. I *prevented* that. There is a very unfortunate rumor about now, but it is *wrong*. We need only announce the truth to set the record straight."

"The record will still say that he showed up and demanded me," said Edgiva quietly. "And that is your doing too."

"What?" Leofric kept his voice low but his face was turning purple.

"You did not know? She wrote to him and told him to abduct me."

"That is not true!" Godiva protested.

Leofric was so outraged his wife could see the veins on his neck even from horseback.

"Why did you have to bring her here?" he demanded through clenched teeth. "Why did she leave the abbey? And why exactly did she depart at the same moment that you did? It must have been at the same moment, the same *heartbeat*, or there could not have been this confusion."

That he was willing to do this in front of the entire population of Coventry was a deliberate shaming. He was furious at her.

"Of course there was confusion, people were very frightened, they had been told—mistakenly, by someone else—that the Welsh were attacking, the bells were ringing, everyone was hiding in the church . . . but there was chaos and confusion inside the walls *before* he ever reached the gate."

"But he would not have been *at* the gate were it not for you," Leofric snapped. Turning to the abbess, "Do I have that correct, Mother Edgiva?" he demanded.

She nodded anxiously without speaking. She looked as if she might swoon.

Leofric made a wordless sound of exasperation. He turned to face the villagers and monks and servants, and something in his movement and his expression startled the lot of them; they leapt back together. "All of you go home!" he said. "Leave! Now!" Immediately the wave of people melted back behind the buildings.

Leofric turned back to the two women. "I cannot turn you away," he said curtly to Edgiva. "I cannot fathom why she brought you or why you agreed to come. It is close to a disaster that you are here. You do not look well—"

"I am not, sir," Edgiva said with quiet urgency.

"So come inside and we will have you tended to, and I must have a few words alone with my wife." He said this without looking at Godiva, his teeth so clenched he could have cut an apple with the sharpness of his tone. Without a glance at her he turned and briskly led his horse back into the village. His housecarls followed.

When it was just Edgiva and Godiva, and the men who had ridden with them, the abbess released a shaking breath that bordered on a sob. "Oh, Lady Virgin," she said softly. "What will happen to Sweyn now?"

"Nothing," Godiva said, sounding surly. "'Tis just a big mistaken rumor. I will explain the truth to Leofric. Everything will be fine."

Edgiva gave her a horrified, disbelieving expression. "Everything will *not* be fine. Everything will never be fine again. How ignorant are you that you don't see that, Godiva?"

Edgiva urged her horse forward into the village as the monastery bells began to toll None.

Godiva, shaken more than she wanted to allow, dismounted in the manor yard, then went to the hall and asked for a basin to wash the dust of the road from her face. Clean water had never felt so good on her skin. Merewyn went to fetch her a more proper dress and veil, ones that did not make her look like an abducted abbess. She chose her blue-and-rose Easter outfit again, in the wan hope of appearing innocent to her husband and therefore hapless, rather than meddlesome. Leofric was in their room and Edgiva in the guest chamber, so she stood near the kitchen screens to change. The sensation of the silk brushing smoothly against her skin was so lovely after days and days of the drab woolens she had been wearing.

Their chamber was off the far end of the hall. Taking a deep breath to ready herself, she crossed through the hall, went to the door, and rapped upon it.

She heard the bolt slide. The door moving slightly in the jamb as it released. Then his footsteps walking away from the door. He was not even opening the door for her.

She pushed the door and stepped inside.

"Close it behind you," he said tersely. "Bolt it."

She did. The entire manor population would, of course, within moments be hovering on the other side. She stayed near the door.

Leofric was seated on the bed. They had one window in this room; it was still covered with parchment, but the curtains were open, and diffused daylight filtered in and gently lit his haggard face. He looked at her without a word for a long moment, his expression that of a disappointed father.

"Is there anything you can say to me that will change my view of what has happened here?" he asked, in a rhetorical tone.

"Yes," she said defiantly. "Edgiva is pregnant with Sweyn's child."

New astonishment wiped all other expression from his face.

He went nearly white. "God's wounds," he said, pushing his hand hard against his temple and then up through his hair. He clutched a handful of hair as if he would tear it from his scalp.

"So you see," she continued, in his silence, "I am not the only one who has misbehaved here. I am not even the one who has misbehaved the most!"

"This would bring me to an early grave were I of a lesser constitution," Leofric said, almost philosophical in his shock. "I would prefer the heat of battle to the mess that we now face."

"You do not mean that," she rebuked him.

"No, but very nearly," he snapped back. "And do not use that voice with me, Godiva, I am the *only* one in this who does not deserve scolding. You are certain of her condition?"

"Yes. And that Sweyn is the father. Beyond that, I know very little. Everything happened so fast. I went there to get her advice about Edward's punishment, and I had been there not an hour when Sweyn arrived."

"But he arrived there because of you," he said sternly.

"Not exactly," she said. She moved to the foot of the bed but did not dare—not yet—to sit beside him. "I told you at the Council I saw them falling for each other, do you remember that? She rode back north with his party when the Council adjourned, and stayed the night in Hereford with him. Just one night, but that is all it took. That happened *without* my meddling, Leofric—I was not there; we were on the road home. Edey went back to Leominster, realized she was with child, and wrote to me in a panic. But I did not realize the import of her message, I thought she was merely in love, and so I wrote to Sweyn—who I thought was in Hereford—telling him to pay her court."

"Godiva!"

"Not to show up armed outside her gate with half an army, screaming for her!" she protested. "I knew that he was pining for her, he had told me that bluntly, and when I knew it was re-ciprocated it seemed right—it seemed my calling—to encourage them to pursue it."

"She is an abbess!" he thundered.

"She was *made* an abbess, she has no *calling* for it. I am not saying she lacks faith, but she surely lacks *vocation*. She uses her power and position constantly the way a countess might. You have seen it. She has no native interest in a cloistered life. She is accustomed to it, she is adept at it, but have you ever seen her pray or lead a service with a quarter of the passion she gives to her work as a healer, or even, by heaven, a *calligrapher*? It was political convenience that put her in her position, not vocation. God knows well what her strengths are upon this earth, and she need not be an abbess to make the most of the gifts the Lord has given her."

He had grown quiet during her speech. Now he said, much calmer, "That is very eloquent, Godiva. Moving, even. Unfortu-nately it has nothing to do with attending to this crisis."

"You're right, I am sorry," she said. She finally sat down on the bed beside him. "If you are thoroughly finished shouting at me, let's you and I talk through and see if we can best determine what to do now."

He flopped back heavily onto the pillow. "I should have guessed you were responsible for all of this as soon as I caught wind of it . . ."

"I am not responsible! 'Twasn't I who ploughed her furrows!"

He laughed ruefully, briefly, with frustration. "Do you know? The punishment for rape is a fine paid to the woman's guardian, but Leominster Abbey is in Herefordshire, so I suppose he owes himself the fine."

"You are patron of the abbey, so he should owe it to you—no, what are we saying, Leofric, he doesn't owe it at all, because he did not rape her."

"It might have been better for her if he had."

She glared at him. "I did not hear you say that."

"While you were changing I wrote to Sweyn and told him to keep his head down for a while."

"He knows she is here."

"I assumed as much. I told him not to come."

"He has already promised me he would not," she said, desperate to show she deserved credit for something.

"That was before there were condemnations and threats being issued against him by the bishop and the king," he said. "Were I in his position, the first thing I'd do would be to put out a letter to all of England informing everyone that I had not abducted the Abbess of Leominster, because Godiva of Coventry had got there first. I would also use that opportunity to deny I was the father of her child—unless he decides politically it is in his interest to claim it as his, which, now I think of it—"

"He knows nothing of that," she said, standing up with agitation. "He does not even suspect."

He opened his eyes wide and looked up at her. "You mean you kept out of something?" he said. "Praise Woden and pass the mead."

"Not funny," she said sharply, and lightly kicked his foot. She was relieved the rage had passed and he was willing to speak to her—actually speak *to* her, not *at* her—again. "In fact, he said that even if the two of them were to wed—"

"Which will never happen."

"He said even if the two of them were to wed, they should have no child until Edward has an heir. Otherwise it would appear to be political maneuvering on his part—maybe even on Edey's—and he did not wish to put her in that position."

"And you fell for that?" he said, making a face. "Surely you are too savvy to fall for such nonsense."

"I did not *fall* for anything. He meant it. He," she informed him, "is besotted. He may not mean it half a year from now, but trust me, he means it now. Anyhow, he knows nothing about the child."

"So." Leofric took a breath and sat up again. He patted the bed where she had just been sitting. "Come here. Let's talk this through. What will Edgiva do?"

Godiva sat. "She needed to get away from Leominster even to consider it. She was in distress the whole ride; it would have been wrong of me to push her to speak of it, especially with the men around us. The one thing she has determined is that she will carry it to term. She nearly aborted it, but found she could not."

"And we know this is no trick of hers, to elevate herself from abbess to future queen mother?"

She smacked his knee. "I cannot believe you would even entertain that notion."

"We must contemplate every possible angle. Few people know her so well as we do—nobody knows her so well as you. Others will look to unsavory motives. If we cannot anticipate those, rumors will get out of hand. And we have already seen what rumors can do."

CHAPTER 21

They had given Edgiva the small room beside their own. She had retired there instantly, attended only by Merewyn, who understood at once what was going on but put her hand over her heart in a silent, spontaneous vow not to speak of it. At the abbess's request, a quill and ink were brought, and Edgiva busied herself awhile, writing soothing prayers and charms into her diary.

When Godiva went in to her, she was curled up on the bed, ink blots on her fingers.

"Edey," Godiva said softly, and sat beside her. Edgiva did not move. Indeed, if Godiva could not see the side of her body rise and fall slowly, she would not be sure her friend was living. "Edey, we have your saddlebag with the herbs in it. If you are not well enough to prepare a concoction, guide me to prepare one for you."

"This is not entirely a sickness of the body," the abbess said in a low voice. "There is an ailment here that drugs cannot cure."

Godiva grimaced, then put a hand on her shoulder to comfort her. "Everything happens according to God's will," she said, citing the abbess's own words from many past occasions. "Somehow hidden in all this is a blessing, or at least a lesson, waiting to be found out."

A strange sound came from Edgiva then, almost a derisive laugh. Godiva waited, but there was no other response. She pressed on.

"Leofric and I have been speaking. He knows everything, and hopes you will soon determine your course, so that we in turn know what to do to help. We do not want to confuse the situation by doing anything without your blessing first."

That same sound, but now louder, barking, more derisive; she shrugged the hand from her shoulder and sat up heavily, her back still to her friend. "That is rich," she said, her rich voice heavy with venom. "Did you have my blessing when you instructed Sweyn to show up at the abbey and carry me off?"

"I did not tell him—"

"And then," she went on, rising unsteadily, "did you have my blessing when you took it upon yourself to repair *that* situation by issuing orders that only worsened the confusion?" She turned to Godiva, her face a color Godiva had never seen before. "Oh, there you are in your pretty little gowns of seduction," she said with impatient dismissiveness, gesturing angrily at Godiva's Easter tunic. "I would never have given my blessing to anything you've done so far! And will you acknowledge that you have entirely interfered with and possibly ruined my life—as well as

Sweyn's? Heavens no, you pat my shoulder with your delicate little fingers and speak to me as if you were a considerate friend whom I should feel appreciative of, rather than enraged at!" Tears of fury sparkled in both eyes and from the right eye spilled down her mottled cheek.

It was a poisonous anger. She had carried it with her all these days, words of rage she had not had the energy or will to chastise Godiva with, all the way from Worcester.

"Edgiva—" she began in her most honeyed tone.

"Do not use that voice with me!" Edgiva hissed. "I know that voice. That is the voice you use with men to wilt them according to your convenience."

"I use it with women too," she said without thinking, in pathetic defense.

"Do not use it with *me*," Edgiva said with the same furious whisper. "Do not soften the edge of my anger, do not rob me of this fury. You have already mismanaged my life beyond repair; you will not manage my sentiments as well. You have done unspeakable damage to me and to Sweyn, and no amount of *charm* can save you from accountability."

"I warrant you that," Godiva said, chastised. "But your rage at me solves nothing. I do not deny I helped to cause the problem, but you are the only one who can resolve it now."

"But that is so like you!" It was a whispered shriek. "*You* have caused a problem, but some *other* soul must fix it. You are marvelous at causing problems that you have no power to fix! You have done it from the moment you could *speak*."

"You act as if I am the only errant party here," Godiva shot back, then lowered her voice to a whisper to demand furiously:

"Whose child are you carrying, and how did it get inside you? Am I to blame for that?"

Edgiva reddened and her breath caught. "I have already punished myself for that sin, and offer penance every day for it. That is why I do not take the herbs that would make me feel better—I do not deserve my own succoring—"

"God's wounds, that's absurd."

"That is not the point," Edgiva said, pushing on in a pained voice. "I know that I have sinned, and I am in a constant private dialogue with God about it. I knew I must take responsibility and I was trying to find the time to meditate upon how. You blithely trampled over everything, and now Sweyn Godwinson will be excommunicated and robbed of his land and title for an action he did not commit."

"What, abducting you? He committed a far worse act than that—"

"Which nobody need ever have known about!" Edgiva seethed.

"Are you content that a sin should go uncorrected? What kind of abbess does that make you?"

"A confused one! Trying to navigate her way through her confusion! Meanwhile my name is being bandied about in confounding ways among the entire population of the Council—"

"They were already talking about you as a tax resister."

"And now they shall be talking about me as a whore!" she returned. "And so I lose all credibility, *all* credibility, *forever,* in a way that no secular lady ever would, for the Church will condemn me and cast me out—"

"This is fearful passion speaking," Godiva said to calm her, holding out a reassuring hand; Edgiva snatched her arm away angrily. "Rest and eat and take your mind from it but for a day, and you will see that none of this may come out as you fear. Everything can be rectified—"

"How? By deceit?" Edgiva demanded venomously. She was regaining herself, and adopted now the voice of the all-seeing abbess Godiva always loved and sometimes dreaded. "There are three choices here, Godiva," she said, as if suddenly she were mentor and the countess student. "First, to let these errant rumors run wild, leading God knows where—"

"All Sweyn need do is open his home to show he does not have you, and he is out of danger."

"Unless somebody implies that he has killed me or is hiding me away somewhere. Where else should I be? People saw *me* being taken away *by him*. So either he is suspect in my disappearance, or you and Leofric become suspect yourselves, for why would you set up an occasion in which Sweyn appears to have abducted me, unless you had some plot to get him into trouble?"

"We will speak to S—"

"And even if you resolve things with Sweyn, this is an *incident*. Everybody is aware of it. Whereas, if I had simply come with you to Coventry, nobody would have cared. Whatever choices I made from there, they would be difficult, and I would deserve the difficulty, but they would be *my* choices; *I* would be responsible for them—not Sweyn, not you, not Leofric, not the Church. It is now impossible for me to be mistress of my fate. You have made it impossible."

Godiva lowered her eyes and fidgeted with the edge of her veil, the gold thread feeling brittle to her fingertips. "I am deeply, deeply sorry for that," she said. She tried to look up and meet Edgiva's gaze, but found that she could not. "You said there were three options. One is to do nothing and see what happens, and yes, of course that is not the way. What are the other two?"

"The other two are no better," Edgiva said with patient impatience—a trick of delivery she excelled at since becoming an abbess. "One is to speak out against the rumors by lying, and the other is to speak out against the rumors by telling the truth."

Godiva was comforted by Edgiva's scolding now; it meant the passion was under control and the abbess was, at least, thinking clearly. "Let me call for Leofric," she said. "He loves you as a sister, and he is as upset with me as you are, so the two of you should peck at me productively and sort out how to handle this."

Edgiva glared. "You have not taken in my chastisement in the least," she complained. "Like water on parched ground, it rolls off down the hill instead of penetrating."

"What do you mean?"

"You are making it the responsibility of myself and Leofric to resolve a problem you have created."

"Yes, I am," Godiva said. Edgiva looked startled at the concession. "I do not know how to resolve it myself. If I did, do you think I would not, given how endlessly I like to make everything my business? And what is the more important: that you teach me a lesson by making me try to resolve it on my own, or that it is resolved as efficiently as possible?"

"There is no resolving it!" Edgiva said, her voice breaking with frustration. "That is what I am trying to tell you. What is the point of reviewing all my woes with Leofric, when there is no way to heal them?"

"Perhaps he will think of something we have not thought of," Godiva said blandly. "He does have *some* experience surviving crises."

Edgiva took a breath, trying to contain herself. "Summon him, then, if you must," she said. "I am sure the three of us together cannot imagine a way out of this without damage done to somebody who does not deserve it."

"Who of us does not deserve it?" Godiva asked rhetorically. She opened the door and sent Merewyn for Leofric. He was there within moments, in no better a mood than when she left him.

"I understand," Leofric said from the door, in lieu of greeting, "that you are as much to blame for these troubles as my unruly wife is."

Edgiva reddened.

"That does not help, Leofric," Godiva said. "The poor woman has weight enough on her shoulders without your condemnation."

"I am to blame for my own sins," Edgiva countered. "Godiva is to blame for all the rest of it."

So much for sisterhood, thought Godiva.

"Edward will outlaw Sweyn for this," the abbess continued, anguished.

"He does not have that power," Leofric said reassuringly. "He must ask the Great Council for a sentence of outlawry, and by the next convening of the Council, all of this will be resolved."

"But in the meantime, we cannot ignore the rumors," Edgiva said.

"Obviously," said Leofric impatiently, still not stepping into the room.

"However," Edgiva went on, "if we address the rumors, if we send out a message to all concerned that they have not got the right story, then we must decide if we correct it with the truth or with deceit. I am sickened by my own duplicity and can abide no more of it, so I ask you now, what happens if we tell the truth?"

"This is not a catechism lesson, Edgiva," said Leofric tersely. "I am not accustomed to being spoken to in such a voice, and I will not brook it. Obviously if we speak the truth, the question is, how *much* truth. Do we tell the world what even Sweyn himself has not heard? What does the truth profit us? You come out looking the worse for it, Godiva looks almost as bad, and Sweyn will still be severely punished for corrupting a religious woman."

"So we must not tell the truth," Godiva said decisively. "That means we lie."

"And what lie shall we tell?" said Leofric. "And how may we control that lie as it works its way across England?"

"I will not lie!" Edgiva shouted, raising her voice for the first time. "My secrets blot my soul enough, do not make me a liar too! I *curse* you, you *Ananias*, for putting me in this position!"

Godiva leapt away from her, astonished by her fury. She moved toward Leofric instinctively for comfort. He closed one large gloved hand around her arm—a gesture as much of control as of comfort, but she welcomed his touch, and relaxed a little from her panic.

"Mother Abbess, you do not mean those words," she said, sounding shaky.

Edgiva looked unnerved by her own rage. "I do not," she conceded, strained. "But I will not agree to any resolution that requires me to nurse deceit. I will not do it. I have already fallen far enough; I will not throw myself deeper into the mire."

Relieved by the recantation of damnation, Godiva immediately regained her humor. "We must say that it was a *complete* misunderstanding," she said firmly to Leofric, putting her free hand on his hand that grabbed her arm. "Sweyn was only at her gates to bring her the welcome news that the Welsh borders are now secure. Edgiva had already expressed an interest in coming with me—as she told the sisters, in fact—to gather herbs—"

"That lily-white tale does not explain why you rode to Hereford with Sweyn, disguised as a nun," Leofric said, releasing her and pulling away.

"I was not disguised as a nun," Godiva protested impatiently. "I was dressed modestly and I took my jewelry off! Other people were hysterical and . . . *misperceived* me."

"Very well. You were not disguised as a nun. You still rode to Hereford with Sweyn rather than coming directly to Coventry with your friend the abbess, who was obviously ill. Why did you do that? In this version of the story, where nobody has done anything wrong? Why not cleave to Edgiva from the moment you left the gate?"

They both stared at Godiva expectantly.

Clumsily, inspiration struck: "I was asking Sweyn's advice regarding the ride," she said.

"Which would be tomorrow," Leofric said, rubbing one temple with his hand. "As if we did not have enough crises to contend with."

"What ride?" asked Edgiva.

Leofric blinked. "What did you just say?" he asked her.

"What ride?"

Leofric released a grunt of frustration. "All of this," he said to his wife, gesturing as if to imply the whole room, the whole world, "all of this, and you have not even *mentioned* to her the reason you went to Leominster? The king is on his way here. And now you have put yourself in the middle of a scandal with a woman of the Church. The bishops will be sharpening their legal knives to eviscerate you. My coffers have arrived from Brom Legge; I trust there is enough to pay this perversion of a tax bill, although it may leave us nearly penniless. You cannot make the ride." He turned toward Edgiva. "For the love of all saints, tell her not to make the ride."

"What ride?" Edgiva repeated.

Leofric looked at his wife.

She pursed her lips together and thought a moment. There must be some way to tell this tale so that Edgiva would realize Godiva was not entirely devoid of merit. She was championing Edgiva's cause, after all.

"The king has manipulated the law to levy the heregeld against the residents of Coventry, and no one else," she said. "What he really wants is either to take the estate from me, or to punish me—or Leofric, really—with a very heavy penalty, as I would naturally pay the tax myself, which means Leofric would pay it, as I have no such means. But Coventry is mine, and I refused to pay the heregeld on the grounds that the heregeld should not exist."

She paused a moment, to let Edgiva digest the news that her silly friend Godiva had in fact taken a brave stand on something of weight.

Edgiva blinked rapidly a couple of times, and the muscles in her face changed—not that she looked less tense, but now she looked tense in a different way.

"And what did Edward say?" she asked.

"Edward threatened me, of course. He cited Harthacnut's treatment of Worcester, although that was for the murders, not just the tax revolt. He will not harm the town, as long as I agree to be the scapegoat and suffer humiliation in its stead."

"What humiliation?"

"I am amazed you did not discuss this with her," Leofric snapped.

"She was traumatized and ill," Godiva snapped back at him. Then to Edgiva: "He wants me to ride through the town on horseback, naked."

Edgiva blinked in astonishment.

"What a . . . bizarre and perverse demand," she said after a moment.

"He wants her to do it on Kalendis Maia," Leofric added. "May Day."

"It is not such a large concern, that it is May Day," Godiva said.

"Of course not," said Edgiva. "On the border, the Welsh farmers and peasants observe the old traditions, without even trying to disguise them as Christian as at Rogationtide, or for the Land Ceremony. We look the other way."

"You see?" Godiva said to her husband, taking his hand and trying to stroke the back of it.

"Would you look the other way if the most powerful countess in the kingdom were to participate?" Leofric demanded, snatching his hand away.

"I think you are reading too much into it there," Godiva insisted.

"He wants her to make the ride on May Day," Leofric pressed. "Specifically on the Kalends of May. *Not,* please note, *not* as part of any church ritual. He wants the rumor of it to be misinterpreted, misperceived, to imply that the lady of Mercia is openly practicing pagan ritual."

"I assume he did not say that," said Edgiva.

"No, he did not, because it is not true," Godiva said. "And even if Edward in his own twisted mind thinks so, it would require the collusion of the Church."

"And that is why," Leofric said in a long-suffering voice, "Godiva traveled to Leominster. To ask your opinion on where the Church would stand. Would the bishops leap at the opportunity to shame our family, and decry her for something so scandalous? Would they commend her for resisting an unfair tax and yet also accepting the punishment for doing so? Perhaps lionize her for protecting her people at the expense of her own dignity? Excommunicate her for participating in unholy rites? What do you think, Edgiva? She should have asked you days ago."

"I am not a bishop," Edgiva said crossly. "Ask a bishop what a bishop would do."

"We asked Worcester," Godiva said. "Bishop Aldred. Leofric believes Aldred wishes to avoid being held accountable for any position. But surely anyone associated with Worcester must rally to a protest of the heregeld."

"He has not rallied to me," Edgiva observed.

"Ah," said Leofric, conclusively.

There was a silence.

"So," Godiva said at last, awkwardly. "If you desire a moment's distraction from your own dilemma, Edgiva, I would be most obliged if you would turn your brilliance, insight, and intuition on mine."

Edgiva considered her a moment, steely-eyed.

"No," she said.

"Pardon?" said the countess.

"I said no."

"How can you mean that?" Godiva asked with a sweetly confused smile. "I am distrustful of my own counsel, and seek to lay down the secrets of my—"

"Do not use those wiles on me, Godiva," Edgiva said, sharp.

"We are trying to help you with your dilemma, Edgiva, how can you not help us with ours? I am in trouble because I was trying to champion *your cause* by standing up to Edward."

Edgiva gave Godiva a look of incredulity, even as Leofric sighed at his wife's ineptness. "There is nothing parallel in our circumstances," the abbess scolded. "We must, both of us, make a deal with a devil, but in your case, your enemies have set you up for a fall, for political gain—while in my case, my closest friend has put me, and somebody else, and my *unborn child*, in a horrific position for no gain to anyone at all."

"I acknowledge that, I understand it . . . ," Godiva said, faltering. "So please, Edgiva, advise me how to repair your situation."

"Make one of my unacceptable options acceptable. Nothing less. Please leave me, Godiva; all of this talk is pointless and dismaying. This interview is at an end." Trapped between them and the door, she turned her back on them decisively.

Leofric made a gesture of finality, as if flicking water from his hands. He turned and walked out of the room without a word.

Godiva knew his moods. He would go out now, to ride until the sun was setting. He would imagine to himself he was not yet a husband or a father or an earl, just a young man enjoying the beauty of his surroundings and the company of a few friends—or in this case, housecarls. Leofric no longer had friends. Godiva sometimes wondered if he noticed that.

CHAPTER 22

H er pulse drummed sickeningly in her chest, in her throat, along the insides of her arms, as Godiva walked with brisk dignity out of the room, out of the hall, out of the manor court-yard, to her favorite spot in Coventry.

An ancient, gnarled apple orchard, a haphazard constellation of trees, stretched just outside the newly built manor walls, near the kitchen post-door. It had survived centuries, in turn domes-ticated and feral, as this area had been built up, razed, built up, razed, from tribal settlement to Roman fort to Christian nun-nery . . . this apple orchard on the eastern outskirts of the current hamlet always remained. Generations of trees grew and aged and withered, to be felled or uprooted and new ones seeded in their place. Theirs was an uninterrupted lineage of fruitfulness. England herself could not say as much.

Beneath one ancient tree, fringed with bluebells and anem-ones, she had placed a wooden couch, a gift from her stepson

Alfgar. It was a sweet place to bring Leofric in an amorous mood, but mostly she kept it for contemplation. She hated contemplation, so at least here its unyielding stillness was softened by ever-altering beauty. She often found that when she retired there, either Merewyn or Temman the steward had somehow guessed she might, and in anticipation brought felt cushions out, something to eat or drink, and a little bell for summoning. This time, Merewyn had placed her green mantle on the bench.

She reclined now on the cushions, gratefully, and tried to empty her mind as she gazed out across the flowering trees, the bark dull under the clouds. Edward would arrive tomorrow. She would not concede the town.

So her choice was between paying the heregeld or making the ride. No, actually: between Leofric paying the heregeld, or Godiva making the ride.

It was infuriating that there was no way she could smile her way out of this. She levied tolls herself within her estates, as Leofric did throughout Mercia. But such tolls were for mutual benefit—folk *used* the mills and roads and bridges. The heregeld was different. It was an abuse of power. Harthacnut had extracted money with no benefit to those he taxed—in fact, it was often to their detriment. To pay the heregeld would be to let Edward continue his brother's tyranny.

"So I must not pay the heregeld unless there is truly no alternative," she said aloud to a wary robin, who had landed nearby in hope of crumbs. "But that means Edward will make an example of me." Her strength was equally her weakness: she required an audience. There was no satisfaction to be got from being clever or profound or wise if nobody was there to witness it. She needed eyes upon her. How fitting, then, was Edward's demand. "He may be Saxon like the rest of us, but he spent years enough in Normandy to hold their view of women. He does not like how I accomplish things, and he would punish me by forcing me to overdose on that which I usually sip. Well. Let him try. I can survive it," she assured the robin.

But for the aftermath? The ride itself was only the beginning. For the remainder of her days on earth, she would be the countess whom King Edward had forced to ride naked in front of her own peasants. That stain would cost her, and Leofric, in so many ways. How high the cost?

Was it a higher price than the heregeld?

Possibly.

The robin tired of waiting for crumbs and began to spade the earth with its beak for grubs. She felt a pang of envy that the bird had only itself to look out for. She gazed over the orchard, which was almost unnaturally still in the heavy, damp air, and wondered how many people had sat here before her, pondering their lives' woes. She grievously desired Edgiva's counsel. She knew Edgiva would not give it.

"Never mind, then, I shall *conjure* it," she informed the robin. The robin had lost interest. "Heathen witch that I am, I shall spirit myself into Edgiva's soul so thoroughly that I shall divine her judgment. Are you ready?" she asked the robin, smiling sadly. "Watch this. I shall conjure her."

She had no idea how one was supposed to hold oneself while conjuring. Experimentally, she kneeled in the exact center of the couch, closed her eyes, and pressed her palms together, prayerfully, in front of her chest.

"Edgiva of Leominster Abbey," she chanted in Gregorian tones, "show me the proper form of indirect resistance here."

With a vividness normally reserved for her most intense dreams, she recalled at once an unusual moment from their childhood.

Edgiva—very unwontedly—was misbehaving with her. To protest Abbess Berthe's harsh treatment of a terrified novice, Edgiva had determined to skip afternoon mass (something Godiva did quite often, but Edey? Never). Godiva, of course, joined her. Mother Berthe sent her prioress after them, one Sister Agatha, and Agatha was not a friendly woman. She used a willow stick liberally for even the most minor infractions, and not with the compassionate regret that was, according to St. Benedict, supposed to accommodate such lashings; Godiva the grown woman still had faded scars to prove it. Agatha was the sister Berthe had used to terrify the novice, so young Edgiva was particularly disapproving of her. Agatha meant to drag them bodily into the church to make an example.

But she had to catch them first. Knowing young Edgiva's fascination with herbals and healing, she sought them in the drying shed. As she approached, the girls giggled nervously, sensing her proximity. She pounded on the door with a heavy, calloused hand. "Unbolt this door and let me in!" she thundered.

They giggled more. Sister Agatha threw her considerable weight against the door, and the board shivered in the braces holding it in place.

"Do you think that is wise, Sister?" Edgiva queried from inside. "This little shed is likely to fall over before the board breaks."

"Open! This! Door!" Agatha hollered, pounding her fist against it with each word.

Edgiva, usually so serious and dutiful, looked at Godiva with mischief in her eyes. It was bewitching to see her in this mood. She put her finger to her lips, and then pointed with her free hand to each end of the board. Together, moving carefully in silence, they lifted the bolt up out of the bracing—if they had slid it open, it would have made a sound. They lowered it to the ground as Agatha, assuming the door was still bolted, again threw all her weight against the door.

The door fell open and she tumbled smack onto the floor. Edgiva clapped her hands with pleasure.

The story did not end well for them, but that moment had been priceless.

And Edgiva—so typical of Edgiva—used it as a parable years later, as Godiva the Conjurer remembered now:

Just married, the new lady of Mercia had ridden tearfully all the way from Leofric's court of Brom Legge to Leominster Abbey, and begged advice on deflecting her new stepson Alfgar's temper. To the earl's dismay, whenever his wife and his son were in a room together, surly adolescent Alfgar would taunt Godiva, saying execrable things about her family, declaiming she was ugly, declaring Leofric would never love her as he'd loved Alfgar's own mother. Godiva, stung, would snap back at him, which only egged him on until he reached decibels of cruelty that overwhelmed her, ignoring his father's threats of punishment.

"Recall how we used Sister Agatha's own strength against her," Edgiva, new-minted abbess, reminded her distraught friend. "If she had not been hurling herself at the door that way, she would never have landed on her face. Fighting anyone gives them something to fight back with. Letting them rage at you—in fact, inviting them to rage—gives them an opportunity to fall on their face at your feet."

"And then lash you and send you to bed without supper," Godiva had argued sardonically.

But she took the advice to heart. Back in Brom Legge at Christmas feast, Alfgar—furious his father had ever remarried—had beset Godiva with verbal abuse before the entire court, including the king, who was visiting for Christmas. Only his mother had ever been able to rule him, and since her death years earlier, Leofric had given up trying to curb his tongue. His visits home from his fosterage in Northumbria were unpleasant for everyone, including him, but over the past decade, Leofric's court had grown inured to it.

Young Godiva had not, however. She was spirited, and everyone in Leofric's household had heard her tussle with Alfgar verbally. It felt unnatural to check her tongue now, to refrain from all the witty barbs he lay himself open to. But she kept Edgiva's words foremost in her mind, and this time, let him rail. She even said, as graciously as possible, "I regret to cause you such offense, young master, please continue to instruct me on my shortcomings," wondering how this could possibly turn to her advantage. Her words dampened some of his spark, but not enough for her to feel as if she had somehow triumphed.

As the bread pudding was being cleared away, King Cnut turned to Leofric and declared, loudly, "Your lovely bride already pleased me with her face and her comportment, but without your son's outrageous cruelty I would not have had the chance to see how dignified she is."

That shut Alfgar up completely.

"I would like to honor her extraordinary poise with a gift," continued the king. "I will have my chamberlain send relics to her favorite abbey and the necklace my mother always wore to the lady herself, for her own keeping. I applaud what I am sure is Alfgar's desire to make a gesture of recompense as well."

The entire hall was speechless. Godiva realized this was more to instruct Alfgar than to reward her, but still she smiled with relieved pleasure, thanked the king profoundly, and asked that the relics be delivered, at His Majesty's convenience, to Leominster Abbey, "where I learned all the grace that pleases Your Majesty."

Alfgar, astonished at the benefit of her restraint, began to practice some himself. When he came home for Easter and kept his tongue civil, Godiva smiled at him warmly for the first time, and he softened. After a brief, predictable period of his lusting for her (which she and Leofric had simply pretended not to notice), he eventually became her most devoted kinsman.

She opened her eyes now and looked around the silent orchard. A fog was creeping in, pearling on the newly opened blossoms; the air grew heavier and colder. The robin was gone, which made her lonely. *What does this conjuring advise me?* she wondered. *The message seems to be: give in, and trust that giving in will yield a benefit. But does that mean I should surrender, then, and pay the tax? Is that what my private angels tell me now?*

But that did not feel right. That made it Leofric's burden. And by extension, the burden of all Mercia.

Some part of her wanted to give another part advice, but did not know how to speak in words, only in examples. If the advice was—as she sensed in her gut—against paying the heregeld . . . what was it in favor of?

The ride.

In demanding the ride, Edward was actually doing exactly what Edgiva had counseled her. Despising her displays of femininity, he would force her to display *all* of her femininity. He was felling her with her own ax.

And so . . . she should allow him to shame her? As with Alfgar's torment, was there a way not merely to escape abuse, but to somehow *gain* by welcoming it? Was it possible to make Edward wish heartily he had never even tried to punish her?

She got up, shivering, and began to pace, avoiding the campion blossoms just beginning to open around the edges of the orchard, rubbing her clammy hands together briskly. Riding. Naked. That was the insult she must embrace. He wished her to ride naked through the streets in order to mortify her with shame. Could she possibly embrace the punishment without suffering the humiliation?

How?

"It is not humiliating," she heard her own voice say, startling her. As if the words were someone else's, she carefully repeated them: "It is not humiliating."

And now, tasting the idea, examining it: "I need not be humiliated. One assumes an ordeal is a humiliation. But the first is an action, and the other a spiritual state . . ."

". . . Do you see?" She doffed the mantle. "There is no immutable law saying one incurs the other. One kisses a beloved, and feels contentment. One defeats a foe, and feels triumphant. We assume these are always true things, but they may not be," she declared, nearly jumping on top of Leofric as he lay on the bed with his boots off. He shuddered at her cold fingers on his neck but did not push them away. "You might kiss a loved one without feeling contentment—if they are on their deathbed, or about to leave on a long journey. You might strike down an enemy, but if he is also your child or your brother or your oldest friend who has turned on you, you might feel more grief than triumph. We perceive that a certain action requires a certain response, but 'tisn't always so. There is no law says I *must* feel shame for riding naked through the streets. There is simply an assumption that I *will*."

"Is it not a correct assumption?" Leofric asked sardonically. He began to rub one of her chilled hands between his large warm ones.

With a conspiring grin, she bent low over him and whispered, "What if I am *delighted* by it?"

He dropped her hand and gently pushed her up away from him. "If you are delighted about riding naked through the streets on the Kalends of May, then you surely are a harlot or a pagan or both."

"No, no, I mean what if I am delighted about doing what my king demands of me?" she said. In the presence of her favorite audience—her husband—she glowed with playful energy again. "What if my response is: Thank you, Edward, for this command! I am so honored to be given the opportunity to follow your royal will. I am the most fortunate of ladies in the kingdom, that I am singled out by His Majesty with this opportunity to look out for my people's well-being."

"There is no proof the king ordered you to ride naked through town on May Day," Leofric said bluntly. "There is no evidence you are following any orders. There is only the evidence of your behavior. The archbishop—or any prelate—could call that heathenism and condemn you for heresy."

"What an alarmist you are!" she said with a nervous laugh, climbing off the bed. "Aldred counseled it was a good thing to do."

He sat up and took a deep, steadying breath. "Godiva," he said. "You cannot prove that. Understand me: If I am right about this, they may excommunicate you and annul our marriage."

"An excommunication can be reversed."

"Not quickly. If you are excommunicated then nobody— including your servants, your people, and your husband—*nobody* may have anything to do with you, or the Church will claim we risk contamination from your sinful state. And then do you see what happens? Edward will help himself to Coventry. They require a ruler whose stained soul does not endanger theirs, and if I remain with you, I am just as tainted as you are."

"Are you telling me Aldred of Worcester and the King of England are conspiring in a plot to steal Coventry from me?"

"No," said Leofric, "Aldred's not that clever. But if Edward gets some other bishop to condemn you, you cannot turn to Aldred for defense. Aldred will not hold himself accountable for what he said to you, he is too much the coward. And Edward will take advantage of that. You shall be censured, and then I must either shun you or be considered tainted with you, which undermines my rule."

She sobered, considering this. "So as you have said: Edward is trying to strike at you through me."

"Yes. That means you should not make the ride."

"No, it does not. If you pay the heregeld, he still wins. In fact, it is a more dangerous victory, for not only does he take your gold, but he leans upon a tyrant's law to do it. I believe he must be counting on me not to make the ride—what is my brief humiliation worth, against his ability to take power at his will from any of his lords?" As Leofric began to answer her, she put a gentle finger to his lips. "You learned your statecraft, Leofric, in a chaotic age, so I understand you assume the most underhanded scheme is always at play . . . but really, love, I do not think this is a subtle matter. He wants the money. He wants to bully you. He thinks he is about to achieve that. Surely his spies have reported that you've summoned your entire treasury here." She gave him a generous, indulgent smile. "Tomorrow, I will prevent him from taking it from you. The heregeld must be ended."

"But not by us. Let Edgiva attend to it, it is her cause." He made a pained face. "Edgiva. I almost forgot. Good lord, Godiva. If only there were a way to breed headaches for profit, you would be richer than Charlemagne."

"What I have learned from Edgiva herself," she said, "is that the problem contains within itself the seeds of the solution."

"I fail to see evidence of that," said Leofric. In the distance, the monastery bells tolled Vespers.

"I must remind Edey of that moral immediately, in case she has forgot it. That will help her to solve her own dilemma."

"Have we solved *our* dilemma? Somehow I missed that," Leofric said.

She kissed him on the cheek and went to the guest room.

Edgiva was on the bed, lying on her back. That was an improvement over lying on her side, curled up like a springtime fern, which is what Godiva had been expecting.

"I have come to talk to you—"

"There is no use in talking," said Edgiva wearily.

"Your options are acceptable," said Godiva, "if you stop resisting them, and just accept them."

"That," Edgiva said flatly, "is nonsense."

"No, it is not. Our problems are alike, yours and mine. When you strip away all the trappings, the only real obstacle is this: we each fear humiliation."

"I do not fear humiliation. I am a woman of the Church. The Church preaches nothing but humiliation."

Godiva laughed. "The church preaches *humility*! That's different! *I* am the one telling *you* this?"

"If you ever fail in your humility, you will be humiliated. One is just the other with a pretty rosary and pentatonic scales to decorate it."

Godiva stared at her friend. "So you are having a crisis of faith."

"I am having a crisis of *life*."

"It is not a crisis," Godiva promised her, sitting beside her on the bed. "It is an opportunity."

Edgiva sat up and stared at her as if Godiva had three heads. Her fingers were worrying her pink rosary beads, dirtying them with the ink still on her fingers. "Where do you get such ridiculous notions?" she demanded. "It is a crisis. I cannot go back to the life I had before. I was a good abbess, a very good shepherdess, no matter how hounded I sometimes was by my own private wolves. How else might I be useful? What else am I good for?" Her voice cracked.

"You might make an excellent lady of Hereford," Godiva said. "I know an earl there who would certainly agree with me."

Edgiva paled, crossed herself, and lay back down on the bed. "Do you know the havoc that would cause?" she finally said.

"No. And neither, Edgiva, do you. But yes, there will be havoc, no matter what you do. Would you like to discover what the havoc will be if you go to Hereford? Or would you prefer to discover what havoc is caused if you go back to Leominster?"

"Those choices are equally unacceptable," Edgiva said heavily, sitting up again, and then getting off the bed to pace the tiny room with agitation.

"Then they are also equally acceptable," Godiva insisted. "If you decide to accept them, they are *both* acceptable. Know that you will live through the consequences of either choice— because you *will* live through them, whatever they are. The worst thing about the consequences is that you do not know what they will be. You are terrified of the undiscovered."

"As is everyone. We cleave to what is known, that is how human beings *work*. We crave what is established, what is *regular* and *ordinary*."

"Except when the irregular or the extraordinary happens, and society lurches forward anyhow," Godiva argued. "Edward's ascendancy to the throne was irregular. The Church telling priests they must no longer have wives was irregular. Sleeping with your neighbor was irregular—"

"It was a *sin*!"

"And yet the world did not end," Godiva observed. "Nor will it end if you marry him, nor will it end if you go back to the abbey with a big round belly and carry on your mission there of healing the sick and instructing your nuns in beautiful calligraphy. You are scared of doing something irregular. That is all it is. If you had no fear of defying what is considered regular, would you feel so stuck now?"

Edgiva considered. She sat on the bed again, and slowly rested a thoughtful hand upon her diary. "*Perhaps* not," she said at last. Grudgingly.

"Well then," Godiva said, "see what I will do tomorrow."

CHAPTER 23

She stayed up very late that night, a pile of parchment to her left, an inkwell, quill pen, and the brightest lamp in Coventry to her right. She would not let Leofric see what she had written, although when her cheerful humming kept him awake, she managed to silence herself.

Her right hand was cramped the next morning; she had not written so much in an instance ever in her life, not even when she lived in the abbey and spent every morning working on calligraphy. She had been squinting in the candlelight for so long, there were creases around her eyes that she was sure would never subside. *Never mind,* she thought, *today is not a day for beauty anyhow.*

She was wearing her lovely set of dark and light blue tunics, girdled with the green-glass belt, her hair contained by a gold fillet and a sky blue veil heavy with embroidery. Everything about her whispered feminine beauty. The silk felt soothing and delicious against her skin.

Edgiva looked much improved when Godiva saw her in the chapel at mass. The abbess did not meet her gaze, but neither did she shun her.

Her husband, as they exited the chapel, gestured to two large carts freighted with locked chests. "There it is," he said, low in her ear. "The treasury. Let me pay him, and this is over. We have more than I reckoned. He will not beggar us."

She wondered if this was just a reassuring lie. She turned to look at him. "Are you commanding me, my lord?"

There was some part of her she did not like that wished he would say yes.

His gaze softened and he kissed her cheek. "I can command you when you are my subject, but in this matter, you are my wife, and so, my partner. I may ask you, beg you, cajole or bribe, chastise or even threaten you—but I cannot command you."

She felt her throat tighten. She wanted to bury herself against him.

She did not move.

They were breaking their fast when a messenger arrived: that same obsequious fop of a man whom Edward had sent earlier. He was announced by the steward and entered as if he were the hero of a parade. He walked straight to them at the high table, bowed almost mockingly, and declared, "His Majesty the King awaits you at the far end of Coventry. If you wish to pay the levy or yield the village, he will come here to receive from you coin of the realm or a piece of town sod as proof of land-grant. If you wish to defy him and take punishment instead, he awaits evidence of your own person, and nothing but your person, at the far end of the high street."

Leofric to one side of her and Edgiva to the other turned expectantly to look at her.

"I do not defy him," Godiva said. She sensed, more than saw, their surprise.

The messenger looked triumphantly satisfied. That proved to Godiva she had been right: Edward expected her compliance after all.

"Excellent, my lady. Shall I tell him to expect gold, or the town charter?"

Leofric was shifting beside her.

"Neither," she said. "I do not defy him, but I rather accept his third offer. I shall meet him at the other end of town. You may tell him to expect me." She took a sip of wine.

Suddenly Leofric was still as stone. She reached toward him and covered his clenched fist with her free hand. His skin was frigidly cold. To her other side, Edgiva crossed herself.

The messenger blinked. "Very well," he said. The corner of his mouth twitched.

"I will go ahead of my wife," Leofric informed the smarmy man, without a glance at her.

"You will?" she said quietly.

"Oh, yes," he said. "I will prepare the way for you. I think I know what Edward is up to, and he shan't have his way." Back to the man: "You may tell His Majesty we will arrive after we have broken our fast."

"I shall announce you," the man said with a smile, and added meaningfully, "to everyone." He bowed, turned, and flounced out of the hall.

"What does that mean?" Edgiva said.

"What I anticipated," said Leofric. "Edward has summoned the population of the town to either view his victory promenade, or, as will apparently be the case, gawk at Godiva as she rides. I shall ride out ahead to tell them not to gawk."

It was as if he'd wrapped a warm protecting blanket round her shoulders. "Thank you, Leofric," she said.

"It is not nearly enough to stem the damage of your choice," he replied, coldly, almost a grunt.

She found suddenly she could not eat. Her hand trembled holding the bread; she did not trust herself with her own dining knife. Excusing herself and fighting a terrible sense of agitation, she went back to her room.

She sat on the bed, knees pulled up before her, rocking slightly.

It was the wrong choice. She should not have said it. She should have let Leofric pay the heregeld. He was strong and wealthy enough, and wanted to protect her—she should have let him. Let someone else protest the heregeld. She did it only to please Edgiva, but there was no pleasing Edgiva now. *What a troublesome, foolish woman I am*, she thought.

There was a rap on the door.

"Enter," she said.

Edgiva came in, in her abbess's modest robes, which made the thought of what Godiva was about to do that much more sickening.

"*Benedicite*," said Edgiva, with compassionate formality. That offered as much warmth and intimacy as the dark of the moon.

But then she said: "Do you need somebody to lead your horse?"

Godiva almost gasped. "You would do that? Even though you judge me?"

Edgiva looked genuinely startled. "I am not judging you," she said. "How could I judge somebody stuck between Scylla and Charybdis, when I am stuck there myself? The making of a choice at all requires so much soul-searching and sacrifice, and I have not accomplished that. You have. I would be the worst kind of Greek harpy to *judge* you."

"You do not think my riding naked through town is just the extremity of my comportment?"

Edgiva blinked in amazement and even laughed. "Are you jesting, Godiva? I think it is quite the opposite. Edward harries you by robbing you of coquetry, which is your greatest weapon. If you make the ride, you lose that power, and my heart rides with you in sympathy."

"Even though you are cross with me for other things?"

"Even though I am cross with you for other things."

That was not actually what Godiva had been hoping to hear in response.

"So you *are* still cross with me for . . . other things?"

Edgiva gave her friend a warning look. "Have those other things miraculously resolved themselves overnight? No? Then, yes, I am still cross."

"I am not the one who put or allowed a child in your belly—"

"We are not revisiting that conversation," Edgiva said sharply. "You are not responsible for my sins, but you are responsible for your interfering, which has endangered Sweyn and complicated everything."

"I would say you complicated everything, as soon as you spread your knees for him."

Edgiva's face instantly went crimson, and Godiva wished she had not said it. "Are you trying to convince me to retract my

offer?" Edgiva demanded. "Because you are just about to suc-
ceed in that."

"I'm sorry, I'm so sorry," she said hurriedly. "I need you beside
me now, Edgiva. I am sorry I am such an ass. You are a better
woman than I am, you have always been so; please be so now. I
did not realize how terrified I was until moments ago."

The abbess softened. "You are my oldest friend; of course I am
not going to desert you in a crisis. Even though you brought it on
your own head."

"I thought you were not judging me!"

"That is not judgment," Edgiva said briskly. "It is fact." She
stepped back and gave Godiva an appraising look. "Let us sort
out how to get you through this."

That was deeply reassuring: Edgiva, in charge, gently pushing
things to happen as they ought to. That was an Edgiva Godiva
knew from her other life, her regular life, before things had
gotten complicated.

"Disrobe here, in this room, in private," the abbess suggested.
"There is something about disrobing that is even more . . .
fraught . . . than actually being nude."

"You speak from years of experience, do you?" Godiva asked
wryly.

"I speak from one experience, but it was recent, and enough to
educate me," Edgiva said pointedly. Their eyes met, and Edgiva
blushed. Unexpectedly, they shared a sheepish grin.

"It has been so long since my undressing before Leofric felt . . .
fraught . . . that I would not have considered that," Godiva said.

"So disrobe here, in private."

Godiva nodded. She unpinned her veil. Edgiva held out her
hand for it, and Godiva yielded it, and the pins.

"Wrap your longest, fullest mantle round yourself, and go down to the stable covered. Get on the horse, and stay cloaked to the manor gate." She reached for and received Godiva's wimple and fillet, and watched long pale tresses spill over the slender shoulders.

The countess took a steadying breath, then lifted off the three heavy gold necklaces gracefully, hooping them down the length of her hair. These too she handed to Edgiva, who continued, abbesslike, to instruct: "I shall carry the mantle as we walk to the far end of the street, then I will give it back to you. Come now, off with your tunic."

Godiva felt clammy, and still trembled, as she pulled off her clothes. Edgiva glanced away, not as if she were ashamed to see her friend's nakedness, but as if she were concerned Godiva stood in fear of her judgment.

Never since her first years with Leofric had Godiva undressed with such awareness of her body's appearance. Everything she liked about it—the smooth skin, the curves at her hip, her slender arms—seemed diminished as she watched herself, as if she were another person undressing another body. Everything she found fault with—a brown spot on her neck where sunlight had poisoned her perfect paleness, her buttocks that did not sit so high as once they did, her ridiculously skinny ankles and bony knees—all of these things suddenly seemed to be what her body was made from. The buttocks would be mostly hidden under her hair, she was sure, but the knees and ankles would be the most visible parts of her. They would be what people would remember of her from this ride.

Not that many people would see her, anyhow. Coventry was but a hamlet, and Leofric was going out before her to tell people not to look.

All the same, surely somebody would catch a glimpse of her bony knee pressed against the horse, perhaps some serf, and he would tell some cousin of his who had migrated to someone else's estate, who would mention it so that it would make its way up the ladder until the thane or carl of that particular area heard about it, and the next time Godiva fluttered her eyelashes at him, he would laugh mockingly and say, "I hear you have bony knees, Countess," and that would be the end of—

"Godiva, are you listening to me?" Edgiva's voice broke through her unhappy reverie.

"Pardon?" she said hurriedly, and took a moment to review herself: she was down to her shift. She had ungartered her stockings and removed them without paying attention.

"I asked which mantle you prefer," Edgiva said. "Merewyn has brought you two." She pointed to the bed. One was dark blue-black, the color of Edgiva's robes; in fact, it was the mantle that had caused a confusion about who had gone to Hereford with Sweyn. The other was a lighter blue, shot through with red and emblazoned with Leofric's catamount, which stood for vigilance.

"Which would you pick?" she asked Edgiva uncertainly.

"I would wear the one that looks like a nun's robe," she said, "because I am a nun. You are nothing like one."

"I shall wear it anyhow," she said. "If Edward has brought a chronicler with him, I do not think Leofric would want me to remind anyone I am his lady today."

"On the contrary, he might be very proud of you," said Edgiva.

"I do not think it."

Godiva pulled the shift off over her head. Now she stood entirely naked, except for the cascading shield of hair that fell to below her waist.

"Must I pin my hair up?" she fretted. "I am sure he wants that, to make all of my flesh completely exposed."

"If he said you must be nude, then you cannot wear any hair ornaments," Edgiva said smartly. "Your hair must be as unadorned as you are, so no hairpins." She smiled conspiringly. Her smile convinced Godiva she could go through with this. Her smile made everything seem almost normal. Almost.

Godiva wrapped the mantle protectively around her and pinned it tightly at her shoulder. "Let us go, then," she said.

Edgiva held the door open for her. They walked out into the hall.

The housecarls and servants must have heard what was happening by now, for everyone paused, as if suddenly they were posing for a mural, and then hurried to continue their rounds. All of them were straining covertly to glance at their mistress.

If her closest subordinates were willing to behave that way, what awaited her out among the stranger, ruder populace? This was a new hamlet, and the people did not know her well.

The two women walked across the courtyard to the stable. Godiva could feel her pulse throbbing in her neck, at her temple. She could hear her blood rushing through her, as if it were a thing outside herself, the murmur of the sea on the Northumbrian coast.

The day was dry, as too many had been this spring, and it was sunny. The stable was absolutely empty, with only one horse remaining in it. With a stab of panic Godiva realized she had made no provisions for her horse—she would ride the mare, of course,

but how was she to control it? Should it be bridled? Edward had
said it should be naked too. What if she used a bridle and then,
having survived all of this humiliation, the king claimed it did
not count because she had defied him by bridling the horse?

Edward's harrying the town would have been easier. The villagers could have taken refuge in the manor and Godiva would
have paid to rebuild all their houses. It would have cost far, far
less than the heregeld. She opened her mouth to make this point
to Edgiva, but by then they had reached the stable, and Edgiva
pointed almost cheerfully to Godiva's mare, a broad-boned
palfrey, waiting just inside, haltered by the mounting block. A
slender horsehair cord—the mare's own, by the color—was tied
around the horse's nose, with enough length to it that Edgiva
could hold it and guide the mare with nothing else.

"Thank you, Leofric," Godiva said softly. Edgiva nodded.

They were alone in the stable. The smell of horses had never
been so sharp in Godiva's nose. Perhaps because she had never
breathed it in combined with her own wakeful nervousness.

"I am frightened," she told Edgiva.

"No, you're not," the abbess said, sounding wise and calm and
abbesslike, and not at all like the distraught woman who was so
upset with her. "If Leofric's life were dependent upon your not
falling off and making a fool of yourself, or if you had to survive
being dunked, or walking along the edge of a canyon without
falling, then you would be frightened. This is not fear. This is
something so much smaller that is fooling you into believing it is
fear. Do not be fooled."

There was the mounting block—the same mounting block she
used every time she was in Coventry, a block identical to every

block she used at every stable in Mercia. She looked at it now, felt the grain of the wood as her bare toes trod upon it, and it became the most unusual and fascinating of objects ever under her feet. The strange sea-murmur had not subsided; it was as if the air around her had its own pulse.

She rested her hands on the mare's low withers, leaned her weight forward slightly and swung her right leg over the mare's broad back, pushing off from the mounting block with her left foot. Her cloak swirled heavily with her as she moved.

She was astride the horse.

It felt, to her surprise, comfortable and unremarkable. The mare had been well groomed that morning, was warm from standing in the sunlight; its bare back was softer than a saddle, and the skin of Godiva's thighs and shins, used to woolen stockings and wraps, was indifferent to the smooth horsehair. It hardly felt different from riding bareback in skirts.

She nodded to Edgiva, who pressed her hand against the horse's far cheek to turn its head. The mare could feel Godiva's unease; it was a very gentle palfrey, but its rider's anxiety made it fussy. It tossed its head in disagreement and ignored Edgiva.

"Come, my lady," the abbess cooed firmly. With her left hand holding the lead of the horsehair halter, she once again reached under the horse's neck and rested her strong fingers on its cheek to turn its head out.

This time the mare stepped with her. Godiva felt an uncomfortable thrill at having no direct control over the animal. They walked out of the shade of the stable, across the small courtyard that suddenly seemed smaller than ever.

They reached the gate almost instantly. With a nervous sigh,

Godiva reached to unpin her brooch, but Edgiva held up a hand, and she paused. The abbess listened intently to something that Godiva could not hear, because again her pulse was throbbing too loudly in her head. Edgiva glanced over her shoulder with a slightly alarmed expression.

"What is it?" Godiva asked, feeling helpless.

"Keep your cloak on," she whispered, and pushed at the gate. It gave a little, then paused, and then with some fitful movements, it opened slowly.

Edgiva saw them all a heartbeat before Godiva did, and took in an audible breath. Godiva marked Edgiva's reaction, then Leofric—who sat on his horse there outside the gate, awaiting them—looked toward her, and his gaze pulled her away from Edgiva's startled expression. He was horrified.

Coventry was overrun with people. From their dress they seemed mostly farmers or serfs, and by their numbers they must have come from dozens, perhaps scores of miles, in all directions. Every hamlet, village, farm, and manor within two days' ride or three days' walk—they all must be emptied of inhabitants except those too old or sick to travel. They were all in Coventry. There were at least a thousand people here. The crowd disappeared out of sight down the road, and probably went all the way to Edward, waiting at the monastery. They had not been here yesterday, and there had been no sign of them at dawn today, so they must have come all at once, which was too extraordinary to conceive. They must have arrived almost silently, like an army. That meant they were here under somebody's direction.

Edward's.

There was anonymity in their drab dress, their lack of pen-

nants, decoration, or livery. They were Everyman and Every-
woman. They had been sent for, and they had arrived. Most
likely, they were Godiva's own people and maybe Leofric's, summoned by the king's messengers to bear witness to . . . something.
Did they know? What did they know?

Leofric, moments earlier, had come out here thinking he
would speak to a few score villagers. He was still recovering from
the shock of this enormous massing.

Godiva felt herself grow pale, felt her mouth fall open, and
fought to keep her balance as a heavy dizziness immediately
pushed down on her from the cool spring air.

"Who are you?" Leofric demanded of the crowd.

That was a useless question: very few of them answered, and
those that did spoke over each other in sheepish voices revealing
nothing: "Alred," said one. "A serf from Evesham," said another.
"A freeman tenant of yours, milord." Voices created a mumbled,
apologetic cacophony of no good information.

"Did King Edward summon you?" asked Edgiva's strong
voice, more loudly than ever Godiva was used to hearing it.

"Yes, lady," came the nearly unanimous response.

"Thank you, Mother," Leofric said softly, and then even more
softly, cursed. Raising his voice again: "*Why* did he summon you?"

The response was untranslatable muttering.

Leofric scanned the crowd and then pointed slowly with one
gloved finger to an older man with the leather apron of a farrier.
"You, fellow. Tell me for what purpose the king has collected you."

The man bowed, calmly, and shook his head. "My Lord, he
gave no reason, just sent his men round to tell us that if we appeared here today we would witness something wondrous."

There was nodding and assenting grunts near him, and the phrase "something wondrous" was repeated three or four rows deep.

"I see," said Leofric. "Something touching my lady wife?"

The man bowed again. "Not that he said, my Lord. I guessed it must be, as this is her hamlet, but the king's messenger said nothing."

With a grimace, Leofric glanced at the two women.

"Look closer," Edgiva said, reaching up with her free hand to tug Leofric's sleeve. "Look how many children there are in this crowd. And look at the farmers."

There were at least three dozen lambs—very young, a few days old—hoisted over the thick necks of ruddy-faced men. But stranger than that, fully a third of the crowd—hundreds of people—held clay pots or small leather bags, and they seemed to be holding these toward the gate, as if in offering.

"You there," Leofric said gruffly to a young man near the front. The fellow held a wooden box, the size of his head, out before him. He was dressed like a farmer, but cleaner than most, and groomed enough to suggest personal industry. "What is in that box?"

The young man blinked at him a moment; unlike the farrier, he was nervous to be singled out. "Sod from my farm, milord," he finally said. "For the lady to bless."

"Ah," said Edgiva. "Of course. Ask the closest man with a lamb—"

"Fellow, with the red hair," Leofric called out. "Why have you brought livestock to stare at my wife?"

"So she could bless the creature and so bless my flock," said the fellow, trying to bow without dislodging his mewling burden.

"Did the king tell you to do this?" Leofric demanded. He glanced briefly back at Godiva, almost accusingly.

"No, milord," the fellow said, surprised. "It was obvious. Given the hard years we have had it is only right. We all heard the lady performed the Land Ceremony and then it rained for the only time in weeks. So when we heard there would be something wondrous, I knew it would include her blessing."

"Woden's knees, this will play right into Edward's hands," Leofric muttered with barely contained fury.

"Why?" said Edgiva. "It has nothing to do with what happens in a church. This is to make sure the crops grow and the live-stock multiply. Render to Caesar the things that are Caesar's, and render to the gods of harvest and herds. Godiva already proved she was game to help them by performing the Land Ceremony charm. Now they hope she will intervene directly, without the bother of the Church."

"That is just what Edward will want," Leofric repeated. "A suggestion of paganism. If the countess does not willingly give him Coventry, he shall take Coventry from the witch."

"Never mind that," said Godiva, shivering beneath her cloak. "How do we keep them all from staring at me while I'm naked?"

"I think I can help you there," Edgiva said. "If I may have leave?"

"If you think you can possibly improve things," Leofric said with resignation.

"Good people," Edgiva called out. She was not on horseback and many could not see her. Scores—hundreds—of people were frowning and craning their necks.

"Talk louder," Godiva recommended.

"Talk for me," she countered. "Talk for yourself. Repeat whatever I say. Good people—"

"Good people," Godiva called out.

"Louder."

"Good people!"

"Look upon me for a moment."

"I thought we were trying to make them *not* look—"

"Look upon me for a moment."

"Look upon me for a moment!"

"I will gladly bless each of you, and your offerings, at the far side of the village—"

Godiva repeated this, uncertainly.

"—but I will only bless those who keep their gaze averted while I am disrobed."

"Oh dear God," Godiva whispered. "Do they even know I am about to do that?"

"Find out," said Edgiva. "I will only bless those who keep their gaze—"

"I will only bless those who keep their gaze averted while I am disrobed!" the countess declared hurriedly.

No, they had not known that. The immediate uproar was proof.

"Silence!" Godiva shouted. "All blessings come with a price! The price today is that I must see proof of your devotion before I give you proof of mine!"

Edgiva looked over her shoulder, up at Godiva, startled.

Godiva suddenly felt exhilarated. "Turn your backs on me at once, and march all together to the green that lies just on the far side of the monastery walls, past Coffa's Tree. I will be there moments after you, and at that time you will each be blessed. But until every one of you has removed yourself from the main street of Coventry, I shall stay here and there will be no blessing!"

"That's enough," Leofric advised. "You sound like you believe yourself."

They watched.

There were a few moments of hovering uncertainty. The people on the outskirts of the group did not want to further distance themselves, and they did nothing. However, the men whom Leofric had called out for questioning fixed decisive grimaces on their faces and turned to push their way through the crowd. That turned it; suddenly the entire wave of visitors and residents wanted to reach the far side of the monastery, and now those on the outskirts, suddenly on the front line of the new receiving area, very nearly ran down the road and out of sight.

In the time it takes to draw water from a deep well, there were only a handful of stragglers before the gate. These were all youths, just barely sprouting beards. It was obvious why they had stayed.

"I am no fetching young virgin," Godiva called out to them. "It really is not worth the wait. I have the boniest knees in Christendom."

They giggled, looked at each other, at their feet, and did not move.

"I will send my housecarls to smack you with clubs if you do not find other entertainment," said Leofric with contained, almost bored, annoyance.

The youths left at once.

They were alone now, the three of them, before the gate.

"Thank you," Godiva said to both her companions, with a shaky sigh.

"I'll ride ahead," said Leofric grimly. He tightened his heels against his horse's sides and it skitted forward, tail swishing and knees lifting high; like Godiva's mare, Leofric's mount felt his agitation.

He looked over his shoulder and said quietly, almost grimly, "Know that I love you, Godiva, no matter what follows from this," then immediately faced forward again and clucked his horse into a trot.

Edgiva looked up over her shoulder. "Are you ready?" she asked.

Godiva felt her breath catch. She nodded, and reached up to undo the heavily jeweled brooch that nestled by her shoulder. She had pinned the mantle so snug across herself that even with the brooch unpinned, it stayed around her shoulders. With a shaky breath, she shrugged it off, first her right shoulder, then her left. It slumped down around her waist, heavy and warm, and in its place the cool air slid under her hair and chilled her skin.

"Take it," she said, and pushed the whole mantle off of herself, down toward Edgiva. The abbess turned just enough to catch and collect the yards of dark wool, then, with the whole of it in her arms, she faced forward again. Two fingers held the mare's lead. She had deliberately avoided looking at Godiva.

Godiva breathed in slowly and willed herself to sit up straight on the horse.

Her hair covered most of her upper body, although she had to round her shoulders slightly for it to entirely cover her breasts. She was not used to seeing her own body in direct sunlight. Most distracting felt her knees and shins, for they were entirely bare; breeze and sun felt alien upon them. How much exposure, she wondered, before one was as dark as a shepherdess? And how absurd was she to be worrying about that at this moment?

"Oh dear, look at those bony knees," Edgiva said suddenly.

Godiva giggled, nervously. The abbess grinned—Godiva could actually see her grin although her back was to her; her whole body took on the spirit of the grin.

"So this is all it is," Godiva said. "Here I am, naked, on a horse. I am still me, the horse is still the horse. The sun has not gone out. I have not been struck blind by lightning. The end of the road is just barely out of sight, and then this will be over. I will survive this."

But will I survive what comes after? she wondered.

Edgiva threw the unwieldy heft of the mantle over her left shoulder. "Let us go, then," she said and, standing at the level of the horse's eye, tugged gently on the lead. Abbess and mare both walked forward.

The rocking sensation of riding bareback—essentially bareback—was familiar to Godiva from her early years. She had only to squeeze her thighs against the horse's barrel of a body to feel secure; its warmth was comforting, sending a message between two living beings, in a way she never felt when riding a saddled horse. In the abbey, she had managed to slip out now and then to "borrow" a horse from the stable, without a saddle and frequently without a bridle. And usually horses not so gentle as this one.

It was not the sensation of being on the horse, but the sensation of her own nakedness in the world, that lifted her out of her body. She had never been such a stranger in her own skin, for she had never been made so aware of her own skin. Not since the first time Leofric took her as a wife; and then it had been dark, and she had been so young, and so innocent of all the things there are to be self-conscious of. Then, she had simply lain back and let him do with her what he wished to do; her simply being undressed was enough. If she had left her body then, she left it in the hands of somebody who knew exactly what to do with it, who could protect and master it. Now she had to remain conscious and attentive; Edgiva could not catch her if she fell.

Her nipples were hard, as they always were when she was chilled, but now she felt the brief drift of breeze upon them, and the strange hard silk of her own hair, which created almost a shawl of protection. She thought briefly Leofric might find it enticing to see her like this, but it did not *feel* enticing. It felt strange, and she wanted it to be over.

Her senses were heightened. Besides the extreme awareness of her breasts, she heard the sounds of springtime, the rhythm of the insects and small animals scurrying unseen on the earth around her; along with the reassuringly familiar scent of horse, she could *smell* the grass growing, and the earth overturned, beckoning seeds to come to it and give it life to feed upon. She now noticed the sunlight tease and dazzle every thing it lit upon, even birds, even rocks on the side of the unpaved road. She saw how it lit up the sky, as if there were no tomorrow to save itself for. It gave itself completely to the day, this day, this moment. *We should all do as much,* she thought. *I sound drunk,* she thought next. *I wish I were drunk. Why did I not overindulge on wine at breakfast, so that I could have done this in a stupor of disregard? No, instead I am doing this cold and dry and too aware of what awaits me when I reach the far side of the village.*

Despite her heightened senses, although she could hear every flap of bird wing, somehow at the same time the throbbing of her blood muffled her, placed a sphere of soundlessness around her. Everything was either too loud or too soft, or somehow both at once—nothing sounded normal. The monastery bells were sounding—Terce? Sext?—they did not toll for her now; she existed outside of time.

They walked on. They passed the small huts, wattle and daub, thatched roofs, no windows, opened doors. She wondered if anyone lurked within there, old women or little children, watching and wondering what they were seeing, trying to make sense of it. She had never noticed how cleverly the thatch was laid onto the roofs before. She wondered if there was a trick to it.

This was so simple. All she had to do was ride, with her hair so thick about her, below her waist, that she hardly felt unclothed at all. Edward thought this was a punishment? Ha! The more fool Edward! She could not wait to arrive at the other side of town and tell him so, show him so.

No, she did not want to ever reach the other side of town. Then all the throngs would be there, and she would have to either bless their bags of earth in front of the king, which surely would be damning, or send them all home fretful and disappointed, disgruntled, and if there was yet another year of drought and bad crops . . . they would lay it on her head.

Much easier to keep riding in this strange altered state where she watched herself, as a different person. There is Godiva, lady of Mercia, she thought, pointing her out to herself. She is riding naked through the town. She felt compassion for that woman, for all that she would have to face when she came to the other side of Coventry.

For that was the real moment of crisis, after all. Not the ride itself—that was easily done, the proof was that she was *doing it now*. The hard part was what followed after. She had no control over that. She could not guess what Edward would do. She could not guess how the mass of people would behave. She could not choose Edgiva's next actions, or Leofric's. The hardest thing about taking action was accepting that there would be a reaction, which one could not control. She tried to think of exceptions to this. Had she ever done anything in which she had power over somebody else's response? One could offer food to a hungry child, and there was no guarantee she would taste it. One could lift one's skirt to one's adoring husband, and there was no guarantee he would lift it higher. One could write a letter to a friend encouraging him to pursue his lady, and there was no guarantee about anything at all.

She thought about Sweyn and Edgiva as she rode. Nobody would remember much about these madly intense few moments of her life, for the kingdom's gossip was focused so much on the two of them. Theirs was the story that would echo infamously through history. How silly to make a fuss, Godiva thought, and wondered to herself if she meant a fuss over her ride or a fuss over them. How silly to make a fuss over anything, really, she decided. How silly to make a fuss.

They came to the deserted market square.

"Halfway," said Edgiva.

"Yes," Godiva said.

They continued. Moment by moment she was less absent from her self; ordinary senses resumed: sound became normal, her nostrils were filled only with the smell of the horse, she was once again aware of living within her own skin. She found that mildly disappointing. But even as her skin braced itself against the cool morning breeze, even as her mind tried to pretend there was nothing strange at all about the sensations it was feeling, the sun on her knees, the yielding warmth of the horse beneath her thighs and buttocks, a breeze dancing at her toes and elbows . . . even as she began to believe these things were good and natural, just as her forefather and foremother would have ridden in the Garden, just as she was almost ready to convince herself of that, she saw, a bowshot away beyond the monastery, the dark crowd that was the host of farmers and shepherds and villagers. It was time to return to humanity. To cease feeling nude and instead feel naked. For the first time ever in her life, she did not want an audience.

A handful of men on horseback waited much closer, at the monastery gate. *I built that gate,* Godiva thought, *and now I am made to pay for their jealousy of my accomplishment.*

A high, thin glaze of clouds was paling the blue of the sky. "We approach," said Edgiva gently, as if testing to make sure Godiva was still conscious.

"Yes," she said.

"Are you well?"

"Of course," Godiva said, as if she did this all the time.

"When do you want your mantle back?"

"Hand it to Leofric and let him drape it over me. He feels powerless right now to protect me."

"You don't need protection," Edgiva said, in an approving tone. "He should be proud of you for that."

"Husbands like the idea of such things, but in reality it is much easier for them when they can protect you, or rescue you." They were close enough now to make out the individual figures, although not their faces. "I'm telling you that so you know how to manage your own husband," she said, "should you elect to take one."

Edgiva said nothing.

Leofric was plain now, and it was easy to discern the king: he was surrounded by the others, on a tall horse, dressed in purple.

Amazingly enough, it was almost over.

Or: it was all about to begin.

"Now that I have done this," Godiva said, "will you tell me what you think the Church will make of it all?"

There was such a long pause she thought Edgiva was either ignoring her or had not heard her. "I think," the abbess said at last, "it depends on what you mean by the Church."

"Do not be obscure," Godiva scolded.

"I do not mean to be," she said quickly. "I no longer know what that means, that term: the Church. Not even for myself, let alone for another. If it means a set of uncompromising beliefs and principles, then I know how to answer you. If it means something gentler and more human, that comforts and succors—in that case too I know the answer. But if you mean the Church as we know it today, where everything is manipulated and twisted for political gain or personal vendetta, then no, I do not know. But I think you are about to find out for yourself."

They were nearly there. The sky was whitening—no clouds rolling in, just a general glazing-over of the blue. She could see the expression on Leofric's face. He looked ill. She wanted to reassure him. She wanted to tell him that she was well, perfectly well; that she was better than well. She had slain the beast, and she was not brought down by it. Coventry was saved and Edward squelched, and she had done it, at no cost to herself.

She could not say these things in front of Edward and his men, however, so instead she smiled as warmly as she could at Leofric without appearing foolish.

When they were not three yards from Edward and Leofric, Edgiva stopped and tugged on the mare's lead. The mare pulled its head up slightly in protest, but halted.

"I am here," Godiva said simply. Edgiva released the horse, crossed under its neck toward Leofric, and offered him the great rumple of mantle. He understood at once, and nodded to her with grim thanks. Edward and Aldred blinked in confusion at Edgiva's presence, as Leofric lifted the mantle by its shoulders out of her hooped arms and then, expertly steering with his weight and legs, sidled his horse alongside Godiva's mare and draped the heavy wool around her shoulders. She remained unmoving until he released it, and then—her eyes boring into Edward's without a blink—she pulled the mantle closed, overlapping, across her breasts. "It is done," she said.

"It certainly is," said Edward, his nasal voice sounding unnervingly pleased. "I was expecting the money, of course, or perhaps the town instead, but this suits me well enough. I do not like having to humiliate my people, because it means they have been misbehaving. But that, at least, was less unpleasant than most forms of punishment." His smile became dangerous, his voice sleek. "And the harbinger of so much more to come."

"What do you mean?" Godiva said stonily. "That is it. We're done."

"You and I are done," he agreed. "You have fulfilled what I required of you. But, Godiva, my ravishing and ravishable lady, your humiliation is only now beginning. I fear news of this day will travel far."

"It already has," Godiva said. And smiled.

He looked startled. So did Leofric. So, glancing over her shoulder, did the abbess.

"I wrote to every one of my peers and superiors around the kingdom," Godiva said pleasantly to Edward. "Last night. This morning, I emptied our stable of messengers, all of them laden with multiple scrolls and orders to relay them to the far reaches of your realm."

"What did you write?" Leofric demanded—not angrily, but shocked.

"I alerted everyone they were likely to hear strange unsavory tales of what had happened recently in Coventry, and I wanted them to know the truth of it straight from me."

"And what," asked Edward, threatening, "did you present as truth?"

"I told them," said Godiva, unthreatened, "that I had struck a deal with the king, that in exchange for one fairly minor and peculiar ordeal, I had completely overruled his intention of taxing my people oppressively. I encouraged them to do likewise. Refuse his tyranny, I counseled all of them, and for a very small price, you will be free of it. I am not humiliated, Your Majesty. I am exultant. I have paid your price, and it has not diminished me."

Never in her life had she felt more triumphant.

The shock on Edward's face elated her. How she would celebrate with Leofric and Edgiva tonight! She had accomplished the impossible: used Edward's own power against him, made his attempt at tyranny the very thing that would take away his power. It was a delicious moment.

But no more than a moment. Edward collected himself, gave her a small, dangerous smile. With his gaze locked onto hers, he gestured with one hand. Behind him, another horseman stirred, and urged his horse up beside the king's. She recognized his pudgy face.

"Godiva," Leofric said sorrowfully, "Bishop Aldred has come to censure you."

CHAPTER 24

Godiva stared at Leofric. He looked away. She stared at Aldred. He smiled sheepishly.

"Your Eminence *recommended* that I do this," Godiva protested. "You said a little penance would clear me of any transgression associated with it. You lauded me for resisting the heregeld."

"Did I?" said Aldred. "Forgive me, Lady Countess, I do not recall that."

Mother Edgiva made a distressed sound.

"Such a shame you did not keep His Eminence's letter to remind you," Leofric said with resigned sarcasm to his wife. Godiva felt her skin grow clammy under the mantle. "I believe you have also misplaced the king's written declaration that your riding naked through Coventry would be punishment enough for defying him."

Edward looked incredulous. "I am sure I never wrote such a thing," he said.

"In which case," said Aldred, looking uncomfortable but

grimly determined, "perhaps you will explain to us your actions. I see that you have used your influence to convene a mob expressing pagan beliefs, among many hundreds of your people who are otherwise devout Christians."

It was the first declaration Godiva had ever heard him utter.

"This is, of course, a jest," she said. "And in terrible taste."

"I would never jest about something so serious, my lady," said Aldred apologetically. Turning to Edgiva, he said nervously, "Sister? Be kind enough to quote scripture to the countess, as she may be ignorant of the holy text and therefore the consequences of her actions."

"I grew up copying and memorizing the Holy Writ, you hypocrite," Godiva nearly snarled.

"Then perhaps," said Aldred, "you would recite the second book of John, chapter one, verse ten."

Godiva had always found the Book of John by far the dullest of any in the Bible, and besides: "I was never given that to copy," she said.

"Then I shall recite it," said Aldred, sounding bizarrely obsequious. "'Whosoever transgresses, and abides not in the doctrine of Christ, has not God.'"

A pause. Godiva smirked impatiently. She wondered what he would demand of her for penance, now—and why he was playing this game in the first place.

That Edward had even brought Aldred surprised her. It suggested the king knew there was a possibility she would make the ride, and wanted to milk advantage from it if she did. But why would Aldred—indecisive, passive Aldred—agree to such a stratagem?

"Verse eleven," Aldred continued. From the corner of her eye, she saw Edgiva tense and cross herself. "'If there come any such unto you, receive him—or her—not into your house or family. Neither bid him God speed: even he that bids him God speed is a partaker of his evil deeds.'"

Edgiva dropped the horsehair cord and took a step away from the mare, shuddering. "I must not be a party to this," she said. Her tone alarmed Godiva more than anything that had happened so far on this already alarming morning, and she looked quizzically at the abbess. "God forgive this," Edgiva said in a cracked voice, her eyes suddenly full of tears. She held her hands up in a submissive gesture. "He is casting you out. He is telling us we must all cast you out." She crossed herself again.

"But you will not do such a thing," Godiva said, trying to smile, and failing. Her chest felt hollow when she attempted a laugh. "Edey, you will not shun me, surely."

"It is not a choice, Godiva," Edgiva said. "I have very difficult choices ahead of me. This is not one of them."

To Godiva's astonishment and alarm, Edgiva turned away and then suddenly broke into a run, with a frantic earnestness that belied her fragile physical state, back toward the manor house.

"Edey! What are you doing?" Godiva cried out. The abbess ignored her and continued to flee. The image of her oldest, dearest friend's receding form chilled her. The sky, she noticed with a shudder, was darkening from white to grey, abruptly now.

"She is but the first of legions," said Aldred sadly.

"You will not do this," Godiva said. "You will not do this to me, and to my husband, and to my people."

"Daughter," he said, looking at her horse instead of her, "if only you had not transgressed, you would not be doing it to yourself and those you care for."

Confusion clouded her; she was almost dizzy, she could not make sense of Edward's seduction of Aldred. "You are saying that I am to be shunned from my own home? That my subjects must not even greet me?"

"Sadly, yes."

"Because of what I just did? Just that? Now?"

"Because what you just did reveals a deeper stain in your soul."

Annoyance and panic fought for precedence. Annoyance got the upper hand. "What atonement must I perform in order to have this heinous sentence lifted from my shoulders?"

"For such a grave offense against the Church as you have just committed now," said Aldred regretfully, "we must begin with your publicly declaring and renouncing your wrongs. And then a pilgrimage will cleanse your soul."

"And after that Edgiva—for whom I got myself into this mess—will talk to me again? To Canterbury then, is it?"

"For a transgression such as this one? Jerusalem, I should think," said Aldred heavily.

"What?" Leofric nearly shouted. "You are not sending her to Jerusalem because she rode a quarter mile naked on a horse."

"You are right, of course, milord," said Aldred, almost pleadingly. "I am sending her to Jerusalem for practicing paganism under the Church's very nose. She even had a nun beside her—she was attempting to corrupt a woman of the cloth."

"This is a farce!" Godiva shouted.

"That particular woman of the cloth has already been corrupted," Leofric snapped. "Stick your ecclesial proboscis into *her* affairs. Those are actually affairs."

"She is safe, at least," Godiva said bitterly. "She did not even bid me *adieu*." She used the French deliberately, glaring at the

Normandy-raised king. She was stunned by Edgiva's abrupt abandonment. "If I go on pilgrimage—"

"Godiva, you are not going on any pilgrimage," Leofric said crossly. "This is all appalling political posturing."

"If I were to go," she pressed on, ignoring him, "would this sentence of excommunication be conditionally lifted so that I might practically prepare for such a trip?"

"No," said Aldred, apologetically.

"So you are saying I must somehow prepare for a dauntingly dangerous and extended voyage, without any means to make those preparations? That makes the trip impossible!"

"Then you will not be going? Such a shame to see you so truculent," said Aldred, glancing nervously at Edward the way a childhood bully glances at a cohort. "We had high hopes for your repentance."

She looked over her shoulder. Edgiva was gone. *Gone.*

"It is the monastery," Leofric said suddenly, in a voice of discovery.

"What do you mean?" she asked—but even as she heard the words, she knew.

"Edward wants Coventry, so he has offered Aldred the monastery that is the center of it. That is the arrangement, isn't it?" he demanded of the bishop, who lowered his eyes. "You will never fill Lyfing's sandals, and you know it, so you are staking claim in new territory, where you cannot be compared to the better men who came before you. If Godiva is excommunicated, her estates are masterless—they do not automatically come to me. Edward takes her land. Except the monastery. You'll get that."

"Well, it certainly cannot be patronized by a woman who is excommunicated," said Aldred.

"Or by her husband," added Edward. "I believe the good bishop just quoted scripture that implies you are as much a sinner as she is, now. Unless you remove yourself from her sinfulness."

"Or if she were to repent," Aldred said helpfully.

"By going to *Jerusalem*?" Leofric said furiously. Godiva was feeling too ill to speak. She could not believe Edey had run away from her. Again she looked back toward the manor. The vast sky was darkening quickly, turning an angry purple. How could any sky turn so quickly? The breeze had died completely; the air was so still it felt unnatural.

"You could go with her," Edward said pleasantly. "I will keep my eye on Mercia while you're away."

Leofric turned to look at his wife. She could not read the look on his face; was it accusation at her, or outrage at them? Or both? He closed his eyes and sighed heavily. Then, opening them: "If I do not shun you, then others must shun me. My servants, my thanes, my housecarls, my serfs . . . I cannot explain to all of them that this is a sham, a political manipulation. They will believe I am imperiling their souls, and they will seek to cleave from me and turn to someone else to rule them. King Edward, for example."

"So you will shun me," Godiva said, not believing it.

"I must," said Leofric softly. "For now."

Godiva took a moment to consider that. The wife in her wanted to shriek at him in fury, pound her fists against his chest until he relented in a shower of kisses. But the countess understood, and so she grimaced and said nothing to him. "All right, then," she said, to Edward and not to Aldred. "Since you are the puppeteer, Your Majesty, give me your conditions."

"I have no idea what you mean."

"Stop that," she said irritably. "You have set all of this up so that you may get Coventry and Aldred takes control of the abbey. If we let you have those things without a fuss, will you tell him not to excommunicate me?"

"If Aldred does not excommunicate you, Edward does not get the town nor Aldred the abbey," said Leofric.

"Let us say you excommunicate me, you take the town and the abbey—so it's done. You have won that round," Godiva pressed on, to Edward. "Given that, is it necessary to send me to Jerusalem? Could you not have him send me to Canterbury? Or flagellate myself a few times and be done with it? I could do that right now, I am already undressed. And then at least I can start to put my life back together before dinner."

"You are in no position to be making any demands at all," said Edward mildly. "Follow His Eminence into the church, where monks await us to bear witness to the ritual of bell, book, and candle."

That phrase tore through her like a disease, and suddenly the full impact of this moment hit her. She almost vomited. They really would do it. She would lose everything. Her people, her home, Leofric, Edgiva . . . although she had already lost Edgiva. Despite her fallen state, she was a good abbess, a devoted woman of religion, and she would not speak to Godiva if Godiva were cast out. She had already run off at the threat of it.

And all those shepherds and farmers and villagers waiting under the still, strangely angry sky, who had come so far to be blessed—what would happen to them now? They would be told, in a few moments, that the woman whose blessing they sought was a creature of Satan, an apostate, and that if they had anything to do with her, they themselves would be cast out from the Church. And so they would believe their traditions were tainted and dangerous, and they would cease to follow them, and then have only the Church—this Church, led by men such as this— for spiritual guidance. A dismal future for all. And this time, truly, there was nothing she could do to stop it. It was all a chess game, and she had not seen until now how inevitable it was that she should lose.

The bishop beckoned her toward the church. The king dismounted and let his horse's reins drop to the ground. "Come, lady, let us go in," he said.

"*Wait!*" a woman cried from the market square.

They all turned.

In the purple-blue glare of the strange sky cover, Edgiva came running toward them, her veil flying back, one hand holding up her long loose skirts, the other hand gripping a small leather- bound codex. "Your Eminence, you have mistook the situation! I beg you, be advised!"

She reached the group and stopped, panting for breath. She leaned over, red in the face and nearly retching from exertion, but she held up the small book.

"I have brought you evidence," she managed to gasp, "of your misapprehension of this whole affair."

She stood straight again, pushed her veil back over her shoulder, and looked around at all of them.

"What are you talking about, woman?" Edward said sharply.

"The reason for Godiva's ride," said Edgiva breathlessly.

"She made the ride to entice good Christians to embrace heathen ways," said Aldred. "The evidence is the superstitious populace waiting on the other side of the abbey."

"I cannot account for their appearance," said Edgiva. "But I can tell you why she made the ride. Although you have not

greeted me as such, Your Majesty and Your Eminence, I am still
Mother Edgiva, Abbess of Leominster, and I command a certain
authority over this woman, who came to me at my abbey seeking
spiritual counsel. She has committed a grave sin, a terrible sin,
a sin so great I recorded it in the abbey's diary, which I brought
with me. I have in this same diary recorded the penance that I,
as abbess, gave her."

"What?" Edward said sharply.

"Were you not aware that abbesses can issue penance?"
Edgiva said sweetly, still getting her breath back. "You have
spent too much time in Normandy, uncle. I prescribed to her the
penance of riding naked through the town of Coventry."

Both Edward and Aldred blinked convulsively a moment,
before Edward said, "And for what sin, precisely, was she required to perform such an egregious penance?"

"She abducted me from my abbey, and then made it appear
that Sweyn Godwinson was the one to have done so," Edgiva
said promptly, offering up the codex. "She will confess as much
to you herself, and as I said, I have recorded it here in the abbey
chronicles. I have placed a strip of vellum in the page to mark it.
Please read it for yourself."

Godiva pressed the fingers of both hands over her lips to keep
from shouting or laughing or perhaps both. Bishop and king
stared at her, stupefied.

Edgiva gave them a quizzical smile. "What puzzles you so,
gentlemen?" she asked. "Were you not aware of the rumor that
Sweyn had abducted me from Leominster? Or perhaps you were
simply not aware that the rumor is false? It *is* false, as you can tell
by the fact that I stand before you here in Coventry. As I am in
Coventry it follows that I am not, of course, in Hereford."

Godiva lowered her fingers and allowed herself a smile, which was far more impish than she knew was proper. "The poor dears," she said quietly to Edgiva, "that's *two* earls in one day whom they now cannot rebuke."

"What do you mean, Godiva abducted you?" Edward demanded.

Edgiva waggled the codex at him. "You may read about it. She and five armed men appeared at the abbey and brought me back here, although I had no intention of leaving the abbey and never once acquiesced to the journey. And then she created a diversion that made it appear as though Sweyn had taken me back to Hereford."

Edward and Aldred angrily exchanged looks. "Why would she do such a thing?" the king demanded.

"Because she wanted to besmirch Earl Sweyn's name. She and Leofric felt threatened by Sweyn's rising influence, and she felt it was necessary to undermine him by creating a scandal that would envelop him."

"Did you really?" Edward demanded sharply of Godiva.

Godiva was so astonished to hear Edgiva lie—so fluidly, so comfortably, as if she did it all the time—that she almost could not collect her wits enough to speak. But: "Yes," she said. "It's true. It was evil and meddling of me. I begged Edgiva for a penance, and she—"

"That is not what happened!" Edward shouted furiously. "That is not why you rode—"

"Isn't it?" Leofric asked with a grudging smile. "What could it be, then?"

"If it were a punishment for not paying taxes," Edgiva pointed out, her breath fully recovered, her voice modulated and abbess-

like, "then the letters Godiva has sent around the kingdom will
be perceived as truthful, which is not, I think, in His Majesty's
interests. How fortunate, then, that His Majesty did not order
Godiva to ride naked through Coventry." And pointedly to the
bishop: "I am the one who did that. And she has performed her
penance, as you have witnessed. Proving what a faithful and biddable Christian she is." Pause. "Are there any misunderstandings
still to be addressed? Would you like to read the book?" She
offered it up again. Edward looked at it in angry disgust, then
swatted it away into the dust. Edgiva's pleasant expression did
not waver. "We have cleared Sweyn, Godiva, and His Majesty
of all wrongdoings in this matter, and of course His Eminence
would never attempt to excommunicate someone who has done
no wrong simply as a political maneuver—"

Aldred looked sincerely relieved by this turn. But Edward was
not done yet.

"Why did you choose such a horrendous penance?" he demanded.

"Do you think it is really so horrendous?" asked Edgiva
charmingly, stooping down to pick up the codex. "I think she
was quite successful in surviving it, and considering she is just a
fragile woman, it could not have been so difficult."

Sudden in the electric-silent air, an orange streak of lightning
split the purple sky to the west. They and the horses all startled,
and the horses nearly shied when a high-pitched crackle jolted
them. Then silence.

"Sweyn did not abduct you from Leominster?" said Edward
at last, gloomily.

She shook her head. "I have never been in Hereford but by my
own volition. And that not since the Great Council concluded.

Again, I offer my codex for perusal." She held it up to him—a brazen thing, thought Godiva in wonderment, for while much of what she said was true, and written, plenty of it was not.

Edward and Aldred had pushed Edgiva too far, and made her into a liar—at least to Edward and Aldred. She seemed strangely liberated for having succumbed to the sin she hated most. It was a necessary ordeal to survive in order to escape the crushing hypocrisy that now defined the Church she once had loved.

A pause.

"Would you like some dinner before you head back to your respective palaces?" Godiva asked, pulling the mantle even tighter round her shoulders. "I believe our cook is dressing the lamb and plucking the cocks even now."

"We will dine at the monastery," said Edward in a disdainful voice.

"Less work for our cook," Godiva replied agreeably. "If Your Majesty and Your Eminence will excuse me, I shall ride home and dress."

"And attend a celebratory mass for having completed your due penance," Mother Edgiva amended.

"If I must," said Godiva with a tiny grin.

"What are you going to do about the farmers?" the bishop demanded unhappily. "They have come expecting your blessing."

"There is surely no harm in a fully clothed lady giving a benediction to her serfs," said Edgiva quickly. "The lady countess already did as much at the Land Ceremony. But if you have any theological qualms about it, Your Eminence, I will be happy to bless them in her stead. As an abbess I certainly have the qualifications to do so."

"Why don't we let the bishop do it himself?" suggested Leofric. "They've come all this way, they deserve the highest-ranking prelate we can offer them."

"I'm not going to dole out pagan blessings!" Aldred said nervously.

Edgiva, with a knowing look, said then, "There is not such difference between a pagan blessing and a Christian one, as long as the blessing is sincerely given. They want to believe somebody with more power than they have is looking out for them. That's all. I often feel the same way myself. Do not you? Would you deprive them of the succor they need? What kind of shepherd does that make you?"

"They want a heathen blessing," Aldred said, looking slightly desperate.

"And lo, the bishop arrived among the heathen, and they received him and accepted his blessing, and when he departed, they were again amongst the righteous," said Edgiva beatifically.

"Or even, lo, the *king* arrived . . . ," Godiva suggested.

"Now *that* sounds like a chorale in the making," Edgiva said heartily. "Shall we send them to you at the monastery?"

And then the rain began.

The rainstorm, sudden in its outbreak, was gentle, unseasonably warm, and lasted just long enough to wet the thirsty soil without pooling into floods. The farmers returned to their homes in a state approaching ecstasy, welcoming the pearls of rain on their faces, considering this miraculous shower to be Godiva's blessing on them. The earl, his lady, and their guest went home to the manor, where Mother Edgiva wrote into her codex that she had sinned by lying, then added that her bigger sin was this: she truly did not see it as a sin, for the good it accomplished.

It was the next morning now, and gently overcast. Godiva's seat was slightly sore, but otherwise the ride had left no residue. At all.

King and bishop had departed, without ceremony; there was no entourage, no extra horses, no loitering curious commoners trying to win a glimpse. Except for Edgiva, the only people in Coventry now were townsfolk.

And Edgiva was not quite in Coventry now; nor was Godiva, nor was Leofric. They sat astride their horses just outside the edge of town, looking down the westward road, listening to the monastery bells ring Terce. Their boots were dark with mud, as were their horses' hooves. Leofric and two of his housecarls had reined their horses away from the women, to give them a confidential moment.

"This road goes to Hereford," said Godiva pointedly.

"It also goes to Leominster," Edgiva replied quietly. "But I cannot go there while I am with child."

"Then you had better go to Hereford."

"'Tis not that simple, Godiva," she said, a little sharply. Then she grimaced and Godiva could see she regretted her tone. "If I go to Hereford *because* of the child, then Sweyn has done a terrible thing that will bring trouble on his head. If I go, it must be a choice, not a necessity."

"What would make it feel like a choice?"

"Knowing that *if* I chose Leominster, there *would be* an acceptable alternative for the child."

Motherhood had never been required of Godiva, and God had never tested her or blessed her with it.

And oh, how she wanted Edgiva to go to Sweyn. Not only for the political benefit to Leofric, but also because despite herself she was in love with the idea of them in love. If the child forced her to be with him, how much the better?

But that was not what Edgiva needed now.

"We would take the child and raise it in fosterage," Godiva said confidently. "We would provide for it and nobody would ever need know its parentage. Not even Sweyn. If you feel called back to that . . . *abbey* of yours, the child will not suffer for your choice. And you may, of course, stay here until you are delivered. I shall tell the abbey we keep you here at our request."

She saw tears well up at the inner corners of Edgiva's eyes. The abbess pursed her lips together hard, as if afraid allowing herself to smile would lead to weeping.

"Are you certain of that?" she asked in a husky whisper.

Godiva nodded. "I may have to coax Leofric a bit, but he will understand." She grinned. "Motherhood would keep me too busy to get into much trouble."

Edgiva let herself smile, and let herself weep too. "Thank you," she said, her voice shaking. "Now I may make the choice with a clear conscience." She reached out to Godiva, who reined her horse over so they could embrace each other round the shoulders. For a moment, Edgiva sobbed. Then she collected herself and wiped her face off on the edge of her dark veil.

She looked longingly down the road. Godiva could not know if the longing was for the abbey or for Sweyn. The countess began to piece together a convincing argument to soften Leofric's resistance to their potential new houseguest.

"Well?" Leofric called out from a stone's throw away. His horse leisurely began to walk toward them, the housecarls following. "Are we enjoying the view or are we saying our farewells? These fellows will ride with you if you are leaving us, Mother."

"I do not think she is going back to the abbey quite yet," Godiva said.

Edgiva took a deep breath. "I am not going back to the abbey at all. I," she said decisively, "am going to Hereford."

In all the years Godiva had known her, Edgiva had never looked so radiant.

Leofric took a moment to consider everything behind that statement. "So our Leominster Abbey no longer has an abbess," he said. "And my most powerful, unruly neighbor is about to have an heir with royal blood. That is the thanks I get for offering refuge to a sinner."

Edgiva looked mortified.

"It means your most unruly neighbor is about to be domesticated virtually into our family," Godiva added, smiling beatifically at Edgiva. "You need not thank me for arranging that, husband."

Leofric gave his wife a droll look, before nodding slowly, with a grudging smile. "Very well then." Turning toward the former abbess, he said, "Welcome to the world, my lady. May it be a better place with you among us."

Acknowledgments

Many thanks to:

My manager and fairy godfather, Marc H. Glick (Esquire); my agent, Liz Darhansoff, and her cohort, Michele Mortimer; my editor, Jennifer Brehl, and her sidekick, Emily Krump, for their critiques and patience with the endless permutations of this project. Never was an author so blessed to have such a tremendous, loyal team.

The eternally generous Alan and (especially) Maureen Crumpler, who introduced me to the story of Edgiva and Sweyn, and (as usual) took me everywhere and showed me everything.

Lindsay Smith, for medieval British equestrian insights, Daniel Donaghue for *Lady Godiva: A Literary History of the Legend*, and Bill Griffiths for *Aspects of Anglo-Saxon Magic*.

John and Janet Aldeborgh (and lovely, gentle Orville), for assisting my . . . field research. And Sarah Mayhew, for documenting it.

The Gorgeous Group, especially Kate Feiffer for quipping, "It's *Sex in the Medieval City*!"

The readers of the original, and entirely different, concept of this story, including Eowyn Mader and Amy Utstein.

Billy Meleady, for more than words can describe.

Barbara Babcock, for providing a winter writing sanctuary.

Alene Sibley, for helping me to stay the course, and Chrysal Parrot, for listening to me when I thought I'd literally lost the plot.

All the good folks at HarperCollins who market and promote this book; all the people everywhere who work to make it available; and all the people who choose to purchase it, or any other book.

All libraries everywhere. This is, in part, a story about the transmission of information, and libraries reign supreme in that regard. Long may they do so!

About the author

About the book

Read on

Insights,
Interviews
& More . . .

Meet Nicole Galland

Eli Dagostino

NICOLE GALLAND is the author of four previous novels: *The Fool's Tale, Revenge of the Rose, Crossed: A Tale of the Fourth Crusade,* and *I, Iago.* After growing up on Martha's Vineyard and graduating with honors from Harvard, she divided the next sixteen-odd years between California and New York City before returning to the Vineyard to stay. During those years she variously made her living in theater, screenwriting, editing, grad-schooling, teaching, temping, and other random enterprises. She is the cofounder of Shakespeare for the Masses, a project that irreverently makes the Bard accessible to the Bardophobes of the world. She is married to actor Billy Meleady. ∾

The History Behind *Godiva*

WELL-BEHAVED WOMEN seldom make history—or legend. This story of misbehaving women combines historical fact with the stuff of legend.

EDGIFU (Edgiva)

Edgifu's real-life tale does not end happily. The *Anglo-Saxon Chronicle* reports that in 1046, "went Earl Sweyn into Wales. . . . As he returned homeward, he ordered the Abbess of Leominster to be fetched him; and he had her as long as he list, after which he let her go home."

In fact, she did not go home—at least, not to Leominster Abbey. She stayed with Sweyn about a year and bore him a son named Hakon. Then the Church intervened (Worcester lore claims Bishop Lyfing "rescued" her, but this cannot be, as he had died by then). She was sent to Fencote, a small farm outside Leominster village. The abbey was closed, and Edgifu spent the next forty years there, outside the sway of politics or religious power (i.e., by my lights, under house arrest), dying at Fencote in 1086. There is no record of her ever seeing her son or Sweyn again. Hakon was a hostage (in the sense of a political pawn) during the intrigues that led up to the Norman Invasion. Nothing further is known about him with any certainty.

Historians disagree on whether Sweyn took Edgifu against her will or she ran off with him by choice. (My curiosity ▶

3

about that spawned a much earlier and very different version of this novel.)

Sweyn was banished for abducting her and lost his lands and title; these were restored to him upon his father's intervention, but his continued rashness got him into further trouble. He was banished for murdering his cousin, and then Edward exiled the entire Godwin clan in 1051. Sweyn went on pilgrimage to Jerusalem and died on his way home in 1052.

Sweyn's younger brother Harold (who—not to coin any conspiracy theories—happened to benefit greatly from both of Sweyn's banishments) eventually and briefly became king of England, but lost the title to a fellow from Normandy we now call William the Conqueror, at the Battle of Hastings in 1066.

GODGIFU (Godiva)

Godgifu was the wife of Earl Leofric of Mercia; the dates of her birth and death are uncertain, but she was considerably younger than Leofric, and was probably his second wife (and possibly Alfgar's stepmother). She and her husband were the prime benefactors of Leominster Abbey while Edgifu was the abbess there.

Coventry is on record as being an estate of Godgifu's, but the story of her infamous ride is not mentioned in print until nearly two hundred years after her death. In the thirteenth century, Roger of Wendover wrote the following remarkable (but historically impossible) account of Godgifu's ride:

The countess Godiva [*sic*] ... longing to free the town of Coventry from the oppression of a heavy toll, often with urgent prayers besought her husband, that ... he would free the town from that service, and from all other heavy burdens; and when the earl sharply rebuked her for foolishly asking what was so much to his damage, and always forbade her ever more to speak to him on the subject; and while she on the other hand, with a woman's pertinacity, never ceased to exasperate her husband on that matter, he at last made her this answer, "Mount your horse, and ride naked, before all the people, through the market of the town, from one end to the other, and on your return you shall have your request." On which Godiva replied, "But will you give me permission, if I am willing to do it?" "I will," said he. Whereupon the countess, beloved of God, loosed her hair and let down her tresses, which covered the whole of her body like a veil, and then mounting her horse and attended by two knights, she rode through the market-place, without being seen, except her fair legs; and having completed the journey, she returned with gladness to her ▶

astonished husband, and obtained
of him what she had asked; for
Earl Leofric freed the town of
Coventry and its inhabitants
from the aforesaid service, and
confirmed what he had done by
a charter.

And thus was born the legend.

It's a great story. It's also, as I said,
historically impossible. It contains one
central error: Coventry belonged to
Godgifu, not to Leofric. Under the law of
the day, the only person with the power
to tax Coventry was Godgifu herself.
Since Leofric could not have been taxing
Coventry, the legend sadly falls apart . . .

. . . Unless there were some *other* tax
Godgifu might have been protesting.
But that could not have been something
Leofric had power over; it could only
have been the heregeld, the one national
tax in existence at the time. I am not the
first to suppose this might be the basis of
the legend. (Edward finally repealed the
heregeld in 1051.)

An interesting note: the couple's
relationship in Roger of Wendover's
version makes Leofric very much lord
over Godgifu. This depiction suits the
era in which the anecdote was written,
but not the era in which the couple
actually lived. Among the gentry of the
thirteenth century, Norman rule had
disenfranchised and disempowered
women. But Leofric and Godgifu were
Anglo-Saxon, and in their era, women
had political and personal power that

their female descendants lost after the Norman Conquest. It takes a Norman writer to affectionately trivialize Godgifu's stubbornness, and to depict Leofric's response to his wife's strength as "rebuking her foolishness" that she "never ceased to exasperate her husband." In the story, he punishes her for the insubordination of talking back to him. That may reflect a Norman perception of gender roles in marriage, but not an Anglo-Saxon one.

The story of Godiva's ride has been retold many times over the last eight hundred-odd years, each time with slight amendments or twists that reflect the era or the teller. *Lady Godiva: A Literary History of the Legend*, by Daniel Donaghue, is an entertaining survey of all these variations (including the addition of the original Peeping Tom, who was invented six hundred years after the first written tale).

AND:

The demarcation between paganism and Christianity was murky in the eleventh century. The Land Ceremony Charm— one of the happiest surprises of any research I've ever pursued—was committed to writing around this time. I have slightly altered it, as recorded in the entrancing *Aspects of Anglo-Saxon Magic*, by Bill Griffiths.

SO:

Two powerful, accomplished women, each the survivor of a shockingly ►

The History Behind *Godiva* (continued)

prurient anecdote subject to misinterpretation—and these two women knew each other! It was too tempting not to intertwine their stories . . . especially in a novel about the relationship between what is known and what is just suspected, what is truth and what is pretext, what is reported and what is merely rumored. ✑

Reading Group Guide

1. Discuss Godiva's use of flirtation as a political tactic. Do you find this to be a positive or a negative trait? Why?

2. If you've addressed the first question from a twenty-first-century vantage point, address it from the eleventh-century perspective, or vice versa. Is there a difference?

3. Discuss Godiva's friendship with Edgiva. They are quite critical of each other regarding their (significant) differences, but they retain a deep bond. What does each of them get out of it?

4. Have you ever been in a friendship with a similar dynamic? Which character did you more resemble?

5. Whom do you find to be the most and least sympathetic characters in the story? Why?

6. Consider the Land Ceremony ritual, which clearly blended paganism and Catholicism in the eleventh century. Why do you think the Church rejected pagan elements over the following centuries? What aspects of paganism has Christianity retained? Why those elements and not others?

7. Do you agree with Godiva's decision to make the ride? Why or why not?

8. Have you ever found yourself similarly pushed into making a ▶

choice in a "no-win" situation? How did you decide what choice to make?

9. What decision about her future do you think Edgiva would have made if Godiva had not shown up at Leominster?

10. What do you think of Leofric's relationship with Godiva? Would he have shunned her if she had been excommunicated? Why or why not?

11. Godiva and Edgiva are fairly vocal about what changes they'd like to see in each other, but if each could change one thing about *herself*, what do you think it might be? ～

Have You Read?
More by Nicole Galland

THE FOOL'S TALE

Wales, 1198. A time of treachery, passion, and uncertainty. Maelgwyn ap Cadwallon struggles to protect his small kingdom from foes outside and inside his borders. Pressured into a marriage of political convenience, he weds the headstrong young Isabel Mortimer, niece of his powerful English nemesis. Gwirion, the king's oldest and oddest friend, has a particular reason to hate Mortimers, and immediately employs his royally sanctioned mischief to disquiet the new queen.

Through strength of character, Isabel wins her husband's grudging respect, but finds the Welsh court backward and barbaric—especially Gwirion, against whom she engages in a relentless battle of wills. When Gwirion and Isabel's mutual animosity is abruptly transformed, the king finds himself as threatened by his loved ones as he is by the many enemies who menace his crown.

A masterful debut by a gifted storyteller, *The Fool's Tale* combines vivid historical fiction, compelling political intrigue, and passionate romance to create an intimate drama of three individuals bound—and undone—by love and loyalty.

REVENGE OF THE ROSE

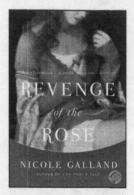

An impoverished, idealistic young knight in rural Burgundy, Willem of Dole greets with astonishment his summons to the court of Konrad, Holy Roman Emperor, whose realm spans half of Europe. Immediately overwhelmed by court affairs, Willem submits to the relentless tutelage of Konrad's minstrel, the mischievous, mysterious Jouglet. With Jouglet's help, Willem quickly rises in the Emperor's esteem . . .

. . . But when Willem's sister Lienor becomes a prospect for the role of Empress, the sudden elevation of two sibling "nobodies" causes panic in a royal court fueled by gossip, secrets, treachery, and lies. Three desperate men in Konrad's inner circle frantically vie to control the game of politics, yet Jouglet the minstrel is somehow always one step ahead of them.

Brilliantly reimagining the lush, conniving heart of thirteenth-century Europe's greatest empire, *Revenge of the Rose* is a novel rich in irony and wit that revels in the politics, passions, and peccadilloes of the medieval court.

In the year 1202, thousands of crusaders gather in Venice, preparing to embark for Jerusalem to free the Holy City from Muslim rule. Among them is an irreverent British vagabond who has literally lost his way, rescued from damnation by a pious German knight. Despite the vagabond's objections, they set sail with dedicated companions and a beautiful, mysterious Arab "princess."

But the divine light guiding this "righteous" campaign soon darkens as the mission sinks ever deeper into disgrace, moral turpitude, and almost farcical catastrophe. As Christians murder Christians in the Adriatic port city of Zara, tragic events are set in motion that will ultimately lead to the shocking and shameful fall of Constantinople.

Impeccably researched and beautifully told, Nicole Galland's *Crossed* is a sly tale of the disastrous Fourth Crusade—and of the hopeful, brave, and driven people who were trapped by a corrupt cause and a furious battle that were beyond their comprehension or control.

I, IAGO

I, Iago is an ingenious, brilliantly crafted novel that allows one of literature's greatest villains—the deceitful schemer Iago, from Shakespeare's immortal tragedy *Othello*—to take center stage in order to reveal his "true" motivations.

From earliest childhood, the precocious boy called Iago had inconvenient tendencies toward honesty—a failing that made him an embarrassment to his family and an outcast in the corrupt culture of glittering Renaissance Venice. Embracing military life as an antidote to the frippery of Venetian society, Iago won the love of the beautiful Emilia and the regard of Venice's revered General Othello. After years of abuse and rejection, Iago was poised to achieve everything he had ever fought for and dreamed of . . .

But a cascade of unexpected deceptions propels him on a catastrophic quest for righteous vengeance, contorting his moral compass until he has betrayed his closest friends and family and sealed his own fate as one of the most notorious villains of all time.

Inspired by *Othello*—a timeless tale of friendship and treachery, love and jealousy—Galland's *I, Iago* sheds fascinating new light on a complex soul, and on the conditions and fateful events that helped to create a monster.

Don't miss the next book by your favorite author. Sign up now for AuthorTracker by visiting www.AuthorTracker.com.